I0716369

MENDED WITH LOVE

Sons of Ishmael
Book 3

UNOMA NWANKWOR

KevStel Group LLC

Lawrenceville GA 30046

Copyright © 2017 by Unoma Nwankwor

All Rights Reserved. No part of this book may be reproduced in any form or by any means without proper consent of the Publisher, excepting brief quotes used in reviews.

This is a work of fiction. Any reference or similarities to actual events, real people, living or dead or to real locales are intended to give the novel a sense of reality. Any similarities to other names, characters, place, and incident are entirely fictional.

First printing October 2017

Printed in the United States of America

www.kevstelgroup.com

Praise for Unoma Nwankwor

"Unoma really is the best kept secret in Christian romance. I love how she weaves in African culture into her stories. Love The Final Ultimatum, love it, love it." **Pat Simmons, award-winning author of Carmen Sister series**

"I loved this story from beginning to end. He Changed My Name has a double meaning and I loved them both."~ **Barbara Joe, author of Forgive Us This Day**

In He Changed My Name, Unoma takes readers on a page-turning, beautiful journey of second chances. This is one of her best. ~ **Vivian Kay, author of Secret Places**

Unoma delivers a satisfying "truth is stranger than fiction" tale every time with her plot twists, plus some godly interventions. Romance isn't a fairy-tale in Unoma's **Anchored by Love**. It's real! **~Pat Simmons, award-winning author of Carmen Sister series**

Unoma has woven a compelling story of regret, forgiveness, love and God's amazing grace in this beautifully written novel. Poignant. Engaging, a great read -that cleverly demonstrates how God is able to use the most horrific situations and turn them around for his grace. Five stars**! ~Abimbola**

Dare, Author of The Small Print and When Broken Chords Sing

This sexy romance weaves forgiveness and love into a warm blanket rich with comfort. Nwankwor writes a well written story with several universal themes of family, forgiveness and love **~ Readers Paradise on A Scoop Of Love.**

"Unoma sets up each scene in **When You Let Go** with an emotional punch that will keep your heart racing to the finish line. Warning: You will lose sleep trying to get there!" **~Pat Simmons, award-winning author of The Guilty series.**

"**When You Let Go** is a true testament of the power of God within ourselves and our marriage. Although, we are tested every day, it is up to us to lean on our faith to get through those difficult times and offer forgiveness to those who may have hurt us in the process. Amara and Ejike's faith was tested throughout this novel but once they learned to put God at the forefront of their household, they were able to weather the storm." ~ **Diva's Literary World**

"I love how Unoma Nwankwor weaves the distinctive, spicy flavor of West Africa into her novels. I feel right at home with the food, pidgin English, quirky expressions, and cultural norms. I'm also enjoying watching her grow as an author. **~Sherri L. Lewis, Bestselling Author and Missionary**

Nwankwor adds more depth with the cultural nuances that could be a roadblock or a gateway to understanding. She expertly intertwines all of these elements, including faith lessons, to make a tightly woven story for a reader's enjoyment.~ **USA Today Review of An Unexpected Blessing.**

"In **An Unexpected Blessing**, Unoma Nwankwor has penned a sweet romance with an important message about love and acceptance. She's definitely a writer to watch." **~Rhonda McKnight, Black Expressions Bestselling**

Author of What Kind of Fool and An Inconvenient Friend.

"What woman hasn't felt the pangs of unfulfilled desire? In **An Unexpected Blessing**, Unoma Nwankwor weaves deception, cultures and the intrigue of love for a romantic journey that spans two continents and challenges the cornerstone of faith."~ **Valerie J. Lewis Coleman, best-selling author of The Forbidden Secrets of the Goody Box TheGoodyBoxBook.com**

"I read **An Unexpected Blessing** and I must admit I loved it very, very much. I look forward to reading your next novel."~ **Diane Ndaba, reviewer Africa Book Club**

"Unoma's writing reads effortlessly. There is the perfect infusion of faith and international flavor. Readers are quickly swept up on a romantic literary adventure. **The Christmas Ultimatum** is a great read for anytime of the year"~ **Norma Jarrett Essence Best Selling author of Sunday Bruch**

"I loved it. **The Christmas Ultimatum** is my first read from Unoma and it won't be my last. I enjoyed the international favor she gave to the story. There is nothing sexier than a Christian man who goes after who and what he wants. Kudos!" ~ **Pat Simmons Award winning author of the Guilty Series**

*To my husband Kevin, and my kids—Fumnanya & Ugo.
Their support is immeasurable.*

Acknowledgments

To my Lord and Savior Jesus Christ. I thank you for paying the ultimate price that I may have life and for your grace which I do not deserve. Thank You for the gift of writing and I humbly pray I continue to be a vessel in this journey.

To my family, my husband Kevin who is my number one fan, cheering me along every step of the way. I love you and thank you. To my kids Fumnanya and Ugo, my gang, my pookies, my munchkins they keep me sane when insanity sometimes abound. I love you both more than words can express. I pray for God's continued protection over you.

A very special thank you to my baby brother Engr. Christopher Osiegbu. He helped me craft Kamal Danjuma perfectly. Even with our time difference, he was always available to answer my soccer questions and talk plot from a technical perspective. I love you bro!

To my parents and mother in-law, *Daalu.* Thank you for your constant prayers and speaking words of life, courage and hope upon me.

To my readers, author friends and sistah writers thank you, thank you. Sometimes support doesn't always come from the people or places you expect but trust in God and He will send the right people to you.

It's the **FINALE!**

The Sons of Ishmael series tells the story of three brothers who should have been sons of favor, but their lives took an unexpected turn when their father made a decision that molded their future. Or so they thought.

Just like Ishmael in the Bible, our circumstances in life can change quickly, and sometimes for the worse. That is when we should draw near to God and seek His wisdom and strength.

We may be tempted to become bitter when bad things happen, but that never helps. Only by following direction from God can we get through those valley experiences.

Follow Rasheed, Jabir & Kamal; the Danjuma brothers as they try to live in the present still harboring pain from the past and the ladies that will finally make them see that it is best to let go.

There are some questions at the back of the book, so you could discuss them with your friends or just read through by yourself. If you have additional questions, you can reach me at www.unwankwor.com

In book one, you met Rasheed & Ibiso. In book two, you meet Jabir & Damisi. Catch up with both couples and get ready for the whirlwind that is Kamal and Ebele. I had so much fun with these two, especially Kamal. He's unlike any male character I've written. I hope you love him as much as I do.

It's a bit emotional for me to see the Danjumas exit the stage, but I've had a blast with them and I hope you have too.

Unoma

October 2015

It was the hour of reckoning. The LA Sun Sides had just lost the Western Conference finals, and the fans needed answers. Kamal Danjuma draped a towel over his head as he headed for the tunnel of the StubHub Center stadium. He'd masterfully dodged questions from reporters on the field but knew he wouldn't be so lucky in the locker room. The season had ended for his team of three years, but making it worse, they were knocked off at home. And to San Jose Dynamos - the clear underdog, according to the Major Soccer League.

Since his transfer from Spain, this was Kamal's most painful loss. He'd given it his all but not his best. Even beating his two goals a game average wasn't enough. His future weighed in the balance. Recent troubles had plagued him, but the team still depended on him, and he couldn't clinch the win.

He rubbed his sweaty hands on his soccer shorts, as he made his way through the pungent smell of the locker room to the wooden alcove that sported his nameplate above it. The lockers made a semi-circle around the room that had the white and red colors of the LA Sun Sides. He looked over to the side and his teammate, Joe Reid, had reporters all over him, demanding answers. The second Kamal's eye connected to one of them, everyone shifted their attention to him. He inhaled a deep breath and sat on the chair in front of his locker. Repositioning the towel around his neck, he waited for the barrage of questions to follow.

"Kammy! Kammy!"

Reporters yelled his name, each vying for his attention while shoving devices into his face.

"Okay, hold on guys. I'm going to answer your questions. Just give me some room." He looked over to the reporter from the *LA Sports Break*, Brent. Kamal always thought the *Break* was fair in their reporting.

"Brent, what you got?" Kamal asked.

"Is there any truth to the rumor that you won't be returning for the regular season come March?"

Kamal removed the towel from his neck and draped it on his knee. He wasn't sure how much he wanted to disclose to the press at this moment because his agent, Pete Summers, was still on the hunt for a loaner club in the United Kingdom. Depending on how long the loan period could be negotiated for, he wouldn't be returning in March.

"We're in October. The season just ended. Who knows what'll happen? I just wanna enjoy the holidays for now."

"The DUI you had was dropped. Is that the reason you're considering going on a loaner?" another reporter asked.

Kamal's jaw clenched. This was why he hated talking to the press. They always tried to be sneaky. He felt they mostly tried to do it to foreign players to discredit them. He reached into his locker, took out a sleeveless T-shirt and put it on.

"I thought I just addressed the loan issue?" Kamal asked.

"Come on now, Kammy. We all know that in the last

couple of months, your game has been off, you've had minor injuries and recent legal problems. First the brawl and now the DUI…"

Kamal eyebrows knit together as the reporter counted off his points with his fingers. He couldn't take it anymore.

"Both of which have been dropped because they were proven not to be my fault." He didn't feel like going into the specifics again. He'd addressed it time and time again. Not only to the press but to his fans and his family. He was done talking about it. The bar brawl was ruled self-defense, and the DUI had nothing to do with him. It was his teammate who was in his car at the time. The police knew they were foul when they booked him. The tabloids took it and ran. By the time his lawyer cleared his name, some damage had been done. It was time to end this. He needed to hit the showers.

"As much as I would love going back and forth with you on something I'm sure you already know, I'm going to have to cut this short." He grabbed his leather duffle from the base of his locker.

"Kammy, any words for your fans out there about tonight?" a female reporter asked.

He paused and faced her. He took a breath. His fans were the people that made him, a fact he never forgot.

"My favorite part of this game is the opportunity I have to play it. I'm grateful to my fans who support me, win, or lose. While I always want to win, I want to thank them for understanding that that's not always possible and rocking with me regardless. *Daalu nu.*" He gave the peace sign and turned around.

"Hmmm, I like when he signs off with his native Nigerian language like that," the reporter whispered.

Kamal smirked. She probably thought her tone was low, but he heard her.

"Becky, it's not Nigerian language. It's Ibo. Ugh," said

another lady, who Kamal assumed was the reporter's colleague.

Kamal chuckled to himself.

The lady continued, "Please, tell me that after all these years you do know that means a simple thank you."

Kamal used his leg to drag the small stool he'd been sitting on to the side. He locked his locker and headed in the direction of the shower and training rooms, where the press wasn't allowed. The only thing on his mind right now was hopping on a plane to Nigeria. For someone who was against commitment, his twin, Jabir, had shocked their whole family. A year ago, he had a small, rushed wedding in Kenya, but now, he was bent on giving his wife, Damisi, the wedding of her dreams.

He was robbed of being the best man before, but now he was going to be standing right there when his twin got married again.

Chapter 1

$\mathbf{D}$*ecember 2015*
"Nna, e di ga ready?"

Kamal Danjuma turned around to see his mother walk out of the house toward him. This woman was his life. As much as she worried about him, he also worried about her.

"Mama, leave this man. He's not a baby," his older brother, Rasheed, teased. He walked over to his mother and draped his arm around her shoulders.

"I don't understand why you keep 'jealousing' the kid." Kamal strolled over to them and lifted Rasheed's arm, replacing it with his.

"He might not be a baby to you, but he's still my baby," their mother answered.

"Haba, Mama, I'm far from a baby, but yes, I'm ready." Kamal kissed her on her forehead as Rasheed grunted and walked around to the driver's side of the car.

"Kammy, *oya o, make we dey go.* I don't wanna be home late," Rasheed said.

"I don't know why you didn't let my driver and I take you to the airport," his mother said.

"Because I don't want you out late," Kamal responded.

"Neither do I," Rasheed said. "Now, Mama, I'll see you tomorrow before my flight to Dakar. Let me take this knuckle-head to the airport."

"Okay." Mrs. Danjuma turned to Kamal. She took both of his hands in hers. "*Nna*, God be with you *o*. Please be careful in this new place you're going to play. *Biko*, the three of you are all I have. Well, now I also have my daughters and grandchildren, but still, I don't want anything to happen to you."

"Mama, I'm good. As long as I can play, I'm fine." Kamal gave her a reassuring grin.

"My son, I know you don't want to think about it, but you have to consider settling down. See your brothers; they're now married. You need someone too. A woman that will see you for you and not the star."

Kamal knew that with Rasheed and his twin, Jabir, married, the pressure would be on. However, he wasn't ready for that conversation. "Okay, Mama, they've started calling my flight. It's time to board."

Rasheed bellowed out laughter.

Mrs. Danjuma smacked Kamal on his shoulder. "You're so silly. They're calling your flight *o kwa ya*? From the front of my house?"

Kamal cupped his ear and looked upward. "Ah, ah, Mama, can't you hear them?"

"Hmmm, okay *o*, that's fine. I'll drop it. Kneel, let me pray for you." Mrs. Danjuma pointed to the patch of well-mani-cured grass in front of the house.

Kamal got on his knees. His mother placed her hand on his head and began to pray. At intervals, she'd blow air from her mouth over his head as she prayed. She spoke in their native language, so he understood some of it but not a lot. He did know that whenever she said, "*na afa* Jesus" meaning "In Jesus name," he should say, "Amen."

When she was done, he got up and hugged her tight.

Kamal kissed her cheek and got into the car for Nnamdi Azikiwe Airport. Destination – East London in the United Kingdom. He was going back to where it all began.

———

THEY JUST COULDN'T WAIT, COULD THEY? KAMAL DANJUMA grunted and leaned back into the plush leather seat of the car. As Rasheed navigated through the streets of Abuja to the airport, Kamal thumbed through the pictures on his team's Instagram account. Once he got in the car and checked his phone, he saw that his notifications were going off. He'd been tagged in some photos. He suppressed the urge to throw his phone out of the window.

This is nonsense. But I got something for them, though.

It was the last week in December, a week before pre-season began. He looked at the picture of his team as they visited the Children's Way Survival Center the day after Christmas. As part of their contractual obligation to some sponsors, the team always did pre-season charity visits. What annoyed him was that the ink hadn't even dried on his deal and already his parent team was doing pre-season promotion without him.

Pete had come through for him, and he was headed to play for Turk West Football Club in Newham for the next three months. After that, he'd return to LA to start the regular season. Kamal had two years left on his contract, after which he'd be a free agent again to play wherever he wanted. His preference would be to return to Europe.

Kamal's irritation stemmed from the fact that it all felt kind of planned. One bad season and management was ready to give up on him. He was so glad he'd taken his agent's advice to get out of the US and play in Europe for a bit. With the way the season ended, Kamal knew that he was on the verge of being cut. He wasn't ready to stop playing soccer yet. What would he do with himself if he didn't have soccer?

For now, he would enjoy the deal he got. The LA Sun Sides would still pay him 100 percent of his salary in addition to what Turk West FC was offering. Turk West FC was a mid-table team in the Premier League based in Newham, East London. Kamal's goal for himself and the team was to help bring them up the ranks in the league and at the same time, remind his fans and LA team management why they fell in love with Kammy Danjuma in the first place.

From the looks of it, his team was scheduled to visit the team owner and commission a playground the next day.

"Kammy!"

"What?" Kamal looked over at his brother.

"I've been talking to you," Rasheed fussed.

"Oh, my bad. What did you say?"

"I asked what you're over there grunting about?" Rasheed glanced over at Kamal and returned his focus to the road.

"Man, my club's management think they're so slick."

"Again, what's the issue? I thought you no longer played for them?"

"For now. If I can get an extension with Turk come March, I won't play for them this season. But technically, they're still my bosses."

"Okay. Does this affect you playing with the UK national team in the Regions International Championship in May?" Rasheed asked.

Kamal turned up his lips in a slight smile. He'd been waiting for this opportunity for two years, and this was the year. Since England was his place of birth, he would be playing with the national team, and it was a huge honor.

"Nah, I'm still good on that."

"Oh, okay, so why are you upset?"

"Look at this." Kamal pointed the picture in Rasheed's direction.

"Kammy, I'm driving. Tell me what's up. I'm not Jabir. I can't read your mind."

"Neither can he," Kamal said. Frustration laced his tone. "How many times I gotta tell you the twin thing don't work like that?"

Rasheed smirked, and Kamal shook his head. Ever since they were kids, Rasheed swore he and Jabir shared the same thoughts. Kamal knew he was trying to be funny but now wasn't the time.

"I have a gut feeling team management is trying to push me out, even after my stint in London," Kamal confessed.

Rasheed glanced at him but remained silent.

Kamal rubbed his hand down his face and looked out the window. "I turned 34 this past September. That's old in soccer years," Kamal sighed. "I've had injuries, recently a heart issue. I—"

"A heart issue? When? Why are you just saying something? Does Jabir know? What about Mama?" Rasheed's terror-filled face almost elicited a laugh from Kamal, but he wasn't ready for the lecture that would follow. He wasn't ready to be told how he never took anything seriously.

"Stone Cold, I'm good. I had an EKG, and it wasn't anything to be alarmed about. Just a slight irregularity." His attempt to lighten the mood by using Rasheed's nickname failed. The frown was still there.

"I'm fine. Mama didn't and doesn't need to know anything. Jabir did, but I swore him to secrecy. But bros, that's not the point."

"I'll kill Jabir for not telling me." Rasheed clenched his jaw. But then his frown softened, and brotherly concern filled his voice. "Why would you think they're worried about your age? Or why are you even worried about it? See that Oguchi guy. He's older than you by a full year, and he's playing, so relax," Rasheed said, referencing a Nigerian-American player, who'd just signed with Philadelphia at thirty-five years old.

"You're right, I guess. I was tripping when I saw this pre-season promotional shoot that I should've been a part of as a star player." Kamal stared at the picture on his phone again and scanned through the comments. It wasn't only him that had questions about why he was left out. Based on what he was reading, the fans had the same questions.

"Leave them in the past and focus on where you're going. The best thing to do is to show them you're not hurting. Success is the goal." Rasheed advised. "Besides, you should be happy. You get to see Coach Grams."

Kamal grinned. Yeah, good ol' Mr. Grams or Coach G, as Kamal called him. He was his first coach. The first person who believed in him. He was the one who noticed Kamal and encouraged him to take soccer seriously. On Rasheed's insistence, Kamal still went to college, but when he decided to go pro, he went in search of Coach G to get in shape so teams could scout him. Whenever time and opportunity permitted, Kamal always visited him.

Rasheed honked and swerved slightly to the right to avoid the bread hawker, who ran across the street without looking.

"Man, where's your driver? Why are you even driving? You know these *Naija* roads need special skills you don't possess," Kamal said.

"You see, just ungrateful. I should've let you find your way to the airport since you want to talk slick."

Kamal sniggered. "I'm just stating facts …"

"Yeah, whatever. My driver took Ibiso and your nephew to a kid's birthday party she's catering." Rasheed's wife, Ibiso, owned an upscale restaurant that catered parties for special clients.

"All right, but stop driving. You've been living here now for about two years. You know these hawkers act like they're immortal. Don't get me started on the way people drive."

Rasheed chuckled. "True, so I'm risking my sanity to drive you to the airport, and you want to call out my skills."

"You don't have any skills. That's the point. And don't front, you know you don't ever miss an opportunity to play my daddy. Even when I told you I'd call Uber, you insisted."

He turned his attention back to his phone. He'd since stopped trying to figure out why Rasheed babied him more than he did Jabir when they were the same age. As long as he didn't push too often, he'd let his brother have his daddy moments. Rasheed was more father to them than the one whose sperm he and his brothers came from anyway.

"I keep forgetting Uber is now in *Naija* now," Rasheed murmured, more to himself.

"But you know *Naija no dey carry last*. Almost everything is in Naija now."

A beat of silence passed between them as Kamal's mind travelled back to his soccer team in LA. What he'd failed to tell Rasheed was, his worry was increased by his knee bothering him again. He'd seen the look that the team's doctor gave his coach the last time he went for a checkup. He was fit to play, but he didn't need anything hindering his plans of a comeback to LA if he decided to.

Several minutes later, the car came to a stop in front of the airport. Kamal put his hood over his head and put on his sunglasses. It was late evening. He would've loved to enjoy the crisp Harmattan air but didn't feel like being recognized by fans at the moment. He wasn't in that head space.

"You ready?" Rasheed asked, with his hand on the door handle.

"Yeah. No need for you to get out. I'll get my luggage real quick and make a dash for the British Airways lounge. I have this PYT that always helps me when I want to go unnoticed."

Rasheed shook his head. "If Jabir could change, there's hope for you. Pretty, young thing, huh? What of Brittani?"

"Bro, don't get it confused. First, Brittani is where she is. Second, all I do with other ladies is flirt. Jabir, on the other hand, dated each and every one of those women while silently crying over Dami … punk." Kamal laughed, and Rasheed joined in.

"You know I'm telling, right?" He wiped the tear that formed in the corner of his eye from laughing so hard.

Kamal shrugged. "And? He knows he was a punk." He brought out his travel documents and put the strap of his duffle bag across his shoulder.

"All right Kammy, be easy. Stay safe, and we'll see you in a few months for Mama's birthday, *abi*?"

"I won't miss it for anything. The old woman is turning sixty-five. *Na wa o.*"

"Jabir is a punk. Mama is old. Well done, I'm so telling them," Rasheed said.

"Oh, don't forget …" Kamal placed his hand on the door to open it.

"What?"

Kamal got out of the car and shut the door. He opened the back door and took out his luggage. After extending the handle to roll the suitcase, he shoved his head through the open window. "Don't forget to add, Rasheed is a snitch." He chuckled and quickly backed up, avoiding his brother's jab.

"My love to Ibiso and tell my nephew I'll Facetime him this weekend." He lifted his hand, made a peace sign, kissed his fingers, and raised them at Rasheed. Once his brother nodded, he turned around and walked into the airport to catch his flight to London.

Kamal kept his head lowered as he made his way through the airport. Thoughts of his new beginning occupied his mind. He hadn't played in Europe in about five years. He couldn't go out like a nobody after all these years, and that's what might happen if he didn't succeed at Turk West. He needed to get one up on them. After all, he was Kamal Danjuma.

Over his career, he had two hundred fifty-four appearances, one hundred four goals, one hundred-seventy-two wins, and only thirty losses. He could comfortably say he was the best-attacking midfielder the LA Sun Sides ever had. The year after he joined them, they won the MLS Shield. He was an integral part of that win.

Off the field, he'd been named MLS's best-dressed player two years in a row. His signature kaftans, and well-tailored suits complemented with Ankara breast pockets, and Ankara loafers that had his initials K.E.D., made him stand out. He had appeared in magazine spreads in Nigeria, UK, and America. He had lucrative endorsements deals, and women loved him. His charity work was known abroad and in Nigeria. If he were going out, it would be on his terms and with a bang.

London would be a blast. He could feel it. Best of all, he'd be reunited with his boy since the sandbox, Tega Lawson. Two *Naija* guys on the same team. With a wicked grin tipping the corner of his mouth, Kamal was ready to have fun, play ball, and give the fans what they loved.

Chapter 2

Saturday evening, Ebele Ashiedu palmed her forehead and let out a labored breath. *This is foolishness.* She rolled her eyes at the clerk at the British Airways kiosk. She was on time for her flight, and they had the nerve to tell her a flight she paid for was overbooked, so they wanted to move her to the next. *Mba.* No. Not going to happen.

She was already two-and-a-half months late for her last year at the University of East London. The school year started late September, but her classes didn't begin until October. Christmas break was now over, and she was desperate to catch up. The next flight out was in two days, meaning she wouldn't make it in time for the first class of the new year, and she couldn't afford any more time off.

"As I was saying, Miss. Ashiedu, the flight is full ..." the clerk tried to explain.

"I don't understand how that affects me. I'm confused." She'd been going back and forth with this lady for ten minutes. She saw that they didn't appreciate her *Britico* side or the proper *"init"* British accent she was using. She was about to bring out her *Naija kolomental.* All she knew was, she had to be on this flight.

"See, look. I bought this ticket months ago. I called to have it moved because of a family emergency. At that time, I changed my departure from Lagos to Abuja …"

"Miss, I understand, but there's no more room. We'll pay for an overnight stay in Abuja and put you on the next flight," the clerk said.

As the clerk spoke, Ebele rubbed her hand on the back of her neck, closed her eyes and shook her head. *They'll pay for an overnight stay, then who will pay for the second day?* She reopened her eyes and narrowed them to zero in on the lady's name tag.

"Valerie?"

The clerk stared at her with frustration in her eyes, but Ebele wasn't bothered. "Listen to me. I. Cannot. Miss. This. Flight. *Biko*, print my boarding pass. I paid for coach, but since BA decided to overbook it, I'll sit with the pilot if need be, but I have to get to school."

Ebele hated getting out of character, but she also disliked being underestimated because of her size and what her friends called her nerdy look. So what if her wild curly hair, bare face, and petite frame made her look eighteen. She needed to be taken seriously because she had to be in school Monday morning.

"Miss…"

"No! Get me your supervisor."

Regretting her decision not to fly out of Lagos, Ebele frowned. The flights from Abuja weren't as frequent as those from Lagos, but she wanted to go through Abuja so she could check in on her friend, who had recently laid her father to rest. Ebele couldn't relate to how close Bintu had been to her father because she didn't share that relationship with hers. But she heard the pain and despair in her friend's voice and wanted to be there for her.

As she waited, Ebele thought about the strained relationship with her father. The issue of her dad was a touchy subject for her. Here she was in her late twenties and had only had her first conversation with him a couple of years ago. She was conceived out of an affair he had with her mother and opted to ditch his responsibility instead of facing it head on. She sighed recollecting the story her mother had told her.

He was an expatriate in Port Harcourt, and she worked for the same company. They started an affair, and he never told her he was married. Ebele often wondered if her mother didn't suspect it at some point. When the company called him back to the U.K, he forgot all about her mother and continued his normal life, not knowing a child had been conceived. Ebele would have understood him not being in her life if he didn't know about her, but he found out later and still wanted nothing to do with her until about five years ago.

Ebele shifted her handbag to her other shoulder and watched as traveling passengers went to other clerks to process their documents. She was beyond frustrated. It was like the enemy was constantly trying to rattle her and stifle everything she did. Her mother's recent illness had rattled her the most. All her life, it had been just the two of them. Her mother was like her best friend. Ngozi Ashiedu made the rejection from her father bearable. She took pride in her, despite the shame her birth brought. Even in her rebellious years, her mother didn't give up on her.

A week before Ebele was to head back to school, her mother fell ill. She was diagnosed with shingles; and then, it was complicated by pneumonia, and she had to be hospital-ized. Ebele thought her world would crumble. Her mother was discharged after eight days, but she was still very weak and unable to take care of herself. Although they were given all kinds of assurances from the doctor, Ebele couldn't leave her mother alone to return to London for school. No amount of Skyping or phone calls could take the place of her staying and monitoring things herself. By the time her mother was better, school was headed into Christmas break; so of course, she stayed. Now it was time to head back to the books.

Father, You said You wouldn't leave or forsake me. Please, I need some help here. I'm already behind.

Her joint honors degree in Physiotherapy and Management meant everything to her. The three-year program was her fresh start, her new beginning. After two years in a funk, she'd fought her way back by God's grace. This was her – turning her mess into her ministry – and nothing was going to stand in her way. Thankfully, the extra credit she'd earned in the previous semesters would keep her from being too far behind.

"Hello, Miss Ashiedu, I'm Mr. Abdul." A man approached her from around the counter and extended his hand to her.

Ebele studied him for a few seconds. "Hi." She shook his hand.

"I have been told about your situation. I sincerely apologize …"

"Mr. Abdul, Valerie has been apologizing too. I don't mean to be rude, but please, what can you do for me?" She'd been there for almost two hours. She stood in the long line to get through customs bag check and another line to get to the kiosk. Now it was about an hour to departure time, and she was tired of everyone apologizing and not doing anything.

"Yes, I understand. I think there's something we can do. Let me see your passport and ticket."

Caution danced behind her eyes as she handed the documents over. She didn't know how it worked, but surely, they could find her a seat. The man snapped his fingers, and another man came from the side, picked up her luggage, and weighed it.

A few minutes later, she heard, "Follow me."

Ebele furrowed her eyebrows in confusion and walked behind the man until they got to another checkpoint. Ebele was happy to see that it looked as though she'd be on the flight after all.

"Miss, I do apologize for any confusion. This woman here

will take you to your flight." Mr. Abdul handed her documents over to the woman instead of giving them to her. The woman checked her documents and looked at her. Ebele wasn't sure, but it seemed like surprise laced her eyes. She was only joking *o* when she said she'd sit with the pilot. Or did the man put her in the back with the hostesses? Ebele's heart thumped against her chest.

"Follow me, Ma. They're about to finish boarding." The woman turned and started walking down the narrow way to the gate of the plane.

"Can I see my boarding pass?" Ebele asked as they approached the door of the plane.

"Oh, yes, Ma. Here it is."

Ebele choked on her saliva when she saw her seat placement.

Chapter 3

"This is definitely a mistake."

Kamal heard a voice that made the hair on his arms stand before the face it belonged to came into focus. It was raspy and silky at the same time. Her tone was soft but laced with apprehension.

"Well, I guess this is your lucky day because you were upgraded. Let me show you to your cabin."

He assumed the hostess responded to her. Their steps got closer; soon she came into view. She wasn't just cute – her beauty was bewitching. Their eyes connected and held for a moment. She lowered her eyes and tried to tuck her wild, black curly hair behind her ears. Kamal concluded she either didn't know how beautiful she was or didn't dwell on it. He stood and opened the overhead cabin to get to his bag to retrieve his neck pillow.

"Here you are," the air hostess said.

It took a second before Kamal figured out the pod she pointed to was right next to his. He glanced at the women.

"Ladies." Kamal nodded and proceeded to put his bag up.

The air hostess smiled while the beauty's face remained stoic. The hostess handed the lady her hand luggage and made her way back to the front. The woman muttered her thanks, which he was sure the hostess didn't hear. She glanced around but seemed stuck in place.

Kamal used that opportunity to observe her features. The first thing he noticed was their height difference. He towered over her. She couldn't be more than five feet, two inches – three inches tops. Clad in jeans and a simple red shirt, her petite frame made her look like a teenager. However, the curves on her body betrayed that theory. Her skin was light brown as though she was mixed with something. Her oval face contained cute freckles that were invisible if she were further away. When she lifted her hand luggage for the overhead bin, her curly mass fell across her face, temporarily blocking her vision. Kamal smiled and walked around his pod to hers.

"May I?" Kamal asked. With her nod of approval, he took the bag from her. As he put it up, she moved past him, untied her cardigan from her waist, and settled into her seat.

"Thank you." That voice washed over him again.

He looked down at her, and for the first time, he noticed the color of her eyes – blue with a hint of brown. He'd never seen that color on anyone, and he'd seen many women in his lifetime. Her skin, hair, and now her eyes convinced him that she was indeed biracial. The mystery of her appealed to him to know more.

"You're welcome," he said. He settled into his seat and placed his hand on the button that controlled the privacy panel. "I could raise this up for you if you'd like."

She frowned and shook her head. She'd been doing a lot of that. "This is first class, right?"

With confusion etched across his face, he responded, "Uh, yeah."

She crossed her hands and rubbed them up and down her bare arms.

"Are you cold? I can adjust the air."

"Err, no, it's fine. I'll put on my sweater." She fidgeted as she put her arms through the piece of clothing. Her eyes darted around the cabin.

"Is something wrong?" Kamal asked.

"Uh, no. Forgive my manners; I'm Ebele." She extended her hand.

"Kamal." He shook her hand. It was as soft as he'd imagined. Her nails were freshly manicured.

Before she could say something else, a hostess appeared. "Mr. Danjuma, would you like me to take care of that for you?" She pointed to the glass of orange juice he'd gotten earlier.

He nodded and handed her the glass. "Thanks."

Kamal tried to ignore the flirtatious grin the hostess gave him when she turned to leave. Earlier, he'd taken a good look at her, noticing she was brick-house built. He'd planned on seeing what she was about during the flight, but the petite mystery that sat beside him had blown that plan to smithereens.

"You're one of *the* Danjumas?" Ebele asked.

"Depends on *the* Danjumas you know." The question always rubbed him the wrong way. He knew his voice held more aggression than he would've liked, but he hated that question. It was the same question Rasheed always teased his wife with. Apparently, she'd asked him the same thing when they met. It was as though the news outlets in Nigeria couldn't get enough of their story.

Ebele eyed the LA Sun Sides towel he had across his lap. "You're Kammy, the footballer?"

He forced a smile. "Guilty."

Ebele pursed her lips. "Hmm."

"Have we met before?"

"Not at all," Ebele said, turning away. Her expression said the conversation was over.

Kamal frowned. He didn't do rejection very well. Normally, he would've brushed her off. She wasn't even his type. He usually liked his women supermodel tall with a lithe body. The more he thought about her dismissal, the more it annoyed and intrigued him at the same time.

"Lady, you're gonna have to give me more than that." He placed his right hand over the left side of his chest. "You're bruising my ego."

"Not likely," she mumbled. She turned and looked out of her window again.

Kamal was beginning to get irritated. She was cute. He thought he'd have fun getting to know her, but they hadn't even taken off yet, and her smart mouth was making her very ugly.

"Oh. I see you're one of those."

She looked at him with fire in her eyes. "And what those are you referring to?"

"Those that sit in the comfort of their homes and judge people they've never met, simply because of their celebrity." His jaw clenched, and his eyes darkened in anger. It was typical – people saw a celebrity and immediately thought they had them all figured out. Before she could respond, an announcement from the cockpit came on. Soon after, they were being advised of safety precautions.

"You're right. I'm sorry. Let's start over." She paused, but he remained silent. "I've had a real frustrating time in the past few weeks and tonight just took me over the edge. It's no excuse, and again, I apologize." She absently twirled one of her loose tendrils. "I keep waiting for someone to tell me I need to get off the plane."

Kamal wasn't expecting her to show remorse. Most people thought that celebrities had no feelings. However, his immediate concern was why she felt antsy. "Why?"

"I have no business being in first class. I know there's a God, but this thing He did tonight is just beyond me." She rubbed her hand on her pants. "I should be happy, but I'm shocked."

The plane began to taxi down the runway. Kamal grunted but remained silent. The way she mentioned God made him want to run. He didn't have anything against the Big Man; he just didn't want to have a Bible lesson on the six-hour flight. His mind immediately went to his brothers and how they got with women who changed them with their Christianity. They'd done a total one-eighty.

Kamal wasn't scared of love, or commitment, but wanted it on his terms. Love? Why was he even thinking of that? He'd just met this woman, and she'd already annoyed him with her judgment. But on the other hand, she did apologize, and grudges were one thing he didn't do a lot. That was Rasheed's former specialty.

"Apology accepted."

Kamal hesitated, wondering if he really wanted to find out what happened to make her act that way. He settled for easing her mind. "We're moving now, so you don't have to worry about being booted off the plane."

She started to respond but stopped and gripped his hand as the plane sped up. Several minutes later, after the plane steadied, she looked over at him. Her cheeks were flushed in embarrassment.

"I thought you were going to break my hand there for a minute." Kamal rubbed his hand in feigned pain.

"I'm so sorry. Did I hurt you? I hate taking off. For some reason, I fear the plane will fall back on its tail. That's my worst part of flying." She glanced at his hand. "I normally grab the seat handle, but your hand was in the way, and I wasn't prepared."

He laughed at her rambling. "It's all good. You want to talk about what happened to you tonight? Why are you scared? You running from the law?"

Her expression ranged from concern to confusion until he cracked a smile. She giggled and over the next several minutes, relayed the events of the evening to him. He laughed when she said she asked to sit near the pilot but feared the possibility of her request becoming reality.

"Now that's one heck of a story," he said. She remained silent but gave him a faint smile.

Moments later, she reached into her bag and brought out a notebook and pen. She reclined her chair, and they relaxed into a comfortable silence. As in-flight service began, he pulled out his Beats headphones and iPad. Locating his playlist, he turned it on. He felt her peer over to his side.

"Mali Music, Damien Marley, and KEM? I wouldn't have pictured you listening to them," she said.

He looked at his playlist and raised his brow at her. "What else don't you picture me doing? As a matter of fact, how many times a week do you picture me doing something?" He raised his eyebrow.

"I didn't mean it like that. Smarty."

"Then what did you mean, Judge Ebele?"

"I figured you'd be a rap or Afro beat fan."

"You assume a lot. And I see you don't know how to mind your business either."

"I wasn't trying to be in your business. I looked over and saw your playlist."

Kamal grunted. "Well, I do listen to those sounds you mentioned, but only on occasion. When I do need an African beat, I listen to Banky W or Adekunle Gold. Something more mellow," he explained.

"Interesting. What's your favorite song from Mali's album?"

Kamal shrugged. "I guess it varies by season. Right now, I like "Ready Aim." I also like "Digital," his latest single."

Ebele placed her right hand across her heart. "Really? I love "Ready Aim," too. What do you like about it?"

"Nosey, aren't you?" He scrunched his brows together.

She laughed. The sound was as smooth as her voice. Kamal chuckled with her. He was normally careful with strangers. He never knew who would try to quote him on something. Ebele made him chuck his reservations. She proved easy to talk to, despite her crazy assumptions.

"Come on, tell me. I'll share something you want to know about me," she urged.

The offer was tempting. There was something about her, and he wanted to know more. If it meant telling her something he didn't often admit, so be it.

"The song, to me, speaks about being fearless." He contemplated for a few seconds. "I'm heading into a situation where I'm going to have to prove to naysayers that I'm more than what they see."

"Why do you have to prove anything to anybody if you know who you are?" She shook her head. "Err, no I take that back. I know exactly what you mean." A beat of silence passed between them, and she continued, "At the surface, Mali was talking about being fearless, but I read an interview he gave, and he was actually talking about spiritual warfare."

"What's that?" The minute the words left his mouth, he regretted asking.

"It's how we as Christians do battle with the spiritual world. You're Christian, right?"

"Yes. A lot of people get confused by my name." The Danjuma name often made people think he was a Muslim.

"Yeah, so as I was saying. Everything that happens to us here in the physical is directly related to what's happening in an unseen realm. So, spiritual warfare is fighting at the root and not only treating the symptoms."

"Okaaaayyy." Kamal twisted his lips at her in disbelief.

"I'm for real. You do believe in God, a heaven, and a hell …"

"I do, but I don't go about thinking about an unseen world."

"Well, what you don't acknowledge, you can't fight. Nobody said you should think about it but know it's there."

"I guess."

"It's real. Even Mali was singing about it." She giggled. "The effects of the war going on in the unseen world manifests in our strained and damaged relationships, emotional instability, mental fatigue, physical exhaustion, and other stuff."

He remained silent, thinking of her words. So, was his fear of losing ball because of something in the unseen world? Yeah, right.

"Okay, I'm going to stop preaching now."

"Really? And I was enjoying it too." He snapped his fingers.

"No need to be sarcastic." She rolled her eyes playfully.

"Now my question."

"Lord, will I regret this?" she asked.

"I don't know. What I do know is, you better tell me the truth. I revealed my deep secret to you."

"No way was that your deepest secret, but thanks for sharing it. I never—"

"If you say you never would've imagined, I'm going to place you in a chokehold," he teased.

"Bullying is never the answer." She giggled, and he shook his head at her goofiness.

"Why did you scoff when I said my name, and does it have anything to with you understanding my need to prove people wrong?"

"That's two questions."

"I know. Answer them."

"Bossy and a bully."

"Nosey and judgmental. Now answer and stop stalling."

"The whole celebrity thing rubs me wrong. And you … I've heard stories. Not good ones," she said.

"Don't believe everything you read."

Ebele studied him. "You do seem different from what I've read."

He glimpsed at the monitor in front of him. "Great, so no more judgment for the next four hours and fifty minutes?"

"We've been flying that long?"

"What can I say? I'm good company." He popped his collar and looked over at her.

She had her hands folded across her chest and stared at him with one brow raised.

"I guess you're all right too."

She rolled her eyes again.

"Keep rolling those eyes, and they might get stuck. *Oya* answer my second question." He noticed her mood change.

She twirled her stray hair. "Some time ago, I was in a funk – kinda gave up on life. People wrote me off, but through His grace, I was able to pull myself together, and prove those people wrong."

"I guess we're two peas in a pod."

"I wouldn't go that far." She smirked. "Just similar stories."

Kamal studied her. Behind her lightheartedness, there was sadness in her eyes. He suddenly felt the urge to beat down all those who made her feel less of herself. To lighten the mood, he changed the subject. For the next several minutes over drinks and snacks, they discussed a variety of topics, from food, music, religious beliefs, to likes and dislikes.

He chuckled when she reached into her bag and brought out *Kuli Kuli*. The peanut-based snack was his favorite to munch on anytime he came home. Apparently, it was hers too.

He found out that her father was British while her mother was from the Ibo speaking part of Delta State – Issele Uku – an area he didn't even know existed. When people said Igbo, he automatically assumed it was the area his mum was from. Ebele was quick to point out the differences in dialect. He was embarrassed when she told him she'd heard of the scandal between him and his brother's wife. He palmed his face at the memory of when all of Nigeria thought he'd gotten Damisi pregnant out of wedlock.

After a while, she yawned and covered herself with her blanket. He took that as his cue that she didn't want to talk anymore or was tired. Quite frankly, he needed a minute to himself to process what was happening. He had a strange feeling in the pit of his stomach. When he first saw her, her beauty captivated him. But for the last two hours, their conversation showed him how beautiful her mind was as well. He hadn't had this in a long time. A woman talking to him without seeing him as a meal ticket had become foreign to him. He knew she was headed back to school, but he hesitated to ask where when she didn't offer. He knew he couldn't entangle himself in any other kind of relationship right now.

Kamal heard light snoring. He reclined his seat, adjusted the overhead light. He put on his headphones and shut his eyes, ready to be carried away to la-la land with the smooth melody. However, one big question roamed his mind. Was he willing to walk off the plane and never speak to her again?

Chapter 4

Monday morning, Ebele burrowed deeper under the covers as her alarm went off. Her body felt like an eighteen-wheeler had rolled over it. She'd spent the day before unpacking and rearranging stuff around her flat. Just like the previous day, the minute she opened her eyes, her thoughts immediately went to Kamal. How could she think of a man so early in the morning?

Ebele extended her hand and hit the snooze button. Taking a deep breath, she stretched and sat up. She rubbed her hands over her face and slid to her knees as she did every morning. When the chilly air greeted her flesh, she felt for her warm blanket at the foot of her bed. She quickly unraveled it and covered herself with it. She remained silent for a few minutes before she began to read from her devotional. The passage was one on peace. God knew she needed that, especially today. John 14:27, *Peace I leave with you; my peace I give you.*

"Gracious Father, thank You for another day. Thank you for Your peace. As I step out today, help me remember that no matter what comes my way, You'll keep me in perfect peace if I fix my eyes on You." After saying prayers for herself, others and observing a few moments of silence, she stood.

Ebele made her way through the living room of her off-campus residence. She entered the kitchen, turned on the lights, and put on the kettle. Her agenda for the day was at the forefront of her mind. Class, meeting with her professor, and later, lunch with her father. Her mother had warned her to give him a fair chance. Did she really have a choice? Since he was paying her tuition, she figured it was the least she could do. Her phone chimed, and she saw that her mother was calling her on What's App video. She placed an empty glass on the counter and answered the call.

"Mummy, good morning?"

"Asa m o, e teshi go?"

"Yes, Ma."

Her mother never used her name unless she was serious about something. She always called her "Asa," which meant beauty in their native language. Ebele thought back to the day her mother started calling her that. She was eight years old, and one of the kids at school had made fun of her because she was biracial. That was the day she also got to know the real deal about her father.

"Have you prayed?"

"Mummy, I'll be thirty in four months, and you've asked me that question every day for as far back as I can remember."

"And it's a valid question so ..."

Ebele chuckled as she put a slice of lime into the glass, picked up the kettle, and poured warm water over it. "Yes, *o* I have prayed." After letting it stand for a few seconds. Ebele mixed the contents and drank.

"Good. God's favor be with you, my daughter. I know it's because of me that you're late getting back to school, but God will do what He does best," her mother said.

"Ha! Mummy, He works wonders, so I'm not worried. *Shebi* I gisted you what He did with that flight thing?"

"*Ehen* now. I told your grandmother, and she couldn't believe it."

"I'll call you when I find out what they say, okay? *Ehen*, later, I'm having lunch with my father. I'll give you that *tafia* later. Let me go." Ebele tried to get off the phone because she knew what was coming next.

"Ebelechukwu…"

"Uh, oh, she's pulled out the full name."

"Ebelechukwu, I'm not joking with you. Behave yourself. Give that man a shot."

"Mummy, what will he use a shot to do? I appreciate him for the school fees and all, but a man who can't acknowledge me in public won't even know what to do with the chance I give him."

"Ebi—"

"I love you, Mummy. Kiss Mama for me, and I'll talk to you soon. Bye." She hung up the phone and made her way back to her bedroom to prepare for her day. She wasn't ready to go through the, "he's doing the best he can considering …" story. She had bigger problems to tackle. Like finding out where she'd be doing her clinicals.

———

LATER THAT AFTERNOON, EBELE SCROLLED THROUGH HER CELL phone as she waited to see the head of the program team responsible for the placement assignments. Her last class ended an hour ago, and she was famished. However, before she met her father for lunch, she needed to figure this out. Out of three-hundred-sixty credits, she had one-hundred-twenty-five credits to go, and she'd walk the stage. Sixty of those remaining credits were attached to the completion of a twelve-week placement. Online registration was no longer an option since she was so late. Now, everything depended on what the program head could muster up for her.

For the past two years, her life consisted of school and her part-time job at a dance studio. Sometimes, when she could, she'd volunteer at the interpretive dance department of her church here in school. She didn't date, nor did she go out much. She wasn't the average student so saw no need to enjoy "college life." She was about a decade too late for that.

As she waited, a smile rose at the corner of her mouth as her mind travelled back to the handsome soccer player she'd shared a flight with. Despite her resistance, he commandeered her concentration.

She was in Nigeria on holidays some years ago when the news of the Danjuma brothers broke. It was a surprise that the late tycoon had sons no one knew of. The media ate the story up. It was all they talked about. It didn't hurt that the brothers were too handsome for their own good. At the time, Ebele wasn't interested. After all, *wetin concern abgero with overload?* Not her circus, not her monkey.

The next time she heard of the brothers, she was in a salon near school having her hair straightened. The lady in the next chair, also a Nigerian, was discussing Kamal and his twin with her client. There was a story about him and his sister in-law, the newscaster, in a magazine she was holding. The look on his face in the photo threw her off. He looked like he'd be so demanding, arrogant, and cheeky.

After spending six hours with him on the plane, Ebele concluded not all her assumptions were true. She so wanted to Google him when she got back to her room but was afraid of what she might find. She wanted to remember him for how he was some days ago.

When he stood to help her with her hand luggage, she got a whiff of his cologne and temporarily lost her ability to talk. The effect he had on her, and the shock she was in about being in first class, made her stand there like she was crazy. Kamal towered over her. As her eyes travelled up his tall, sculpted frame, the first thing she noticed was the diamond stud in his right ear. His black hair had a wavy pattern and was cut low. His thin moustache connected to his thin, low beard. She couldn't tell if he wore it like that regularly or he hadn't shaved in a while. The facial hair gave him a sexy, rugged look. He had on gray track pants and a black T-shirt. Although the shirt didn't hug his frame, it did nothing to hide his well-chiseled chest. His milk chocolate skin was several shades darker than hers. When they began to talk, and she got more comfortable with him, she noticed his dark smoky eyes, which she had to talk herself out of getting lost in.

When she woke up mid-flight, Kamal was asleep. His head was against the compartment, and it took everything in her not to stroke his waves. He looked so peaceful, not that she'd seen him otherwise. As they got off the plane, she half expected him to ask for her phone number, but he didn't. Disappointment rose through her, but she quickly came to her senses. She didn't need the celebrity *wahala*. She didn't need the reminder of its troubles.

Her phone chirped, alerting her to a text. When she saw who it was from, she was forced to remember celebrity troubles. Victor. She rolled her eyes as though he could see her. If she didn't know any better, she'd think he put a tracking device in her brain. Any time she thought of him in the slightest way, he called or texted.

Victor: Hey sweetheart, are you back in school?

How did he even know my movements? Ugh, it must've been his cousin that I thought I'd dodged at the airport.

She shook her head and muttered a word she wasn't supposed to under her breath. It amazed her how Victor was in denial about the state of things between them. They broke up six years ago, hadn't been in any kind of relationship since, and he was still calling her sweetheart and checking on her.

She contemplated whether she wanted to respond to him or not. Her silence always seemed to be the fuel he needed to keep going, so she decided to respond with a simple "yes."

Victor Mordi was part of the reason she was on her present path but not in a good way. He was the first man that showed her attention and everything he'd said was gospel. In hindsight, she knew growing up without a dad played heavily into that. They were high school sweethearts, but love wasn't the only thing they shared. They also shared a love for the arts – music and dance. They formed a band and were a team. He was the lead singer. She danced and choreographed the dancers.

They were so good that in their senior year of high school, they started getting booked for events. First, they were local in Benin; then gradually, they started going on gigs out of state. Soon, they were offered a deal with a record label. As exciting as it was, she still wanted to go to university. Victor didn't. Why should they when they'd soon be popular, he'd said. Against her mother's wishes, she agreed with who she thought was the love of her life. He was right. They signed the deal and blew up overnight.

Over the years, their band topped the Nigerian charts. She also got gigs to choreograph other big Nigerian musicians. The press compared her to Kaffy Dance, the Nigerian choreographer who performed with Ciara when she visited Nigeria. With fame came the press. Everything was good until she got injured and couldn't dance. Victor broke up with her and left her behind as the band continued touring the country.

She hadn't heard from him or seen him for five-and-a-half years. And then one day about nine months ago, while she was home in Nigeria for a quick visit, she'd run into him at Shoprite of all places, unfortunately. He'd been asking her for another chance and borderline stalking her ever since.

"Ebele, Ms. Wright, will see you now," the graduate assistant working in the office said.

"Thanks."

Ebele's phone beeped again. She glanced at the screen. Victor was trying to make idle conversation. She didn't have the time. She silently cursed Toyin, her dancer friend from their band, for giving him her number. She ignored him and shoved the phone in her backpack. She smoothed down her floral dress and walked into the office.

Ms. Wright, a middle-aged Caucasian woman, sat behind the medium-sized, oak desk scribbling away on her notepad.

Ebele cleared her throat to get her attention. "Mrs. Wright."

"Yes, do come in and have a seat."

Ebele sat in one of the two chairs across from the woman. She looked around as her nerves got the best of her.

"What can I do for you?"

"I'm late to school because of a family medical issue, and online registration for clinical placements is now closed. So I'm here to register and get manually placed."

"Okay, give me a minute." The woman pecked away on the computer for a few moments. "What's your school ID number?"

Ebele provided her with the information and other pertinent information she asked for including a letter from her mother's doctor. She silently prayed she'd get something close and not on the other side of London.

The older woman studied her monitor. She moved the mouse and clicked a couple of times with a scowl on her face. "Everything is gone. They're no longer taking students in the NHS or here around Newham."

Ebele's heart dropped.

"We had some transfers from other schools this year, so the class size expanded a bit." Mrs. Wright paused and continued to look at the screen. "I seem to have a rehabilitation center, but it's in Essex."

"I'll take it!" Ebele clapped her hands together. *Thank you, Jesus.*

Essex was about an hour train ride from her Stratford Campus, but she wasn't complaining. She would've preferred a hospital under the NHS, but right now, she couldn't be choosy. Come October; she was graduating by God's grace. The woman signed some papers and handed them to her. Ebele thanked her and exited the office. So far, so good. Now she needed to face the last challenge of the day – her under-cover father.

———

"Nse, I just got to the restaurant. *Abeg*, let me eat quick with this man. I'll call you when I get back home." Ebele stood at the entrance of the restaurant and peered in, looking for her father as she waited on the host.

"Who? Are you holding out on me?" Nse asked. Nse Akpan was her best friend. She'd been with her through everything. They went to high school together in Benin. When they graduated, Nse went off to the University of Lagos to study Global Management, while Ebele decided to tour the country with Victor. After obtaining her first degree, Nse left the shores of Nigeria to obtain her master's degree at the University of Essex. Ebele often regretted being so behind, but her mother always reminded her that no experience was lost.

"I don't have time for that. You know my only goal is to graduate, work a bit, and eventually own my dream rehabilitation and wellness center in *Naija*. The man is my father."

"Oh, I forgot it's time for the monthly meet and greet." Nse snickered.

"*You no well o*," Ebele said. "Talk to you later. Bye and greet that handsome fiancé of yours for me."

"Okay, call me tonight so that we can plan our *waka* next weekend."

Ebele agreed and hung up the phone. Nse lived in Essex, so any time Ebele went to see her, she ended up staying over.

She had so much work to do, but an evening with her best friend was long overdue.

She gave the hostess her name and was escorted to the table. As she approached, her father stood, kissed her on both cheeks, and pulled out her chair. Ebele placed her backpack in the empty seat to her right and glanced over at the man, who'd contributed to her genetic makeup.

"Vanessa, how are you?" Mr. Watson asked.

"I'm fine, father. You look nice," she said.

A smile spread across her father's face. She knew he cherished the compliment, and she genuinely meant it. If she didn't know better, she'd think he was seeing someone new. His wife had died about five years ago.

"Why thank you. So how is your mom? Is she better?"

"You'd know if you called her."

"I did call her. I was trying to make conversation."

"I'm sorry." Ebele paused. "She's fine. I spoke to her this morning as a matter of fact. She even gave me the, 'be nice to your father' speech."

Her father chuckled. "Vanessa, I don't want you to be nice to me because you have to. I want to build a genuine relationship with you."

As she was about to respond, the waiter approached and took their drink orders. She hadn't looked at the menu yet, so told him she wasn't ready to order. When he left, she opened the menu and perused it before lifting her eyes to look at her father. For the last four years, their relationship was built on superficiality. He paid her tuition, so she was cordial to him. The first real conversation she had with him was a year ago. What bothered her then and now, was he didn't try to explain his absence or take some responsibility for the tension between them.

"Father …"

"Why do you call me that? Call me Steve or Dad."

"I can't call you by your first name. My mom would knock

the spit out of my mouth. And come on, I mean, father is the most respectful thing I can call you. It takes a lot more than paying my college tuition to be a dad. I was twenty-five before you and I had our first conversation ever over the phone."

Her father sighed but remained silent. Ebele felt a twinge of guilt as her mother's voice popped into her head. She decided to try again.

"I've never asked you this because I thought you'd explain it on your own. But instead, you keep trying to build this relationship on weak ground by pretending the past doesn't exist."

Tears welled up in her eyes, and she hated herself. After being teased and told the story behind her birth, she'd promised herself she'd never cry over her father again. Her mother was enough for her. But here she was, after braving many of these lunches, crying over a man who was supposed to love her unconditionally. That vulnerable little girl that so badly wanted to understand was back. "Why?"

Her father sighed and took a sip of his drink. His eyes roamed everywhere before finally landing on hers.

Ebele crossed her arms over her chest and shook her head as he started to narrate the history she already knew. What she wanted to know was, after he knew about her when he reunited with her mother during his second tour to Nigeria, why did he deny her?

"Again, what I want to know is why? My mom tried to reach you when she had me, but as you said, you didn't tell her the real you. So, she couldn't find you. When she saw you again, the way you embarrassed her in your denial of me made her quit her job and move us to Benin." She exhaled and clenched her fists in anger. "Why?"

He bowed his head and ran his fingers through his hair. "I was embarrassed, ashamed, and confused. How could I tell my family I had a child with a black woman?"

She raised her eyebrows. The audacity. He laid down with the black woman, didn't he?

"Please, don't look at me that way. I'm not racist, and my views have since changed. That's why I'm trying to right my wrongs."

"Paying my fees is hardly righting your wrong. You waited until your wife passed to even reach out to me. According to you, I have a brother and a sister. And I don't even know them. I go by my mother's surname. So how are you trying to claim me as your daughter?"

"Vanessa …" He started but closed his mouth as the waiter approached. They both placed their orders. A beat of silence passed between them, and he continued, "Vanessa …"

"You do know you're the only one that calls me that. My name is Ebele," she said.

"I know. I like Vanessa. I'm trying." His eyes pleaded with her. "I want us to have a good relationship before I expose you to whatever introducing you to my family may bring."

Five years ago, she knew she had to put her life back together after losing Victor and her status as a dancer/choreographer. She needed a change and a new purpose. So, after fighting her way back from depression with the grace and mercy of God, she agreed for her mother to reach out to him to sponsor her college education.

Ebele was too old to fall for the game he was trying to play now. He was ashamed of her but was trying to ease his conscience. Did she want the unconditional love of her father? Of course, but at this stage of her life, she'd done well without it, and by the look of things, she wasn't getting it anytime soon. She was no fool, so she'd continue to play her role and collect those school fees.

Their food arrived, and the clanking of cutlery cut the thick silence that had developed between them.

"Okay, father, we'll do it your way," she said. She picked up her napkin, placed it across her knees, and prayed over her food. The aroma of the steamed potatoes, string beans, and baked chicken filled her nostrils, making her taste buds jump in anticipation. She'd been so anxious earlier about her loose ends with school that she'd skipped breakfast.

Until her father was prepared to come correct, she'd continue to treat this like a pseudo business meeting. For this month, she'd fulfilled her obligation.

$$\frac{}{}$$

Chapter 5

$$\frac{}{}$$

A little before seven a. m. the next Monday, Kamal was headed to the Turk West FC training facility for his first day of practice. He checked his rear and side mirrors as he changed lanes to get off the exit for the forty-five-minute drive to Newham, the club's headquarters.

His agent had worked with a realtor to get him a four-bedroom, three-bath rental right in the middle of Essex. The Northeastern suburb of London would be his home for the duration of his loan period. The house came complete with a swimming pool, a spacious lanai, and an indoor mini gym. The kitchen was fitted with stainless steel and black appliances. He knew how to cook but doubted it'd get much use. His favorite room was his bedroom. He'd asked it to be done in grays and cool blue. Over the years, he'd come to learn the colors helped him relax. His bedroom was his sanctuary for only positive energy.

The distance from the club to his home was pretty good since he hated driving long distances. Especially in England where they drove on what he considered the wrong side of the road. Kamal meandered his way through the streets, taking in the serene surroundings. He'd spent the last week settling in and familiarizing himself with the club and city in general. He hadn't been back to East London since he left more than a decade ago.

The place once marked a new beginning for his family. A year after his father left them and moved back to Nigeria, his mother and Rasheed went to find him. It was then that they discovered he had another wife and kid. When they returned from their trip to Nigeria, they'd moved to East London for a fresh start. Kamal was six when it all happened, and it was a difficult time for all of them, but together, they made it.

Back then, apart from her day job, his mother also worked the night shift cleaning offices. That's where she met Mrs. Lawson, his best friend, Tega's mother. Unlike Kamal's father, Tega's didn't abandon them. He died, leaving his wife and only son to fend for themselves in the UK.

It was Mrs. Lawson that told his mom about the Boys & Girls Club because she'd enrolled her son there as well. He grinned as he remembered the way he and Tega met. They got into a fist fight because they each blamed each other for their team's loss in a soccer match. Once they settled their differences, they became close friends. He and Tega went to different colleges, had professional careers with different soccer clubs, but they never lost their friendship.

Kamal was brought back from his reverie when in his peripheral vision, he noticed a jogger with wild hair. He turned to look at her and was disappointed when he realized she wasn't who he thought she was.

He could, without a doubt, admit that exactly nine days and forty-six minutes ago, he'd made a big mistake. How in the name of all things good, could he let Ebele walk away without getting her number? By the end of the flight, they'd gotten so comfortable with each other, that he started calling her E. The woman had touched him deeply in a matter of hours, and he let her walk away.

He knew for certain he didn't need any complications in

his already complicated love life. The relationship he was in with Brittani was teetering to its end, but it hadn't officially ended. In the past several days, he'd longed to hear Ebele's voice again. See her roll her eyes. Or observe the concerned look etched across her face as she looked at the scar above his left eye. The way her eyebrows had come together when she first saw it, almost made him forget the injury was almost a decade old.

How could he not get her number? He didn't even ask her what school she attended. He knew the real reason he didn't. She had the ability to turn his life inside out. His recognition of that fact had him running for the hills. But not getting her number was still a big mistake.

———

An hour later, Kamal made his way through the wide corridor toward the Turks West locker room. He gave head nods of acknowledgment to some of the players as he located his space. Shedding his clothes for his training outfit, he made his way to the field. The team had a full-length soccer field, a state-of-the-art medical area, pool, and a gym. Basically, everything needed to keep a player fit. They also had a mini kitchen that kept nutritional snacks and drinks on deck for the players. He rubbed his right palm against his tummy. He needed to work extra hard to stay in shape – a concept his mother couldn't or refused to understand with all the food she'd tried to give him in the last couple of months while he was home.

"Okay, guys, gather round," the coach bellowed through the megaphone. Everyone jogged to meet him in the center of the field. Kamal looked around for Tega. He hadn't arrived. They'd talked last night and planned their schedule, so he should've been here by now. After a few seconds, his friend came jogging in. Tega was a burly, dark-complexioned fellow.

At six-feet-one, he stood two inches shorter than Kamal. He didn't have any hair on his face or head, but like Kamal, he sported diamond studs in his ears.

"Lawson, you're late," the coach said, with a frown on his face.

"Sorry, Coach."

After a little pep talk and information about the upcoming game next weekend in Belgium against Vastatin, the players were divided into groups and spread out across the field. For the next four hours, they did cardio training, sprints, and technical drills. They ended the day in the gym after some tactical drills between teammates. Kamal took a shower and decided to do a few laps in the pool. He was getting out when he saw Tega approaching him.

"Man, what happened?" Kamal inquired about his tardiness.

"It's my girl. It's this morning; she decided she wanted me to look at some last-minute schedule for the wedding."

Kamal sneered. "Man, that's y'all 'in love' folk."

"Whatever, man. Let me go hit the shower; then we'll be on our way," Tega said.

"Yeah, me too." Kamal dried his head as he made his way to the back. They had plans for lunch before Kamal had to go see his lawyer. Having played most of his career either in Europe or the US, he opted for an agency and a law firm that had offices both in England and America. That way, it was easier for him to be taken care of based on where he was. However, over the years, he preferred Pete, based in the US, as his agent; and Adam Shultz, based in the UK, as his lawyer to handle his affairs.

Later, he'd head home for a relaxing evening and resume dreaming about the petite woman who had taken over his mind. He let out a frustrating breath. *I must find her.*

———

Kamal and Tega leaned against his car outside the restaurant. Lunch was over, and the friends were chatting idly about every and anything. Kamal's phone chimed. He glanced at the screen. It was Brittani. He hadn't talked to her since the day after he landed in London.

"Let me get this. If I don't, she'll just keep calling until I do," Kamal said.

"Okay, I'm about to head out …"

"No, chill. I'll be quick. I need to run something by you. She really has nothing to say anyway." Kamal saw the reluctance in his friend's face but was glad he obliged him.

"Hey, Brit. What's up?" he asked, answering the call.

"Hey, baby. I was checking on you. How was your first day of practice?"

"It was good. Same thing, different location."

"I would've been there to help you settle in, but you know my model shoot was last week. Next week, the girls and I are going to Miami. Jade's best friend wants her to housesit his condo, and we decided to make a trip of it." Brittani rambled on, and Kamal reflected on the history of their two-year relationship. At first, she was all about him, and he genuinely cared for her as well. She seemed to care about him, the man, and not Kammy, MVP for the MLS in 2011, and the second highest paid midfielder in the US.

"Kam, baby, are you listening to me?"

"Hmm? Yeah. Have a nice time, and I'll call soon?"

"Okay, baby, love you. Remember this is a new opportunity. Don't mess it up. If you're lucky and don't cause any problems, they'll sign you for a couple more years. I'll let you know when I can come out there so I can take care of you," Brittani said.

Kamal grunted his response. She was laying it on thick, but right now, he didn't have the energy or time to argue or fuss. He'd been up since well before dawn. Now he was full and tired. He still had one more stop to make before he could pass out and do it all over again tomorrow. He told her he had to go, promised to call her the next day, and ended the call. His eyes met Tega's disapproving gaze.

"What?" he asked. Abrasion laced his tone.

"I see you're still on that."

"Who, Brit? Yeah, she's okay. She means no harm." Kamal shrugged.

"Means no harm? May I remind you, this is the same chick that bailed on you after the bar incident. She's the same one who wasn't by your side for a single court appearance with the DUI thing … and she means no harm?" Tega asked.

"Man, you're reading too much meaning into those situations. She had prior engagements."

Tega chuckled. "I know you're acting blind because she's arm candy and comfortable. I'm not denying she's fine. But you need someone who cares about you and not your bank account or the footballer, or as you American's say, soccer player."

Kamal scoffed. "Like I said. We're not the best, but we work."

"This is me, man. Apart from Jabir, I'm the closest person to you. So, I know you."

He'd met Brittani in the US while he was playing for LA. She was originally from the UK but had moved to the US about four years ago. They had met at some party after a game. When he first heard her British accent, sharply contrasted to the American accents, he was still trying to get used to; it reminded him of home. He wanted to know more about her. He struck up a conversation, and they'd been dating ever since.

Kamal couldn't remember exactly when he and Brittani started drifting apart. Was it when he started to get in trouble and no longer seemed to be of value to his team? Thinking hard, he could agree that recently, she never had time or helped him with anything. He, on the other hand, as her man, made sure he provided her every need – from her shopping sprees to her spa days and her girl's trips. He'd even allowed her to move into his home in LA when her condo was destroyed due to a water main break in her building. She had indeed changed, but he wasn't ready to let go.

"I know that, but trust me, we're good."

"Keep telling yourself that. You're getting old, man. It's time to find the one." Tega wagged his index finger at Kamal. "This right here is more than twenty years of friendship, and I know your problem."

"Oh, no, not you too with the marriage thing."

"I never said you should get married. Not that I'm saying you shouldn't," Tega said. "What I am saying is stop wasting time and find the one."

"Just because you're getting married doesn't mean we all should."

"Agreed, but your issue is deeper. You're afraid of being alone. That's why you won't let go of Brittani, even though you're not really into the relationship. But it's better to be alone and wait for God to send you someone who won't only stimulate you physically, but will challenge your mind, soul, and spirit."

"I'm not afraid of anything. Drop it," Kamal said.

Tega raised his hands up in surrender. "So what did you want to talk to me about?"

"I'm about to head to my attorney's office. He says he has some papers he wants me to look over."

"What kind of papers?"

Kamal waved him off. "No, nothing like that." He knew his friend was worried that he might still have some lingering legal problems. "He wants me to start building my financial portfolio. So, he pulled some companies for me to go over and possibly invest in. I wanted to ask you about one in particular. I can't remember the name now."

"Okay, bet. We can discuss it later. You're coming to the house this weekend, *abi*?"

Kamal nodded. "Yeah, I haven't seen that fine fiancée of yours in a minute."

"Watch it," Tega said.

"*Haba*, someone can't pay her a compliment again?"

"Make sure you're on time so she won't get on your case. She's already upset you've been here for a little over a week and haven't come to the house yet."

"She'll be all right. Tell her I'll be there."

The men finalized their plans and Tega got in his car to leave while Kamal headed in the opposite direction. He couldn't help but notice Tega's smile when he talked about his fiancée. Kamal wanted that, but he wanted it on his own terms. He wanted to be able to control his feelings. He didn't want to get so attached to anyone, and they turned around and left. He liked being the carefree Kamal that everyone fawned over. The one who showed enough charm and affection to get by.

Over the years, he'd been very careful not to attach himself to anyone except his family. In his thirty-four years, he'd never been in love. Those he loved always left, so why bother?

His brothers' reaction to their father's abandonment was anger. He was more hurt than anything. There was a time when their father tried to apologize to them and their mother. Kamal was in his mid-teens then. Rasheed was not having it. Neither was his twin, Jabir. Kamal had so many questions, but out of loyalty to his brothers, he followed their lead and shunned their father. Their father never tried to reach out to them again.

Their mother's father, who was at first angry with his mother for marrying a Muslim, began supporting them a little financially. He sent for Kamal and his brothers to spend some summer holidays with him. Kamal became attached to the old man and took him as a father. Then one day, without any illness, he died. His stroke was so sudden that it stunned Kamal and affected his game.

Soccer was the one constant in his life. He had control on the field. That was why he was committed to getting back to his A game.

As he drove to his lawyer's office, his thoughts landed on the wild-haired woman who slipped in and out of his mind. He mentally justified his not asking for her number. Her charisma had the potential to suck him in, developing a deep attachment he convinced himself again he wasn't ready for. Therefore, Brittani worked for him. He'd leave his relationship status just like it was.

Chapter 6

Friday afternoon, Ebele shifted the weight of her backpack as she waited for Nse to open the door. She knew she looked a hot mess, but that was exactly how she felt. For the past two weeks, the days and nights seemed to roll together for her. Between papers, online modules, group study, and work, she couldn't keep up. She rang the bell again.

"Hey, girl, sorry for keeping you waiting," Nse said when she opened the door. Immediately, she turned around and headed back to the kitchen.

Ebele glanced around the house she'd become all too familiar with over the years. She dropped her backpack on the couch and headed to the kitchen where Nse was cooking.

"What's left to cook?" Ebele washed her hands at the sink.

"Cook? The only thing I'm cooking is this goat meat pepper soup because Tega doesn't eat anyone's pepper soup but mine."

Ebele admired the relationship her friend had with her fiancé. Nse met Tega about a year after Ebele arrived in the UK for her foundation year at the University of East London. It was one of the weekends Ebele stayed over in Essex. She'd watched a movie that reminded her of her relationship with Victor, bringing back old, painful memories and leaving her depressed. Nse had suggested an ice cream run.

When they got to the store, Nse and Tega literally bumped into each other. He wore a hood, a hat, and sunshades covering his eyes. At the time, Ebele thought it was because he was drunk, but she later found out he was a star soccer player and wanted to get some ice cream without being noticed. The Christmas they got engaged, Ebele was in Nigeria with her mother on holidays. She vividly remembered the screams when Nse had called her.

"So everything else is being catered?" Ebele looked at the clock that hung on the wall. They had a good five hours before the dinner party started at seven. Nse, who owned an event planning company, loved to put on dinner parties just because. They were intimate events where good friends talked about everything from the latest news to the Word of God.

Ebele loved them. The only drawback was everyone was coupled up, and she found herself the odd woman out. There were times she didn't attend, but Nse wasn't having it this time. She hadn't attended one in several months. This one was special because it was the first one of the new year. Nse held it off until the second week of January to give her time to settle back into school.

"Yes, the caterer will deliver to Tega's place by six." She scooped a little of the steaming soup on her palm and licked it, tasting it for flavor. "Ebele, come and taste this."

"Ah ah, didn't you just taste it? Don't your taste buds work?" Ebele jested.

"If you don't bring your *oyinbo* behind here and taste this…"

"Why do people always feel they can bully me?" Ebele sniggered and walked to the stove. Instead of putting it on her palm, Nse scooped some of the soup into a bowl and handed it to her.

"I'm putting meat in this plate. Tell me whether it's soft enough," Nse said.

Ebele's face flushed, as it always did when she ate anything spicy. She should have enough sense to stay away, but she loved spicy food. Her mother made sure she knew how to cook every Nigerian dish possible. She closed her eyes to savor the flavor and moaned. "It's so good, but you don't need me to tell you that."

Nse placed the piece of meat in her bowl. "Here, and don't think I didn't hear what you said."

"What?" Ebele cut the meat and put a piece in her mouth.

"Who else is bullying you? Is Victor back stalking you again?

Ebele started to laugh. Her laughter turned into a cough. Hurriedly, she got a glass of water. Nse patted her on her back as she drank. Once her coughing subsided, Ebele shrugged her friend off.

"Leave me *jor*. You knew I was eating pepper and you decided to be a comedian."

"Sorry *na*. Ms. Sensitive. But back to my question. Is it Victor?"

"No." Ebele sniggered. "I don't know how many times I'll tell that man no. That chapter has since been closed. If I didn't take my greedy self to Shoprite that day looking for shortbread, I never would've run into him again."

Nse waved her off. "Don't pay him any attention. So, if it's not him, then who?"

Ebele thought for a minute. "No one." She didn't know if she was ready to share her Kammy experience with anyone. Even her best friend. Unknowingly, a grin crept up the corner of her lips. She felt her face become hot. She hated that she could never hide her feelings because of how light her skin was.

"It's a lie." Nse clapped her hands together in her usual over dramatic nature. She turned off the stove and pulled out a chair at the dinette where Ebele sat. "Spill – who is he and where did you meet him? How come you haven't said anything? *Na wa o*, is that how best friends behave?"

Ebele rolled her eyes and shook her head. "If you can be quiet, I can answer at least one of your questions."

"*Oya* go ahead. See hurry up so you can have a nap before we go. You look like you've been run over."

"I have no words for you. Just know some screws are missing."

"I love you too. *Oya* give me the *tafia*."

"There's no *tafia* to give, really. I told you about the first-class thing—"

"*Ehen*, so?"

"Can you let me finish?" Ebele huffed. "I met this guy on that flight. We clicked. I'm not talking about physical stuff either. Don't get me wrong; he's a fine piece of caramel, but I mean we talked like we've known each other forever. It was strange."

"Are you serious?" Nse gasped and put her hand over her mouth.

"To be such a bully, you're so dramatic."

"Leave me *jor*. You might not appreciate it, but I remember how broken you were after Victor. It was like you had nothing to hope for anymore." Nse sniffed, and Ebele remained silent. She remembered.

"No matter how much I, your mom or grandma talked, you stayed in your dark place. Even your father started calling, and you wouldn't budge."

"I came to Christ," Ebele whispered.

Nse grabbed her friend's hands. "You did my friend, and you found hope in Him. But my sis, you still don't fully trust Him."

Ebele frowned. "What are you talking about?"

"You can't see what I'm saying because it's you. But for almost five years, you've refused to entertain any possibility of the opposite sex. You've carried the blame and burden for what happened to you and held on." Nse paused. "What you went through wasn't great, but it was by design. For you to deepen your capacity for God and for others to see His glory through you. That can't happen if you remain closed. The Bible tells us to cast our burdens, but you're still holding on to yours. Until now. Seeing you blush because of a man tells me you're opening a slight window." Nse wiped the tears that welled up in her eyes.

Ebele absorbed what her friend said. Was there truth in her spill? She berated herself every day for putting her trust and self-worth in a man or in her own might, completely obliterating God from the process. But even if she were opening a slight window, there wasn't any need. She had no idea where Kamal was and was still scared to Google him.

"Well, there's no use anyway."

"Why? Please don't tell me you used your sharp mouth and nerdy sense to chase the man away."

"I'm going to ignore that. Besides my mouth and brain are part of the package." She wiggled her brows. Just because she was a homebody who liked to read and was curious about life didn't mean she lacked social skills.

"I hear you. So, why's there no use?"

"We got off the plane, and he didn't ask for my number. So maybe he wasn't interested."

"*Chai Abasi Mbom*! My God! So? Why didn't you ask for his?"

"Stop being dramatic. He's a celebrity, and I didn't want to look like a groupie." Ebele stood and took her empty plate to the sink. She emptied the bones in the trash and washed the dish.

"Celebrity! That changes everything. *You wey dey fear* paparazzi." Nse snickered. "This life *ehen* … I remember when you and Victor loved the paparazzi."

"Well, he did, and I didn't. That was, then this is now." Ebele's tone was curt.

"I didn't mean anything by it. *No vex.*" Nse went to her cabinet and got out a decorative bowl with a cover. She held it as Ebele started to scoop the hot soup into it. "So out of curiosity, who's this celebrity that has my girl cheesing and broke down some of her walls with one conversation?"

"You might not know him. He plays football *abi na* soccer in America. Kamal Danjuma. They call him Kammy *sha.*" Ebele noticed the bowl wobble in Nse's hand. She dropped the spoon to help steady the bowl. "What's wrong with you? Do you want to spill the soup?"

"Err, no. You say you sat next to Kammy Danjuma on that plane?"

Ebele sighed and picked up the spoon. "Yeah, do you know him?"

Nse ignored her and with one hand, reached for a paper towel to wipe a small spill on the counter.

"Anyway, like I said, there's no use," Ebele said.

Once she was done, Nse abruptly placed the bowl on the counter and covered it. She took the spoon from Ebele and shooed her out of the kitchen.

"*Oya* my dear, *you do well.* Thank you for helping me in the kitchen. Go and take a beauty nap. I'll wake you in two hours. You need to wash this your wild mane so we can style it." She paused. Ebele assumed to get air in her lungs. She continued, "*Ha!* What dress did you bring? Don't worry. We'll figure it out when you wake up."

"Nse, are you okay? Why are you being over-the-top extra?"

"I'm so fine, it's ridiculous. Happy that the Lord works in mysterious ways."

"Huh?"

"Nothing, go to the room you always use and sleep well. I'll wake you when it's time to start getting ready."

Ebele looked at her friend, perplexed at her change in behavior. She wanted to dig further, but a yawn escaped her lips. She'd been going nonstop the past couple of weeks. If she was going to be any good tonight, she needed to sleep. And that was exactly what she was going to do. She'd figure out Nse later.

Chapter 7

K amal circled the block three times before finding Tega's home in Loughton. At this rate, he was going to be a few minutes late. He was terrible with directions. That and his legs being cooped up for long periods of time were why he hated driving.

When he pulled up at the gate, he put in the code and proceeded down the long driveway. Tega had bought the six thousand square foot Victorian style house when he proposed to Nse. Kamal always liked that the detached property set on two acres of land and had gorgeous landscaping at the front and back.

He parked his silver Maserati in the corner lot and retrieved the flowers and store-bought pound cake for Nse. He would've gotten a bottle of wine, but with the extensive cellar in the house, he didn't see the need. Tega wasn't a drinker but loved collecting old bottles of wine. Kamal pressed the fob to lock the doors and pocketed his keys.

Tega told him to dress casual for dinner. Kamal, however, preferred to be overdressed than under. Underneath his tweed coat, he had on a gray sharkskin suit paired with a black, cashmere turtleneck sweater. The cold was blistering, so his hands were in leather gloves, and a scarf protected his neck. He rang the doorbell. A few minutes later, the door opened to a smiling Nse. He hadn't seen her since the engagement a couple of years ago.

"Look who we have here." She opened the door wider for him to enter. After shutting the door, she reached up for a hug.

He smiled back at her and put his free arm around her. "Happy New Year, sis. You know how important you are to me. I can't be on your bad side."

"I can't tell. You've been in the UK for almost two weeks now."

"There you go, trying to clock my moves. The only moves you should be clocking are my boy's," Kamal teased.

She popped him on his shoulder.

"Ouch, woman. Here." He handed her the flowers and cake.

"Thank you." She kissed his cheek in appreciation.

"Why do you have my woman kissing on you? How many times must I tell you to get your own?" Tega's voice caused them to turn around in its direction.

"Man, whatever. I do have my own," Kamal said.

Tega and Nse shared a glance and snickered. He and Tega engaged in a man hug.

"Man, you're late, and I'm hungry, so we're gonna leave that 'I have one' comment alone," Tega said.

Nse turned and walked to the kitchen while he and Tega walked into the living room. There, Kamal was introduced to another couple Tega said was from his church. Soon after, they settled into light conversation ranging from the Premiere League and the standing of the various clubs to the upcoming Brexit vote. A few minutes into their conversation, Nse came to usher them to the dining table.

"Let me wash my hands. The bathroom is down the hall, right?" Kamal asked.

Nse responded with a nod and what he thought was a

grin. He wondered for a second what she was up to. He hoped she didn't have one of her friends staged somewhere. Before he started dating Brittani, she'd tried to set him up whenever he visited. She'd done it twice before and both times were disasters. He even told her that he wouldn't come if she did it again. She didn't like Brittani for the same reason as Tega, but she respected the relationship. Therefore, he quickly dismissed the thought of her being up to no good.

He walked down the hallway adorned with pictures of the Seven Wonders of the World. Tega was obsessed with art and collected pieces all the time.

"Mummy, go to bed. I'll call you in the morning. I'm with Nse."

He'd heard that voice before and like the last time, air caught in his throat. The raspy melody stirred his gut. Temporarily halting in his tracks, he filled his lungs with air and closed his eyes. Maybe he was imagining things. He'd thought about her so much over the last two weeks that he could be hallucinating. Kamal rounded the corner and the laughter that he'd replayed in his mind a thousand times filled the air. Slowing his steps, he came face to face with what only could be described as perfection on legs. By the way her mouth dropped, she was equally shocked.

"Err, I really have to go now. Yes, I'm fine. Talk to you later," she said, her eyes locked with his.

Not trusting his owns words now, his eyes travelled to the phone in her hand. He stretched out his hand towards her. She looked at him in confusion and traced the direction of his stare.

"Let me see your phone." The authority in his tone couldn't be ignored. In silent reluctance, she handed it to him.

He looked down at it and smiled briefly at her face as the screen saver. He dialed his number and waited for the vibration in his pants pocket to tell him the call had connected. The only thing on his mind was never having to go through the days he went through without a way to talk to her. He handed her back her iPhone.

"Still bossy, I see," she quipped with a smile. Her lips parted and showcased her perfect white teeth.

He felt a twinge around the area of his heart. "And you're still judging my innocent actions, so we're even."

So beautiful. A million adjectives to describe her came along, but they all boiled down to one word. Beautiful. Unlike when he saw her the last time, she had her wild mane in a poof at her neck. He had to restrain himself from reaching out and removing the bow-like string that held her hair hostage. She didn't have on any noticeable makeup except for brown eyeliner and lip gloss. The pink and brown sweater dress she had on hugged her curves. As he said before —beautiful.

"How are you here?" she asked.

"Tega is my boy. We've been close since we were six years old."

"So he's your bestie?" she smirked.

"Men don't have besties. He's, my boy." He paused. "What about you?"

"Well, Nse *is* my bestie. We grew up together."

He did the mental calculation in his head. How was that possible? Nse had long ago graduated college and was running her own business. Based on what Ebele told him, she was in her final year for her first degree. How could they be the same age? Ebele had to be much younger.

"Wow! This world is too small."

"I know, right? I thought I would never lay eyes on you again," she said in a low whisper. She lowered her eyes. Maybe because like him, voicing that feeling made it a reality. He walked closer to her until she was backed up against the wall. He looked down on her and used his index finger to lift her head.

"Don't bend your head to me, ever." Her perfume tickled

his nostrils, making his senses painfully aware of her feminine appeal.

Ebele looked up at him with reservation in her eyes.

He bent to her ear and whispered, "By the way, I thought the same thing."

The brief silence between them was interrupted when Nse appeared. Kamal looked over at her.

"For once, you got it right." He winked and proceeded to the bathroom to wash his hands.

Kamal walked into the bathroom and rested against the closed door. A few seconds later, he pushed himself up and stared at his reflection in the mirror. He'd never been one to believe in serendipity, but without a doubt that was what he was experiencing right now. He stared a little more to make sure that the riot going on in his mind wasn't visible to the naked eye.

After drying his hands, he reached for his phone and scrolled to the missed call from Ebele's phone. He saved her number as "My E." His gut stirred and he felt a light rumbling in his stomach. He didn't know now whether it was hunger or the acknowledgment that the E, which stood for Ebele right now, had the potential to stand for "Everything."

———

Kamal studied Ebele from across the table as he idly twirled his spoon in the pepper soup. Dinner proceeded smoothly over light conversation. Nse, the quintessential host, treated them to a meal of Jollof Rice, plantains, peppered snails, and fried fish. No matter how hard he tried, Kamal couldn't keep his eyes off Ebele, who was seated opposite him. When their eyes connected, it was as though they spoke their own language. He was surprised Tega or Nse hadn't called him on it.

From the conversation, he learned more about her and

that she was attending his *alma mater*. Inwardly, he rejoiced when she said that. It would make pop ups easier as he knew the layout of the school perfectly. He also learned that her placement would bring her from school to a rehabilitation center here in Essex two times a week for three hours.

All he wanted right now was for them to be finished with dinner, so he could get her alone. As though she felt his gaze, her eyes connected with his and softened with a smile that messed up his insides.

"Kammy, what do you think?"

The mention of his name interrupted their silent communication. He had no idea what they were talking about. He looked at Tega. "What do I think about what?"

"Who is Argentina's greatest player? Maradona or Messi?" Tega's guest, who he'd come to know as Paul, asked.

"Some say Maradona, and some say Messi. Messi is great and has done a lot. However, a lot of people in Argentina don't acknowledge him as the greatest, because despite his accomplishments, he hasn't won Argentina anything," Kamal explained. "But Maradona constantly puts Argentina on the map by winning them championships."

"I told you," Tega shouted. "I don't care how much you do for outsiders. You have to give back to home."

"Sometimes those at home are just ungrateful," Paul said.

At that point, the ladies stood and headed to the kitchen with some dishes. They came back shortly after and began tidying up the table. Kamal and Tega stopped them and shooed them to the living room so that they could handle clean-up. Minutes later, working in a system, the men had the kitchen spotless, and dishes clean, and stacked. Paul excused himself to the restroom while Tega pulled out a barstool at the kitchen island. He gestured for Kamal to do the same.

"You and Ebele?" Tega asked.

Kamal's brow shot up. "Is there a question there?"

"What's the deal? Because you looked like you wanted us all to disappear, so you could have her to yourself."

Kamal ran his hand over his head. Tega was his closest friend, but he wasn't good at the whole "talk about your feelings" thing. The only person he did that with was Jabir. He contemplated for a moment and figured it wouldn't hurt to change his strategy this time. Since Tega had known Ebele longer, he might be able to help him with some information. Over the next several minutes, Kamal ran down the story from the plane to the present.

"Wow, man, talk about love at first sight," Tega said.

"Who said anything about love?" Kamal asked.

"You did, but you don't know it yet."

"So what's her deal?" Kamal asked, ignoring Tega's comment.

"Man, I'm not giving away that woman's secrets. It's her story to tell. I'll tell you this – she cares zero about your celebrity. So to get her, you're going to have to be Kamal Danjuma."

"I kinda figured that out already—"

"No, I mean for real for real. She couldn't care less, and the reason goes deeper than that's how she is. It's personal." Tega gave him a pointed look.

Kamal wanted to speak but couldn't find the words to say. He was back to feeling he didn't need another complication in his life right at this point.

"What I would say though, is that she's a church girl. So, you either come correct or not at all."

"That's the problem. After seeing her again tonight, the not at all part is no longer an option." Kamal rubbed his forehead.

"But what are you trying to do, though? Aren't you going back to LA? You'll be loving across the seas?" Tega chuckled.

"I told you to cut the 'L' word out. As for the other thing, let me worry about that. It might not be a thing after all. I might be staying in the UK." He paused as her face invaded his mind. "I must have her in some capacity. Even if it's as friends."

"Man, yeah, right. Your mouth and eyes are saying two different things, my brother. After what I saw tonight, there's no 'just friends,' but lemme know how that works out for you." Tega patted him on the back and left the kitchen.

Kamal stayed rooted in place. The mystery that was Ebele had just become more intriguing as Tega's words replayed in his mind. *"The reason goes deeper than that's how she is. It's personal."*

"A kobo for your thoughts?"

Kamal was so deep in thought that he hadn't noticed Ebele entered the kitchen. "Dang E, just a kobo?" Kobo was the Nigerian equivalent of a penny. With the exchange rate, it was much less. She walked up to him and took the seat Tega previously occupied.

"Well, a kobo-and-a-half, I guess," she said.

"How about I take you to breakfast tomorrow, so you can see my thoughts are worth much more than that."

"I know they are. I was just teasing."

"I wasn't, so will you allow me feed you?" His eyes pleaded for her not to turn him down.

"Don't soccer players like train or something on the weekends?"

"Yeah, we like train or something, but we still have to eat. Tomorrow, we have half a day, so we'll be done by 9:30."

"I really do have a lot of schoolwork to —"

"But you still have to eat. If I didn't know any better, I'd think you're trying to blow me off." He turned his lips up in a pout. His pout normally got him what he wanted. It was a stretch, but he might as well try it on her.

Ebele frowned at him, shaking her head. Her eyes danced with laughter. "Don't do that. It's not cute, but okay."

He stood and rubbed his hands together. "Cute or not, it worked. End game baby, end game." At the mention of the term of endearment, their eyes held for a long moment. He cleared his throat to get rid of the awkwardness. He never wanted her to feel uncomfortable. "Come, walk me out."

Ebele stood, and he stepped aside for her to walk in front of him. Not only was he a gentleman, but he couldn't resist the view. When he got to the living room, he said his goodbyes to his hosts. His eyes signaled his hosts to remain seated when they tried to escort him out. Catching on, they stayed in place.

Ebele walked him through the foyer to retrieve his coat. She remained silent as he put on his winter apparel. Once he was done, he turned toward her. Again, her eyes avoided his. He used his index finger to turn her head to him. "What did I tell you about that?"

She gave him a faint smile.

"Don't get shy on me. I'll be by Nse's house to pick you up by ten." He leaned down and kissed her forehead. Her hair smelled of coconut and strawberries, driving him completely bananas.

"Okay. Good night," she said, softly.

Kamal opened the door and walked the short distance to his car. He got into the driver's seat and placed his head on the steering wheel. His heart raced. He raised his head and looked at the closed door. Behind the wooden frame was the woman at the center of his peril.

His phone chimed, indicating he had a text message. He opened it up, and it was Brittani telling him to check Instagram. When he opened the app, he saw a picture where she'd tagged him. She was at a pool party surrounded by her friends. For the first time, her half naked body didn't bring him any sense of pride. She'd captioned the picture, "Living it up #footballwife."

He shook his head, tossed the phone aside and started the car. He needed to get a handle on that ASAP. He might not be sure about what was going on with him and Ebele, but he knew for sure Brittani wasn't going to be his wife.

Chapter 8

Later that night, Ebele walked into her bedroom at Nse's. She unzipped her boots and began to undress for a shower. Wrapping a towel around herself, she walked into the attached bathroom. She was finally able to exhale and hear her own thoughts. Thoughts that had been clouded by Kamal's presence and Nse's barrage of questions. The irony of it all was that she didn't have answers to give.

Back when she was in a relationship with Victor, she had never experienced the level of intensity she felt when she was with Kamal. She'd normally run the opposite direction when it came to someone like him. A celebrity. Wealthy. Heart wrenchingly handsome and spoiled.

As she stepped into the shower, she beamed at the mental picture of him. The water cascaded her body as she thought about breakfast the next day. She'd be with him alone. Nse had declined her numerous pleas for them to make it a double date. According to her, she and Tega already had plans that couldn't be changed. Ebele had been alone with him before, but the awareness of what was happening between them now scared her a little.

After her shower, she dressed for bed and said her prayers.

With her back against the headboard, she turned through the pages of her worn Bible. The words between the pages of that Bible had been her saving grace. It was marked up in so many ways. Some of the pages were rumpled, but she wasn't changing it. She flipped through the guide at the back. She needed a verse on being anxious and afraid. She found Psalm 139:23, but she decided to read the whole chapter. *Search me, O Lord and know my heart; try me and know my anxious thoughts. And see if there are any hurtful ways in me. Lead me in the everlasting way.*

Thinking about what Nse said earlier and hanging out with Kamal, made her realize she wanted to step out again. She wanted to no longer be afraid. However, she didn't want the kind of relationship she'd had with Victor. Back then, everything hung on his word. He was the center of her universe. Instead of him bringing her closer to God, he took her away. Or rather she took herself away because of what she felt was his love for her. That was why when he left, she fell to the bottom quickly. Whether Kamal became anything other than a friend to her, she wanted God to be able to lead her. She'd only entrust her heart to him when she was convinced he'd entrusted his to God.

A familiar ding went off. She looked at the timer on the dresser; 11:45 p.m. Confused, she looked for her phone. Opening the text, her lips turned up in amusement at the message.

7778197567: **You still up?**

Her: **Who is this?**

7778197567: **Ouch, that hurt.**

She waited a few seconds before typing another response.

Her: **Since u don't want to disclose your identity, I'm going to bed.**

7778197567: **Y so early? Big day tmrw?**

What was he talking about, early? It was almost midnight. After the second text, she had figured it was Kamal but decided to play with him a little. She giggled. He'd expect an immediate answer, so she delayed her response. *Let him stew a little.*

7778197567: **E? Ebele? Pls don't make me drive over there to get a response.**

Ebele cracked a smile but concluded she didn't know how far his crazy went, and she wasn't prepared to find out. Nse did say that he lived here in Essex as well.

Her: **Stop whining, big baby. I knew it was you.**

7778197567: **Who you having breakfast with?**

Ebele noticed he still wanted to play, so she decided to indulge him.

Her: **One boring jock I just met, nothing important. After that, I have a paper to write.**

7778197567: **E, you playin' with me, right? In fact, I know you're playin'.**

His text came with a side eye emoji. Ebele replied with a series of laughing emojis.

7778197567: **I see you think you're funny now ... Good night, big head.**

Her: **I *am* funny. Good night & sweet dreams.**

7778197567: **They're already sweet b'cos you in 'em.**

Ebele's body tingled as she read his last text. *This man is so corny. Who would've known?*

Things were so easy between them, but she, of all people, knew that easy and sweet didn't last long. She stared at the last text again. She went into her contacts to save him as "Kam." She tucked her phone under her pillow and lay down. As excited as having him close to her felt, she also knew he had the ability to do major damage to her heart. At the end of the day, her need for self-preservation trumped everything. She'd give a little bit, but definitely not all.

———

THE NEXT MORNING, AFTER HER MORNING ROUTINE OF PRAYER and meditation, she got ready for the day. Nse had left, so she had the house to herself. Kamal would soon be here, and she didn't want to be in the house with him alone any more than necessary. She slipped on her size six jeans and pulled her olive-green sweater over her head. She brushed her contoured brows, applied eyeliner, and strawberry flavored lip gloss. From the time Ebele knew what makeup was, those were the only things she used. She put on her stud earrings and fluffed up her wild, curly mane that had air dried. Finishing off her look with her black boots and black leather jacket, she was ready to go. She grabbed her purse as the doorbell rang. Giving herself one last glance in the mirror, she headed for the door.

Ebele inhaled and opened the door on the second ring of the bell. There was no way he could look better than last night. But he did. Kamal looked like he dropped out of a magazine, and he was dressed down. Clad in a navy-blue sweater that hugged his muscular chest with low-slung blue jeans that sat in tan Timberlands, he effortlessly oozed swag. She must have remained frozen in place because the next thing she heard, was him clearing his throat. She needed to get herself together. She'd just given herself a lecture on self-preservation.

"Hi." He glanced over the apartment and returned his eyes to her.

"Hey." She was proud of herself for keeping her voice at a recognizable octave.

"You ready?" He smiled down at her.

Her stomach fluttered at his voice. That stud in his ear probably cost her whole tuition.

"Sure, lemme get the keys." She grabbed the spare from the coffee table, secured her bag on her shoulder, and headed back toward him.

After they exited, Kamal took the keys from her, locked

the door, and handed them back. He escorted her to his Lexus SUV. She let out a sigh of relief that he wasn't driving the Maserati. Those fast cars scared her. He opened the door to the vehicle and helped her in. He reached over and secured her seatbelt. The rich, musky scent of his cologne tickled her senses. She clenched her hands to stop from touching him. Her behavior surprised her because her attraction to him was nothing like she'd experienced before. He tapped the tip of her nose with his index finger and shut the door. She leaned over to open the door for him.

"Thanks, E," he said.

Kamal secured his seatbelt, started the car, and pulled out of Nse's driveway. Ebele's heartbeat increased. She'd been so overtaken by excitement and spending time with him that she temporarily forgot the fact that he was a celebrity and the press factor.

"Where are you taking me?" she asked.

"What are you in the mood for?" He glanced at her and focused back on the road. "I heard of this nice restaurant that has great food. You wanna try it out with me?"

"Sounds good. I hope we won't get mugged by your fans."

"No, but does my celebrity bother you?"

She contemplated how much to tell him and decided she might as well go for it. It might not be a deal breaker.

"Not yours specifically, but any kind of unnecessary fanfare. As quick as the media takes you up and places you on a pedestal, is exactly how quick they are to put you down and crush you." Her jaw clenched as she thought about it.

"Seems like you're speaking from experience. Are you?"

"Yes and no."

He chuckled. "How's that possible?"

"I don't have a problem with your celebrity. I'm weary of the press."

"Okay, I get that. Explain."

"I didn't go to college right out of high school," Ebele said.

Kamal nodded as though a light bulb clicked for him.

She continued, "I was the choreographer and dancer for a popular band in Nigeria. When we got signed to a label, we kinda blew up. After people knew me, I got jobs to choreograph for big names." She paused. "Do you know Flavour or Chidinma?"

"Yeah, I've heard of them." He put his index finger under his chin. "Wow, E, so you're big time? I'm honored to be in your presence."

"Stop it. Anyway, I was … for Naija. I did that for seven years before it ended with an injury. Plus, my partner, the one I originally started the group with, left me in the dust. The press had a field day, and that drove me into depression. The stories they made up were false and nasty."

"Wow, E. What type of injury?"

"It was a compression fracture that affected two of my vertebrae. Right in the middle of my back."

"I'm so sorry. It was your partner's loss. She'll regret it one day," he said.

Ebele didn't want to dwell on that time. It was horrible. She also noticed he assumed her partner was a woman. She wasn't ready to put a damper on their day. They weren't dating or anything, but she felt awkward talking about another guy. So she didn't bother to correct him. She creased her forehead when they turned onto a dusty road.

Where is he taking me now?

As though reading her thoughts, he said, "Don't have that look on your face. I'll never harm you."

"Funny, but somehow I know that," she said, softly.

"Good. I'm going to be straight though; I plan on getting to know you. Dealing with me means you'd have to be in my world to an extent."

"Who says I want to deal with you?" she scrunched her nose up.

"E, the moment you got in my car. That was the deal."

"So spoiled." She glanced at him, and he shrugged.

"Anyway, I want you to myself, so I got you. We're going to another café I know. It's quaint, homey, and the owners always accommodate me when I visit the UK."

"What do you mean accommodate?"

"They put me in the back at a private table, and let me come in and leave through the rear with no issues. And their food is also out of this world." He adjusted his Bluetooth and dialed a number. After a brief conversation with who she assumed to be the owner of the café, he hung up.

Ebele was pleased by his thoughtfulness. Minutes later, they made it to the café. He got out of the car, helped her out, and took her hand in his as they walked through the back entrance, where someone was already waiting. They were shown to their seats, and Ebele was impressed. From the exterior, no one would imagine what the interior looked like. It had a main dining area that could be viewed from the VIP area, but it didn't seem as though those on the main dining area could see through the same glass. Neutral and dark tones adorned the space, giving it a warm feel. Kamal helped her out of her coat and draped it across the back of her chair. He took his off and did the same. The host passed them their menus and left.

"How was practice?" Ebele asked.

"Cool. Same old things – running tracks, cardio, stretches; you know, the whole nine." He placed his phone face down on the table. "We go on the road on Wednesday. I'm excited. It'll be my first game with the team."

"I remember you saying on the plane your team was the LA Sun Sides. So how does playing in the UK work?"

Ebele listened attentively as he explained to her how loaners worked between the US and Europe. It was more common in the winter when the US soccer season was out, and the Premier season for Europe was still in full swing. Players would come over to the UK on loan. Both the parent team and the loan team would agree on terms and how the player would get paid during the duration of the loan. She inquired why a player would want to do that. Kamal told her some did it to keep themselves fit during the off-season. Some needed a fresh start.

"What's your reason?" Ebele asked.

"Still nosey."

"I'm not nosey." She looked over her shoulder. "I'm out here with you. I need to know why you ran away from home."

Kamal's head went back in laughter. "You're back to being a comedian. I still have a sleeper hold with your name on it."

She sucked her teeth and rolled her eyes. "You're just a bully. Answer the question."

"You mean you haven't Googled me?"

She turned her lips up and shook her head. "I don't do Google. Didn't I tell you in the car, the Internet is vicious? People stay behind their electronics and are mean for no reason."

"I get what you mean." He paused when the waiter walked up. They both placed their orders of coffee, juice, baked beans, sausages, eggs, and toast.

"Back to my question. Why did you leave the US?" She kept her gaze on him and pushed her hair behind her ear.

"There was tension between my team management and me." His expression was nonchalant. "I wasn't playing my best toward the end of the season, coupled with the fact that I got into certain situations I shouldn't have. Things were kinda rocky. So before they could cut me, my agent got me this gig." He looked around, then brought his eyes back to her. She saw apprehension in them. She could recognize it because it was the same fear she had when she was injured.

"Why do I feel like you're cutting out the juicy part?" She

waited for a response, but none came. "Anyway, what's your end game?"

He sipped his water. "Huh?"

"Why are you here? You told me what made you come here, but why are you here?"

"To play good ball."

"That can't be it."

"What are you? A psychiatrist now?" His tone was laced with light sarcasm.

"No. But as part of my study of physiotherapy, I don't only deal with the physical but emotional and mental issues as well. Empathy and compassion. Giving the injured a reason to get back to their former quality of life."

"I'm impressed. Really, I am. Beauty and brains. But I told you what it is," Kamal stated.

"Okay, if you say so."

Their food arrived right on time. A thick blanket of tension had developed between them. She missed the light banter they had going on. Why did she have to open her big mouth all the time? After the food was set on the table and the waiter left, she stretched her hands, and he placed his in them. She blessed the food. When she let go of his hand, their eyes connected both, acknowledging without words the energy between them.

After a few moments, Kamal spoke. "You've tried to unravel my deeper issues. Now, your turn."

"My turn for what?"

"Tell me about yourself."

"Oh, Ebele Ashiedu, twenty-nine, student, you already know. British dad, *Naija* mom, and only child."

"So why physiotherapy? You've told me what you're doing, but why are you doing it?" He smirked, using her own words back at her.

Ebele smiled. "That's simple. After my injury, there weren't any affordable methods or facilities where I could've been rehabilitated." She stared off into the distance as she remembered one doctor after another turning her mother away until her mother decided to pursue native means and dragged her from one herbalist to the other. Ebele gave up and sunk deeper into depression with Victor gone. That was when her mother reached out to her father for help.

"When I graduate, my goal is to open one of such facilities in Abuja. It'll be a state of the art rehabilitation center which will also include a wellness center." She paused. "It'll be equipped enough to cater to the well-off as well as those who need some kind of payment arrangements."

"Wow. That sounds fantastic. How are you going to fund it?"

"Thanks. I plan to work in the UK for about a year while I build up collateral before I approach the bank for a loan."

"Nice. Good one, E." A beat of silence passed between them. "I can tell you're close to your mom. What about your dad?" Kamal asked.

"I'm not. I don't know him except that he had an affair with my mom when he was an expatriate in *Naija*. Had me, denied me, and later came back looking for 'redemption' I guess." She made air quotes at the word redemption.

Kamal lowered his head for a moment. "If there's any advice I can give you as someone whose dad abandoned him too, accept his plea for redemption or forgiveness before it's too late," he said, quietly.

Ebele placed her fork on her plate. "I so want to, but how do you build a relationship with someone who's not even meeting you halfway?" She explained the predicament she found herself in with her dad.

"I don't have the answers, but I remember my sis-in-law, Ibiso is always saying forgiveness isn't about forgetting the deeds of the other but not allowing them to dictate yours. When you get to the point you don't talk about him with bitterness, only then have you forgiven and can build anything.

People can't give more than they have. So maybe he's giving you all he has now," Kamal finished in a pensive tone.

Ebele decided she didn't like the pensive Kamal. It showed his depth, and what he said gave her something to think about. She wanted her jovial bully back. She decided to change the topic. "Are you close to your sisters-in-law or your stepsister?"

He lit up in delight. "Yes. Ibiso and Damisi are like sisters to me. They both compliment my brothers. Halima, now that's my baby. She's three years younger than I am and works for my older brother. She's a globetrotter."

Ebele felt a pang of envy as he talked with so much love about the women in his life. They were his family, so she had no business feeling that way, but she did. "So what about you?"

"Me what?" he asked.

"Any plans of getting married or settling down one day?"

"Yeah, once you stop playing." He wiggled his eyebrows.

She laughed softly. "Kam, I'm serious."

"So I'm Kam now? I must be wearing you down. You're giving me nicknames and stuff."

"I see you want to play."

"I'm gonna let you think that for now." Kamal went back to his food.

Without words, they decided to let go of the heavy topics. The rest of their food was eaten with light chatter about much less sensitive topics. On Kamal's insistence, they shared their schedules with each other. Soon after, they were done and on their way.

On the drive back, they listened to Musiq Soulchild. Kamal's choice of music continued to surprise her. Ebele assumed that as playful as he was, he'd like loud music with no message in the lyrics. All her assumptions about him were being shot down, one after the other. Once they arrived, he parked the car, got out, and came around to help her out. Grabbing her hand, he walked her to the door.

"Thank you for breakfast. I had a wonderful time," Ebele said.

"No, thank you for agreeing to spend time with me."

They stared at each other. Kamal took a step closer to her, causing the squeeze around her heart to tighten. She wanted to reach out and touch him. The intensity caused her to lower her head, as she was becoming light headed. He lifted her head with his index finger and caressed her cheek.

"May I?" His eyes fixed on her lips.

Unable to speak, she nodded her consent. He bent down and brushed his lips against hers. He lingered but didn't attempt to invade her mouth. He was so tender. A few seconds later, he let her lips go and pulled her into him. She wrapped her arms around his waist. How she'd imagined this moment was nothing compared to reality.

Her head stopped right at his heart. Ebele relished in the knowledge that she was the cause of its erratic beat. She recognized it because it mirrored hers. She affected him as much as he affected her. She smirked. It was good to know that she wasn't out there by herself. Unfortunately, undeniable chemistry wouldn't be enough to sustain whatever this was if their hearts didn't also beat in unison for Christ.

After several moments, Kamal broke the embrace. "Imma let you go. I'll call you. Don't be screening my calls either, asking who this is."

She chuckled. They held eye contact for a few seconds before she opened the door and went into the house.

Chapter 9

A little after dawn the next morning, still in his pajamas, Kamal lounged on the leather recliner in his living room. The huge, flat screen television was mute on BBC News while a medley of Nigerian praise and worship songs played in the background. Something he did almost every Sunday. Staring at the fireplace lost in thought, he took a spoonful of his cold cereal.

Today was an off day, and he was supposed to be taking a breather, but rest eluded him. Instead, his mind kept wandering to the angel that seemed to come out of nowhere. The minute he saw Ebele, he knew she was different. He'd settled with the fact that he'd never see her again. As the days passed, he attributed the feeling to longing for what he couldn't have.

After seeing her again, he realized he was so wrong. Kamal knew he had no business getting involved with anyone considering his situation with Brittani, but he couldn't let Ebele get away from him. When she asked about his plans for marriage, he'd surprised himself with his answer. Marriage wasn't a thought that crossed his mind. Talk less of getting married to someone he'd barely known a week.

Kamal finished up his cereal and reached for his sketchpad on the coffee table. He'd studied architecture at university, and although he didn't practice, he still loved to draw. It helped calm him. He drew anything from buildings to landscapes to people. He thought about Ebele's future rehabilitation and wellness clinic. He stared at a blank page for a minute, then with light strokes of his pencil, got lost in his imagination.

Sometime later, his stomach rumbled. Kamal smiled in satisfaction as he looked at what he envisioned the center would look like if he designed it. Setting down his pad, he rubbed his stomach. It was time for some real breakfast. He walked into the kitchen, deciding he was in the mood for an omelet and some toast. Setting the items needed to the side, he returned to the living room to pick up his iPad. Steadying it on the island in an upright position, he dialed Halima on Skype. He hadn't talked to her in a while. Rasheed relied on her the most when it came to running Danjuma Group, and that kept her busy.

"What's up, little girl?" Kamal greeted her when her face appeared on the screen. He recognized her living room in Lagos in the background. When she was sent to Lagos from Abuja, she wasn't too fond of the idea but now loved it.

"*Dan uwa na,*" she greeted him back with a smile. She called Jabir and Rasheed by their names but referred to him as "my brother." Her voice was always so soft, and her disposition demure. Their first meeting was when he was sixteen, and she was thirteen. Kamal thought something was wrong with her because she'd never say anything. If she did, her voice never moved above a set octave.

"You can't call your big brother no more?" he asked.

"You love that title, don't you?" she teased.

"What? Of course, it's my entitlement." He took his eyes off the screen to cut up the vegetables for his meal.

"Almost everything you think you're entitled to," she said.

"So what's good? I see you don't have that thing on your head, so you must be staying home today." He felt her auburn-colored hair suited her and would've liked her to wear it out more. However, he understood it was her Muslim thing.

"It's called a hijab, and yes, I'm at home today. I'll be going to Namibia tomorrow, but I should be able to come by and see you soon."

"I get a visit from the jet-setter baby sis. How lucky am I? How's your mum?"

"Don't say it like that. I always have time for you. Mum is fine. You know, ever since Rasheed, the *real* big brother, set her up with those boutiques, she's always in Dubai shopping."

"Real big brother? I see everyone wants to be funny nowadays." He put two slices of wheat bread in the toaster.

"Who's everyone?"

"Huh?"

"*Dan uwa na*, come on. You said everyone. I know you, so who are we talking about? A woman? A new one? Or is this the one you have already?"

Kamal stared at her and laughed. "Detective Danjuma, don't be trying to clock my moves."

"I have no idea what that means, but you didn't answer the question, so I'm going to take that as confirmation."

Kamal shook his head at her. He was forever explaining American or British slang to her. She schooled in Britain, and was well travelled, but stayed proper. He pondered her question. He walked right into that one, and she'd pester him until he caved. They always shared their personal lives with each other, so he didn't find any reason not to now.

"Yeah, there's this girl I met, but I can't, in all honesty, tell you anything because I don't know myself. All I know is she's special," he confessed.

"Aww, you're blushing. That means she's really something. Don't be like the man who fathered us. Before you explore anything with the special lady, end what you have with Brittani."

"That's just it, though. Supposing what I see in Ebele – that's her name – is just a fluke. I don't want to miss out on both ends." He poured the vegetables into the hot frying pan.

"So what? You want to string both women along? I know you hate being alone, but love is a risk."

"Whoa! Who said anything about love?"

"It's all in your undertone, my darling brother. Don't miss out on both ends because you are scared to take a risk. So what if you end up alone?" She paused. "You have me."

"You?" Kamal chuckled. "While you're giving out Oprah advice, have you told your Uncle Musa you don't want to marry what's his face?"

Halima snickered. "His name is Danladi, and Uncle Musa is your uncle too."

"No, he ain't. I don't relate to snakes. I don't care what dude's name is really, but why haven't you told him yet?"

"I don't have the courage."

"Don't worry, 'lil sis. When I come home for my mom's birthday, I'll handle that for you," Kamal promised with a grin on his face.

"Yay, you're coming home. That reminds me, I need to get with Ibiso and Dami so we can plan our clothes for Big Mummy's birthday," she said, excitedly.

Kamal took pride in the progress his family had made over the years. He and his brothers were cordial with Aisha, Halima's mother, and their father's second wife. Halima had also gotten close to their mother, who she called Big Mummy. Although the two older women were not friends, they maintained a cordial relationship.

"Also please don't handle anything for me *o*. I'll get to it. First, you'll be speaking slang that no one understands, then you'll result to bullying if you don't get your way."

Kamal shrugged. "Okay, mess around and next thing you

know, you'll be in the harem, taking turns satisfying Danladi's needs."

Halima furrowed her eyebrows. "I'm hanging up now."

"Don't be mad at me because I'm stating facts."

"Bye, brother…"

"Yeah, bye, little girl, and I better see you in London soon."

"Such a tyrant."

"You love me anyway."

They hung up the phone, and he settled down for his breakfast. He pondered over the words that Halima had spoken and knew she had a point. Love is a risk or the possibility of it. But with him having to deal with a new team, trying to step up his game even more, did he have time for a relationship? Especially one that had the potential to strip away his layers? He didn't have the answer to that, but what he did know was he wanted to see Ebele again today. Next week would be so busy for him that he wasn't sure when he'd see her.

Kamal finished eating, washed the dishes, and cleaned the counter, then headed up the stairs to his bedroom. His Falz's "Soft Work" ring tone alerted him to an incoming call. He looked at the caller ID and answered it.

"What's up, bro?"

"Kammy."

"People get married, can't call their twin no more. I mean, this world is cruel." Kamal joked as he pulled off his pajama top. He put the phone on speaker and placed it on the dresser. With the six-hour time difference, he didn't expect Jabir to be awake by now.

"Be quiet. I talked to you just last week. Always complaining people aren't calling you."

"What? They aren't. The only people that call me are Stone Cold 'cause he's trying to play Daddy and Mama 'cause she's trying to marry me off."

Jabir laughed. The twins chatted about the new club and how Kamal was settling down in London. Jabir told him that he and Dami were toying with the idea of moving back to Lagos permanently in a couple of years. Soon after, Kamal heard Damisi and his nieces in the background, so he hung up, and dialed again using FaceTime. His nephew and nieces, though barely two years old, had his heart and could get anything they desired from him. He *googoed* and *gaggaed* with the twins over the phone for a short while before their mom took them to get ready for church.

"Is Brittani moving over there with you?" Jabir asked.

"Nope."

"What's the plan? You guys will be traveling back and forth?"

"To be real, I haven't even thought that far."

"She's still your woman, right? Why wouldn't you know?"

Kamal became agitated. "Why is everyone trying to check me about Brittani? We're good. We do us. Did I tell you she was my wife? It's not that deep."

"Whoa, calm down, or I'll reach through this phone. Nobody says you guys are *bad*. Is there something you wanna get off your chest? You sound bothered. I can feel it too."

Kamal sighed. He rubbed his hand on his bare chest and sat on his bed. He had been talking about his feelings too much in the last week. Ebele already had him feeling like a sucker, and he didn't even know her favorite color yet.

"Man, I met this girl. I have no words to describe the attraction but to say we're drawn to each other like white rice and stew … magnetic … and it's not just physical."

Jabir looked at him like he'd grown an extra head. Kamal couldn't blame him. In another time, he also would've looked at himself the same way with those words coming out of his mouth.

"Are you for real?"

Kamal spent the next several minutes telling Jabir everything from the flight to when they got back from breakfast the previous day.

"She's fine, feisty with a shape that should be illegal. All the things I like on the outside. Add to that, she's smart, driven, and oh, she's a borderline midget." Kamal grinned.

"Did you touch her?"

"Man, get your mind outta the gutter." Kamal waved him off. "No, I'm not that bad. I got the Brittani thing going on, and besides, I think she's one of y'all."

"Huh?"

"One of those 'have a personal relationship with Jesus' kinda chicks. I did kiss her, though. Her angel must've been working overtime because it took a heavenly force to pull me away from her."

Jabir laughed. "You're so ignorant that I don't know how to even address that comment."

"I keep telling y'all; I deal only in facts."

"Anyway, if she's all that, take it from me – uncomplicate your life and explore things with her and see where it goes. Don't be me, messed around and missed out on seven years with my soulmate."

"I hear you. I wanna take her out today, but it's cold up here. After being in sunny LA for a minute, I ain't built for this weather," Kamal grumbled.

"Get used to it. That's what coats are for," Jabir said.

"Got any ideas for where I can take her out today? You're the Mack Daddy of the family—"

"Former Mack Daddy. Get it right, Kammy. Don't let me fight you," Damisi yelled from the background.

"That's right, baby. Tell him I only mack for you now," Jabir responded.

"Y'all are sickening. Dami, how you gonna fight me? You know your husband was the mack of them all. But you tamed him, sis. Good for you."

"Kammy, keep trying me. Remember what they say about payback," Damisi warned.

"Stop threatening your boy. You know you love the kid."

"Leave my wife alone. To answer your question, you can take her out for a ride. Y'all can probably chill at an ocean-front in the heated car and watch the sunset. Pack some stuff to eat."

"You see, I knew you still had it in you." He paused and brought his mouth closer to the phone. "All those years of macking, you should sell this advice as a side hustle."

"Bye, little brother. Tell me how it goes," Jabir said.

"Little? Man, you're three minutes older than me."

"A lot can happen in three minutes." Jabir shrugged and hung up.

Kamal tossed the phone on the bed and wrapped a towel around his waist before walking into the bathroom. He brushed his teeth again and trimmed stray chin hairs. He didn't want a full-grown beard but liked the idea of facial hair. Therefore, his mustache and chin hair stayed low and perfectly groomed. He turned on the jets and walked back into his room to get his phone. He went into his contacts and found the number he was looking for.

Good morning beautiful, he typed. After hitting the send button, he dropped the phone back on the bed and went to take a shower.

$$\text{Chapter 10}$$

Ebele's mind was drawing a blank. She and Nse had been back from church for a couple of hours now, and while Nse napped, she was trying to tackle her paper in Social Enterprise and Professional Practice. When Ebele first got to London years ago, she stayed with Nse before moving to school. In that time, she got to make Christ the Good Shepherd Church here in Essex her home church. It was nothing like her smaller church in school, and she was thrilled to be able to attend it regularly again.

She'd report for placement in the morning, then head back to school until next weekend. Nse, being the best bestie she was, had given her free access to her house for the three-month duration of her placement. All things being equal, she'd be done by March.

With a pencil lodged in her hair and another between her lips, Ebele adjusted her reading glasses. She needed a thousand words to meet the required twenty-five-hundred-word count, and the words were not flowing. She sat "applesauce, crisscrossed" with her laptop on the bed and stared at the blinking cursor for the umpteenth time. She tried to will the words to fall from her brain but no such luck. Feeling her eyelids droop, she got up and stretched for a few minutes. Getting back on the bed, she plugged her earplugs into her phone.

Maybe some music would loosen my mind. She searched her playlist, got the song, closed her eyes, and leaned against the headboard. As the melody of Glowreeyah's "Miracle Worker" started to come through, her phone buzzed, alerting her to a text. She opened her eyes. Kam. She froze for a moment. A wide smile curved her lips at his words. Her heart pounded with excitement and fear.

She texted back, **Hey you. It's almost afternoon. Just getting up?**

Ebele waited for a few minutes and didn't get a response. She began wondering what he was doing. Why was he taking so long to answer her? Before her thoughts could fully mount the runaway train, she reeled them in. This man had the ability to make her lose all sensible thought. She was going back to her playlist when he responded.

No. Been up since dawn. You miss me?

She could almost imagine his smirk. She wondered if she should be truthful. She did miss him. Since that kiss, she'd thought about nothing but him. She had to summon all the willpower within her to banish him from her thoughts during service so she could concentrate.

A little. A shiver ran through her anticipating his response.

Why you lying E?

Intrigued by his assumption, she typed back, **How do you know I'm lying?**

The dots indicating Kamal was responding kept wiggling for a tad longer than she expected. She wondered what smart thing was going to fly out of his mouth.

Because I missed you a lot. So, I know you missed me too. How you gonna lie and you went to church today?

Her breath caught at his candid confession. She'd pegged him as someone who enjoyed playing games. She was quite impressed. Self-preservation, however, had her trying to hold on to her made-up perceptions of him. She decided to make a candid confession of her own.

Okaaay, I missed you a lot too. How do you know I went to church?

Better. Let's make a deal. He ignored her question.

Ebele leaned back against her headboard. Her pulse quickened.

Should I be worried?

Unless you plan on lying to me, no.

This was the serious Kamal. She could tell in the tone of his text. She imagined him creasing his forehead the same way he did when he told her about proving himself at breakfast.

With caution, she asked, **What is it?**

Let's promise to always shoot straight with each other. We're both grown. Deal?

She didn't know if that was such a good idea. She didn't trust whatever this attraction was to be vulnerable to him just yet. She thought of a better compromise and responded.

Let's work on trust. Then there won't be a reason to lie.

His response didn't come quick, but it came.

I can work with that. Deal.

She grinned like a stuffed Cheshire cat. She wanted to ask him about practice, but Tega didn't have any; so she knew he didn't either since they were on the same team. She asked him about church instead. She knew he believed in God from their conversation on the plane. However, believing and keeping His commands and precepts in love, and acknowledging Christ as his Savior, were different things.

He responded he didn't go. Ebele frowned in disappointment but quickly remembered that warming the pew on Sundays didn't make you more Christian than another. She should know. That used to be her. Before the accident, it never failed. She was in church every Sunday. But it was just a ritual, more of a tradition. She normally left just as empty as she came. She had nothing against formal worship. She loved her church, but from her experience, she'd never try to force Kamal or anyone to go to church just because. Through her actions, she hoped one day he might go with her. Ebele was more concerned with him having a relationship with Jesus.

You just gonna ignore me?

E, whatchu doing?

Lost in her thoughts, she didn't know he'd texted her a couple of times.

No, not ignoring you. Nothing much. Trying to type this paper. Words not flowing. It's due tomorrow evening.

How many words left?

1000

That's a small thing to a giant like you. Step away from it.

With a dreamy sigh, Ebele plopped back on her pillow. Kamal believed in her. She touched her cheeks, and they were hot. She knew that her face was flushed and red. She couldn't stop herself from swooning. As much as she wanted right now to throw her paper out the window and skip around with him in the imaginary garden, she knew this paper was ten percent of the final grade for this class. She had to get it done.

I can't. I have clinicals in the morning. Then back to sch. Once I get off the train, this class is next. I have to make sure it's done.

Stop whining. It'll be done tonight. I promise. Just step away from it for a minute. As a matter of fact, get dressed. I'm coming to take you for a ride.

To where?

She raised her brows as though he could see her questioning him. Typical Kamal – always demanding. This was one initial assumption she'd had of him that had proven to be correct.

Trust me. I'll be there in 30 mins.

Trust me, he says. I'll smack him if I don't get this paper done.

Ebele saved her unfinished work, closed her laptop, and got out of bed. Giving herself a once over in the mirror, she decided to change her clothes. She had no idea where he was taking her, but it was Sunday. Not a lot of places were open, and he knew how she felt about notoriety. After rummaging through her roll-on luggage, she found something comfortable but chic to wear. She re-applied her lip gloss, grabbed her black satchel, and headed to the door.

She wasn't trying to hide Kamal from Nse, but she didn't want to discuss what she wasn't sure of yet. She preferred to sort out her feelings before she shared them. The day before, she did give her a brief overview of breakfast with him, but she had nothing else to add. She grabbed a pen and paper and wrote a quick note for Nse, which she put on the kitchen counter. The doorbell rang a few seconds later. Making sure her keys were with her, she headed out.

"Hey, you," she greeted.

"Hey, yourself." Kamal placed a kiss on her forehead. "Ready?"

She nodded.

He grabbed her hand, ushered her to his parked car, and helped her in.

Once Kamal climbed behind the wheel, she asked playfully, "Are you now gonna tell me where you're taking me, Mr. Danjuma?"

"Nope, you'll see when we get there." He glanced at her sideways. "Relax, E, I got it."

Minutes later, they eased down the curb and onto the open road. She relaxed as he advised and turned her head to him. "Tell me something about yourself I can't find on Google?"

"What did you find on Google?"

"Haven't you heard not to answer a question with a question?"

"Yep, but it doesn't apply to me." He grinned.

"Kam, be serious," she huffed.

He chuckled. "Okay, don't cry." He remained silent for a few seconds. "I love to draw. It calms me. The ability to put down on paper what I see in my mind's eye. It's not what anyone tells me it ought to look like. It's what I imagine it to be."

She digested his answer and realized it held many under-tones. "It must be hard living by the expectations of others?"

He shrugged. "It has its moments. I'm not ungrateful, though. Soccer saved me, so if I have to play by certain rules, I will."

"Saved you?"

He gave her a brief look and reverted his eyes to the road. It was as though he had something on the tip of his tongue but decided to hold it in.

"What do you like to draw? Just buildings?" she asked. He had mentioned studying architecture.

"Nah, I design some of my clothes, landscape, people, but I love taking a building and recreating it with that African element." He paused. "You know things from ancient African history."

"You've got to be kidding me," she said. She could tell he wasn't used to talking about himself, but this was amazing.

"Tell me you didn't think I was really a dumb jock?" He glanced over at her.

"No, it's that … well, I guess I didn't figure you were this talented."

"I thought we agreed no more assumptions. Besides, I just do it as a hobby. No big deal. Nobody knows but my family and now you."

"I feel honored." She blushed.

"What about you? Tell me something no one else knows."

"I see what you did there, but you get a pass," she said, referring to his avoidance of her question about soccer saving him. "Hmm, let's see. I stopped celebrating my birthday after I turned eight."

"What? Why?"

She shrugged. "I mean my people, like my mom, grandma, and Nse always wish me a happy birthday, but I don't celebrate it."

"When is your birthday?"

"May thirteenth. Until I was eight, I believed in the fantasy of my dad coming back. One day, I was teased at school so bad for the way I looked. Hair wild, almost white – I was so different from everyone else. My mom couldn't afford private schooling, so I went to a local school in Benin. I cried all the way home." The painful memory made a tear form at the corner of her eye. "That was the day my mom sat me down and told me the circumstances of my birth. She taught me the importance of standing up for myself. However, I decided that if he didn't want me, there was no need celebrating the day I was created."

Ebele waited for Kamal to speak. He didn't. His jaw was tight. An awkward silence passed between them. She began to regret sharing so much so early. She was secure in who she was, but it had taken a while to get there. She felt the car turn onto another road. They were at Promenade Park. He pulled over and parked. He turned to look at her. She avoided his eyes for fear she might see pity in them. Her heartbeat accelerated.

"Look at me." His tone held authority.

She brought her eyes to his. He cupped her face and stared into her eyes. "I'm sorry you went through that. You're the most beautiful woman I have seen. Your beauty glows from the inside out. From now on, you *will* celebrate the day you were born."

Tears rolled down her cheeks as her skin tingled. This was

too intense. His stare pierced her soul. She was unable to voice the emotion she felt. He thumbed away her tears. She expected him to kiss her, but he drew her into a hug. His comfort chipped away at her resistance.

"What do you want to do this year? For the big 3-0?" He asked once he released her.

"I hadn't thought about it."

"Hmm, okay." He started the engine and drove them to a secluded spot in the park. There was a group of private, heated cabins facing the park's lake. It gave the perfect view of the horizon. Kamal got out and grabbed a basket from the back; she hadn't even noticed. He put his sketch pad under his arm and helped her out. He gave her two blankets to carry and led the way to one of the cabins.

"Come on. I got the perfect spot," he said.

When they entered, Ebele gazed in delight at the homey, rustic cabin. It wasn't a regular cabin for lodging. She figured it was designed so people could still enjoy the park during the winter. There was a wooden porch swing, a table, and a fire-place in the corner. Ebele set the blankets down as Kamal started a fire. She retrieved the detachable swing cushions in the corner, attached one to the backrest of the swing and another to the seat.

These people thought of everything.

"Nice job, Mr. Danjuma. This is amazing."

"I figured you'd like it." He smiled, watching her. "It's nothing fancy—"

Feeling bold, she walked up to him and held his hand. "It's perfect. Simple. I like it. I want to know Kamal the man, not Kammy, the soccer player. I don't need fancy."

His smile deepened. "Whatever the lady wants."

They settled down on the swing. Kamal covered them with the blanket, and they enjoyed the view. There were people taking brisk walks along the trail. For a few moments, they enjoyed the comfortable silence between them.

"Why didn't you go back to dancing after you healed?" Kamal asked.

Ebele swallowed hard. "I do dance, just not professionally anymore. I teach it and dance in church. Dancing is something I'll always have a passion for and enjoy. But I no longer want it how I had it. I want to enjoy it and use it for God's glorification. It's not about only me anymore but worship to God and service to others."

"Break it down for me?" Kamal swung them gently back and forth.

"I've turned my trial into triumph and from there, found my purpose which is not only about me anymore. You know all men were created for a purpose, a plan He has for you. Some people walk in it; some don't. To know it though, you must first have a relationship with Him."

"So what's yours?"

"To motivate, educate, and teach a holistic approach to overcoming a physical injury. There's a lot that goes into healing. Along with the body, I'll concentrate on the mind and soul."

"Don't you miss the fame?"

"Oh, no, I'm content with where I am."

Kamal remained silent. He absently swirled some tendrils of her hair around his finger.

"I've learned to trust God's plan. It's in Him I have true value, so dance doesn't define me. It's who I am in Him and what I do to His glory." She paused.

His face held a confused look.

"In whatever season I'm in, He has something for me in it. Helping others get back up gives me joy."

Kamal studied her for a minute and drew her closer to him. She put her head on his shoulder. "That's big stuff and so admirable. I'd like to watch you dance one day."

"Come to church and you just might."

"Hmm, I might."

She didn't want to press the issue. Him saying that was enough for now. "What about you? After soccer, then what?"

"Honestly, I don't know. Haven't thought about it. I'm not planning to give it up soon, so …"

"You can't play soccer forever."

"Says who?"

She laughed, reaching up, and touching his hair. "Says these gray hairs sprouting on your head."

He raised his brow at her with a smirk on his face. "You're too funny. Don't be mad when I get you back." He rubbed his hand up and down her arm. "You hungry? I got some things in the basket."

"Sure."

Kamal tapped her, motioning her to sit up. She watched as he walked over and set up their lunch on the table. Little sandwiches, pastries, small fruit platter, and cheeses. He had a thermos and some sparkling wine. While he was setting up, she remembered his pad and picked it up. She turned to the page that had the pencil. As she was about to look at it, Kamal jumped up and snatched it from her.

"Why? I want to see." She pouted.

"No, nosey." He held it above her head.

"That's not fair, after all, I shared with you." She jumped up to reach for it.

"No." He wiggled his brows at her.

She folded her hand across her chest. Her hair fell in her face. "Fine. Keep your nonsense drawing book."

Kamal let out a boisterous laugh. "Oh, it's now a drawing book? You big mad or small mad?" He used his other hand to gently tug her hair.

"Go *jor*." She pouted and swatted his hand.

"But she calls me spoiled. Tell you what, if you can reach it, you can look at it."

Ebele looked at the pad he held above his head. She didn't

have on heels. Even if she did, who was she kidding? She still couldn't reach it.

Then she heard her mom voice *"Ebelechukwu, use your brain. That is why God gave it."* Ebele smirked and walked up to Kamal. He looked down at her; she tugged on his shirt seductively and batted her eyelashes. She pouted her lips for a kiss and stood on the tip of her toes. His eyes became hooded like she knew they would. He bent to reach her lips. Just as they were about to connect, she turned her face away and snatched the pad from his hand.

"Yeah, you can have it, but I'm still getting my kiss," he said.

Ebele turned away from him laughing. She went to the other end of the porch and opened the pad. Her eyes watered at the visual staring back at her. She'd known Kamal for less than a month, and he was slowly tearing her down. He had remembered everything she told him and designed her dream center. He even added things she didn't think about and named it *Mended by E.* She felt his presence behind her. He wrapped his hand around her waist and placed his chin on her head. He began to explain the drawing. When he was done, she turned around. Their gazes held. Electricity passed between them.

She reached up and kissed him. "Thank you. I didn't think of building it. I always thought of renting. This is perfect. Maybe one day, I'll be able to afford building my own space."

"You're welcome. And you will."

She creased her forehead. "I don't want your money, Kam."

"And I'm not giving it to you."

She studied him but didn't counter his comment.

He took her hand in his. "Come on, let's eat. This is all I could get last minute."

Ebele followed him and felt her heart flip. They sat, and

he prepared a plate for her, then himself. They said grace and began to eat.

"Okay, let's talk about your paper."

Between bites, Ebele told him about the topic for her Social Enterprise and Professional Practice class. Kamal chided her, making the point that she shouldn't have any problems. She should use all the stuff she told him earlier about her purpose. He asked open-ended questions, helping her think critically about ways in which she'd apply methods used by big businesses to make an impact socially. They discussed ideas, and she had more than enough material for her paper.

While he was asking her questions, and helping her think through her paper, she knew she was a goner. She just wasn't sure how deep yet. Kamal was showing her how beautiful he was on the inside. His sexy swag and physical dominance were a welcome bonus. The clamp around her heart tightened. She knew she was treading on dangerous ground. She'd kissed him twice now, and he probably had some woman tucked away in America.

Lord, help me rein this thing back in before I fall off the deep end.

Chapter 11

T he alarm blared, jolting Kamal from sleep. He opened one eye and slowly opened the other. He stayed still and stared at the ceiling. He could've sworn he saw Ebele's face. *This can't be normal.* This has been his predicament almost every day. Thoughts of her invaded his mind until he fell asleep, and she was the first person he thought about when he woke up. His mother would kill him if she knew that because she always preached his first thoughts should be thanking his Creator for a new day.

Over the last month, he and Ebele had spent almost every free minute on the phone, either texting or talking. Their talks were so random and easy. They discussed silly topics like the difference between the taste of *Naija* Coca Cola and the British and American versions – which they both agreed the Nigerian one had more sugar. They discussed funny things Nigerian moms did or serious topics like the upcoming Brexit vote. On that, they also shared the opinion Britain shouldn't pull out of the European Union.

Ebele was in Essex on the weekends, so they made Saturday breakfast a thing and took long random drives on Sundays. Kamal couldn't believe he did that considering he hated driving. However, with Ebele, he was doing things he never thought he would. She schooled him on the world of interpretive dance, and he taught her soccer basics. He also found out her favorite color – orange; flower – lilies and meal. Of course, he expected it to be some kind of rice. He remembered her playfully hitting him when he guessed it right – coconut.

When she got the results for her Social Enterprise paper, she sent him a fruit box and raw steaks. It came in a nice arrangement to the Turk West training facility. He, in turn, had surprised her with lunch at the dance studio she taught at part-time. The light he saw in her eyes when she taught the kids to dance was contagious. It was the same way he felt when he got on the field. The trust and friendship between them grew by the day, and they had only known each other a short while. One area they both seemed to avoid was the future.

Kamal dragged his comatose body to the bathroom to perform his morning routine. After a shower and making sure his teeth were clean, he dressed for practice. Kamal walked into the kitchen and headed for the juicer. He plugged it up and opened the fridge to get the pre-cut fruits and veggies for his smoothie. Minutes later, he poured some of the mixture into a glass and the rest into a travel mug. He toasted two slices of bread, sparsely coated them with butter, and sat at the table to eat. He powered on his iPad and pulled up the Our Daily Bread app. He didn't use it every morning, but for a while now, he'd been doing so more often.

One day last year, Kamal was in the dumps over the impending legal issues that hung over his head. He'd called up Jabir, but Damisi answered. She wouldn't give the phone to his brother until he told her what was wrong with "her fun Kammy," as she put it. They talked, and Damisi tried to convince him that he'd find some comfort if he read the Bible.

He had no desire to lug the big book around but agreed to appease her; then he dismissed it.

Some months later, after the twins were born, he went visiting. It took her a minute to convince him, but she installed two apps for him on that trip. A Bible App and the Our Daily Bread App. She made the analogy that as he fed his body, he should feed his soul. Kamal wasn't a stranger to God; he went to church when his schedule permitted. He knew that He was the Creator of heaven and earth. Jesus was His Son and died on the cross. What he didn't get and couldn't seem to figure out was this personal relationship thing his brothers were on.

He inserted his headset and listened to the day's passage as he ate. "Today's Scripture reading from the *Our Daily Bread Devotional* is taken from Ephesians 2:8-9: *For it is by grace you have been saved, through faith—and this is not from yourselves, it is the gift of God not by works, so that no one can boast.*"

He listened as the commentator explained the concept of grace – the gift which God gave through the death of Jesus. As mankind, we're only able to obtain it by our belief; not by anything we do. As Kamal listened, his thoughts circled the concept of being given something by doing nothing. He questioned the possibility of having assured entry into heaven without having to do anything. Therefore, on his own, he gave back in ways that he could. He volunteered in the Boys & Girls Club Rasheed owned at home whenever he was there. He gave to numerous charities and was toying with the idea of a foundation. How could he understand the concept of something for nothing?

He thought he'd read somewhere in the same Bible where it said you reap what you sow. Deciding now wasn't the time to overanalyze it, he said the prayer that was at the end of the day's devotion and stood.

He cleaned up after himself and headed out. He had a home game the next day, after which he'd hit the road for some away games. He tossed his bag in the back of the car. In his world, nothing good came from nothing, so he was going to practice for the win.

———

LATER THAT MORNING, A FRESHLY SHOWERED KAMAL STOOD IN front of his locker after a four-hour practice session. Instead of hanging out, as usual, Tega left to meet Nse for a cake tasting. Kamal was on his way back to Essex to see his old coach, Mr. Grams. After dressing and brushing his hair, he pulled out his phone. He was expecting a response from Ebele. Although they texted every day, it'd been almost a week since he'd seen her.

Hey, Kam Kam, I'm good. And u? Rushing for another class now. TTYL

He read her text in a low whisper. His heart skipped, and his lungs filled with extra oxygen at the endless smiley emoji's that accompanied the text. That's what her smile did to him. Things were so easy for them that he feared what was around the corner. He'd never been so attached to anyone since his dad and grandpa, and even the remotest thought of losing her would cause him to go insane. He headed out of the stadium. He wanted to see her and toyed with the idea of popping up on her at school, but knew she was kinda shy about any unnecessary attention. Instead, he texted her that he'd call later.

Kamal bopped his head to Nigerian artist, Dr. Sid's "Over the Moon" as he made the drive to his old stomping grounds. His head and heart conflicted with each other as Brittani and Ebele crossed his mind. Although the physical attraction between them was strong, and he knew he felt more than just lust for her, he and Ebele hadn't talked about anything romantic. The only day they came close was when he teased her about being his wife. He also noticed she avoided kissing him again. She'd let him hold her hand, play with her hair or hug her, but no kissing.

He'd never gone this long without intimacy, but just being around her – although it drove him crazy – was enough. Despite the intense chemistry and friendship with Ebele, he couldn't let Brittani go.

Suppose Ebele had all these requirements she wanted him to meet first? Like his brother's wives had requested of them. He and Brittani didn't require more than the other was willing to give. Ebele made him strip his layers. He was used to being in control of how vulnerable he allowed himself to be. She took that control away from him. The possibility that she might require him to be what he wasn't and end up leaving him when he couldn't scared him. His sanity was safer keeping her as a friend.

Several minutes later, Kamal pulled up to the address and parked his Lexus 750 LX SUV. He furrowed his brows when he looked at the sign – By His Stripes Wellness & Rehabilitation Center. What was that name supposed to mean? Was he in the wrong place? He'd called and confirmed the location was the same and Coach Grams would be here, but this name was throwing him off.

Kamal walked into the building, and he looked around in awe. The place had changed drastically from when he was here last. To hide his identity, he covered his head with his hood and glasses. The floor was busy with patients and staff – either doing stretches, lifting weights or exercising. Through a glass partition, he saw a group of people taking nutrition classes.

His mind went to Ebele and the expression she made when she saw the design he made for her. This was her dream, and if he could, he'd make it happen for her without that loan. He laughed to himself, imagining her physically trying to fight him if he did that without her knowledge.

He walked up to the reception desk. "Hi, I'd like to see Coach Grams, please?"

The lady glanced up at him. "Do you have an appointment?"

"No, I don't, but I'd like to see him, and I can assure you, he'd love to see me."

She rolled her eyes at him and waved him over to the sitting area. He silently wished her eyes would roll right out of the sockets and onto the carpet. The only person that got away with rolling their eyes at him was Ebele. He had other business to take care of and didn't have time to sit and wait.

"Miss, could you tell him an old student is here?" He tried to plead with her. She was forcing the ignorant Kammy to make an appearance.

"So everyone says. You have to wait." She didn't even have the decency to look at him. He'd experienced a lot in his career, from profiling to ugliness for no reason. It no longer fazed him as it used to, but this wasn't the day. She was rude, and he wasn't here for it.

He turned around and walked straight to the back. Kamal knew where the coach's office was. He heard the lady behind him, hot on his heels. He got to the door, knocked, got a response, and entered. Coach Grams was seated on the loveseat in his office eating what Kamal thought was a ham and cheese sandwich with tea. He chuckled. Some habits never die.

"Kamal, is that you?" the older white man asked. Coach Grams was in his mid-sixties. He stood at about five-feet-seven inches and looked the same, except his dark hair now had streaks of gray. His glasses sat on his nose as they always did.

"Hey, old man." Kamal walked over to help him get up.

"Coach, I knew you were having lunch, so I told him to wait," the receptionist tried to explain.

Kamal took off his glasses and hood and looked her dead in the eye. "Nah, lady, you didn't tell me that. You dismissed me and seeing as I can't stand to be dismissed, I came to get Coach for myself." He paused. "Tell her, Coach. Tell her I don't like being dismissed."

"Kammy, leave that lady alone. Priscilla, it's fine. He's one of my older students and—"

"And star attacking midfielder for the LA Sun Sides, and now he plays for us right here in the UK for Turk West," Priscilla said, in shock when she recognized him. "I'm so sorry. I was having a bad day."

Is excusing meanness with having a bad day the new in thing? Ebele started this stuff.

"You a'ight." Kamal was unbothered by her apology. He couldn't stand it when people wanted to be nice after they recognized him as number eight, as though he wasn't a human being without soccer. Sadly, this was one of the reasons he had to be about his business because, with soccer, there was no mistaking he was somebody.

"So you finally came to visit me," Coach said. He walked over to the double chairs in front of his desk.

"Come on, Coach. Don't say it like that. I was here five years ago."

"And that was too long ago. I worry about you."

"I'm straight, Coach. Trust."

"Uhmm, I don't know about that. You know I keep tabs on you. You're a hothead, so I always pray you stay on the straight and narrow." Coach Grams gave Kamal a piercing stare, daring him to challenge him.

Kamal saw a little disappointment in the older man's eyes. Suddenly, he became that six-year-old boy meeting him for the first time. Knowing he was referring to the incidents that happened last year, he lowered his eyes and inhaled. A few moments of silence passed, then Kamal explained both situations.

"Son, you're so different from your brothers." He chuckled. "Rasheed is so hard and direct. Jabir is so confident that it borders on cocky. You, on the other hand, although confident, still have the need for validation of your worth. No fault of yours; it stems from your hurt. You hide it well behind you humor, or you lash out—"

"Aw, come on, Coach …" Kamal wasn't in the mood for a lecture. Not saying there wasn't truth to Coach's observations. If anyone knew him, he did. But he didn't want to be in that headspace with a game coming up.

"You just told me the reason for your recent troubles was your fear of losing soccer. I understand it's your career, but you can't put your worth in it. If it must end, it must. Don't let fear lead you astray. Think of your mother."

"Aww, man, that was beautiful. Now you gonna make me cry." Kamal laced his voice with sarcasm and stood. He walked over to the wall.

"You see, there you go. But I know you enough to know you heard me."

"Yeah, Coach, I did." Kamal looked at the walls. On them hung many of the kids he'd coached over the years. Some went on to have professional careers, some of them only played as a hobby. Kamal located the picture with him, his brothers, and Tega. He smiled. They looked so young at the time. He also saw different framed Scriptures that adorned the wall.

"Coach, what's the deal? Are you a part-time church now?"

Coach Grams shook his head and chuckled. "Ever the jokester. What are you talking about?"

"All these Scriptures and why are you now named By His Stripes?" Kamal raised his brow.

"Oh, that. I got saved a couple of years ago and felt led to change the name of the place."

"Oh, no, not you too. What does that even mean?"

"What do you mean?" Coach asked.

"Both my brothers are saved. Right after they met their

wives, it was a wrap. Can you believe Jabir won't serve me a beer in his house?" Kamal grinned at the memory.

"Praise God, that's so nice to hear."

Kamal didn't want a full-blown sermon, so he changed the topic. He spent several minutes with Coach Grams chatting about his plans while in London. It gave him a fuzzy nostalgic feeling talking to the man who was so instrumental in molding him one-on-one again. He glanced at his watch and stood. He put back on his hood and his glasses.

"All right. Stay safe, old man. I'll check on you again." He walked out of the office.

On his way to the parking lot, he lifted his glasses and smirked at the receptionist. Getting into his car, he realized his phone hadn't buzzed in a while. He pulled it out and checked; no text from Ebele. He needed to hear her voice.

As he accessed his call log, a call came through. Brittani. He contemplated answering. They talked this morning, so he wondered what she wanted, but he knew that if he didn't answer it would be back-to-back call galore.

"Hey, Brit."

"Hi, baby, I wanted to wish you good luck for tomorrow. I upgraded the cable to the premium package so that I can hold a watch party," she said, in excitement.

This was the kind of stuff she did that he didn't understand. Everything was a reason to throw a party. He had since given up trying to understand her nonchalance for the game but love of the perks. She never attempted to know anything about the game of soccer, no matter how many times he tried to teach her. He wondered why she was paying more money for cable, and throwing a party, and he wasn't even there to explain.

"Okay, Brit. I'm not sure they'll show it but have fun. I'll talk to you tomorrow," Kamal responded. He made up his mind that he didn't have the time or energy to call her on spending money unnecessarily.

"Okay, love you, Kammy." She blew him a kiss through the phone, and he felt an ache of guilt. In two years, he hadn't been able to say those words back to her.

"Good night, Brit," he said softly and disconnected the call. He turned on the stereo, and "Digital" by Mali Music came across the speakers. The song reminded him of his relationship with Brittani. The void he felt leaving Coach's came back, and he turned on his Bluetooth to call Ebele. After the fourth ring, she answered the phone.

"Hey, Kam," she said, her voice shaky like she was agitated.

"E, is this how we doing it? Why haven't I heard from you?" He heard shuffling in the background. It was Thursday, so maybe she was packing to come to Essex since her clinicals were on Friday and Monday.

"Huh? Err ... hold on—"

"E? You okay?"

She didn't respond to him. Instead, he heard what almost made his heart stop.

"Ebele, put down the phone. Let's talk about us." It was a male voice.

Kamal cursed under his breath. Us? Not happening. He hung up the phone and made a U-turn. He wasn't ready, but there would be no "us" with another man. Selfish, yes, but he couldn't let it happen. And why hadn't Ebele told him she was serious or about to be serious about someone? He raced down the street praying he wasn't pulled over.

Chapter 12

E bele leaned against the stove in the kitchen of her one-bedroom, off-campus flat. She removed the phone from her ear and looked at the screen. There was still a connection. She placed the phone back against her ear.

"Hello? Hello?" Maybe he got disconnected.

Ebele shrugged. *I'll call him back when I get rid of this burden in front of me.*

When she got back from her last class, she met Victor outside her place. After he dumped her, she didn't hear a peep from him except what she read on blogs. Those blogs made her sound so pitiful and weak. They compared her to his new partner he was rumored to have an affair with. The media became an expert on Ebele's perceived shortcomings, claiming their failed relationship as her not being woman enough to keep up with a hunk like him. *Hunk ni, hunk ko!*

When she ran into him that day at Shoprite supermarket in Lagos, he acted like he'd seen a ghost. He approached her, and she dismissed him. Joke was on him because from his expression then, he never expected her to make it through. Ebele had been so happy. She was dressed up and had her hair and nails freshly done. She didn't know that with trying to *pepper* him, she'd attracted this harassment she was now facing. The first time he appeared at her front door, some months ago, she was still so bitter that she called the police on him. That was in the past. She was over it. How many ways do you tell a man no?

After she got over her initial disdain on seeing him earlier, she let him in. Apparently, he flew to London from Aberdeen, where he had a show. She wondered why he wasted money like this. There were starving people around the world, and he was here chasing a lost cause—her heart. She walked back to the living room from the kitchen, where she'd gone to answer Kamal.

"Ebi, put the phone down. Let's talk. I know you have feelings for me deep down there somewhere. I messed up, I know. I realize that but I've been asking for forgiveness for nine months now," Victor pleaded. He stood and put his hands in his khaki pockets.

Ebele stared at him with one eyebrow raised. She was trying to figure out how he got the nerve. He was a good-looking fellow. He wasn't as tall as Kamal. He stood at about six-feet tall. His skin was a deep cocoa, and his haircut was very low to his scalp. *Oh, Lord, I'm comparing him to Kamal.* A man who, apart from the light flirtation here and there, hadn't so much as made a move.

Ebele clasped her hands together and rubbed them against each other. "Victor, *Biko nu, ha pum. E nu go. Biko.*" Since he wasn't comprehending the English she'd been speaking, maybe telling him to leave her alone would be better understood in their native tongue.

"*Mba nu.* No. You have to forgive me."

"After all this time? Is it by force? Supposing you didn't see me that day?" He remained silent, so she continued. "In case you don't remember, I helped you build that band. But not up to two weeks into my injury, you left me to suffer alone. Dance was all I had, so you knew how losing it would and did affect me, but you left."

Her eyes misted, but she refused to let one tear fall. Her tears over the years could fill a drinking well. She refused to do that ever again. "Your celebrity shot up, and you didn't need me anymore."

"I do need you …"

Ebele ran her fingers through her hair. "No, you don't. You *want* me because you can't *have* me. Because you see, I'm making something of myself. What happened to all the women you were with when my back was out of commission? When I was being dragged from one herbalist to the other because we couldn't afford the right therapy."

Victor walked closer. She took a step back. "None of them could ever hold a candle to you. All those marriage plans we had then … I'm ready now."

A beat of silence passed between them. Enough time for her to swallow her saliva. She was concocting the most civil response to his assumption that she, Ebele Vanessa Ashiedu, would still want to marry him. After all this time. She opened her mouth to speak but was interrupted by a loud knock.

She should've been in Essex by now, so nobody was supposed to be visiting her. They stood in silence. Maybe she was hearing things. A few seconds later, there was the knock again. She walked over to the door but couldn't make out who it was through the peephole. The person must have moved away from the door. Ebele opened the door and leaned her head around to see who it was. She found herself staring into the face of an angry Kamal. What's his problem? His game wasn't until the next day, so the team couldn't have lost.

"Hey, Kam."

"Hey, can I come in?"

Stunned at his standoffish demeanor, she opened the door wider, and let him in. He entered and stood beside her, making sure she locked the door. She had so many questions, first being, how did he know where she stayed. With measured steps, she walked back to the living room. He followed behind.

Once they got to the living room, she was about to make the introductions when she heard Kamal speak.

"Explain," he demanded, gesturing his head toward Victor.

Ebele shook her head and chuckled softly. She'd bring him to order later about trying to push her around. She opened her mouth to speak when she was once again interrupted.

"Ebi, so this is who you hang out with? Kammy Danjuma? And you're giving me a hard time about celebrity and a good man?" Victor questioned, his disappointment evident.

"Yo, my guy, if you have a problem, address me—not her," Kamal said. "And I don't know you, so calm all that down." He looked over at Ebele. "Your place is beautiful, and I'd hate to break something when I give homeboy a beat down if he keeps talking."

Ebele rolled her eyes at Kamal and looked away. He was in rare form. "Calm down both of you." She faced Kamal, "And you won't be messing up my place. I don't care how mad you get or what you have going on tonight."

Victor cleared his throat. "Is he your boyfriend?"

"No."

"Not yet," Kamal clarified.

Ebele looked at him wide eyed. He hadn't discussed that with her, so she had no idea what he was talking about.

"Victor, as you already know, this is Kamal. Kam, this is Victor—"

"Kam? You're that close?" Victor asked, in annoyance.

"Yep, as a matter of fact, it's Kam Kam." Kamal winked at Ebele. "Has a nice ring to it, don't it?"

"Just childish," Ebele muttered. "Anyway, Kam, this is Victor, my *ex*-boyfriend, and former band mate. Ebele pretended not to see Kamal's neck muscles contract.

"You wanna run that by me again?" Kamal bent down to her mouth and cupped his ear.

"You heard me," Ebele insisted. "Move." She stepped away from him.

"Oh, okay, we'll talk about this later."

The tension in the atmosphere was suffocating as no one spoke for a couple of moments.

"It's Thursday. Go get your stuff and let's go," Kamal instructed.

Ebele didn't like his tone. He was acting like a deranged boyfriend. "No, I'll take the train."

"No, you won't. It's already late. You should've been gone by now." He stared Victor down. It was as though he knew Victor was the cause of her delay. Kamal returned his eyes to her. "I don't want you out there alone."

She folded her hands across her chest and stood her ground." I can take care of myself."

"Yeah, you can, but you don't have to. I'm here."

She stood her ground in defiance.

"E, don't make me act a fool. You're already on the naughty list."

Victor cleared his throat. In their banter, they had completely forgotten he was there.

"Oh, Victor, I'm sorry. I—"

"What are you apologizing for?" Kamal asked Ebele with a frown.

She inhaled deeply and exhaled. He was exasperating. If he weren't so handsome, she would've thrown him out. "Because we both can't be rude like you."

"Look, Victor, we've said all that needs to be said."

"No, we haven't." His eyes begged her to reconsider.

"Yes, we have. I'm no longer angry. I wish you well, but our time has passed. We can still be friends."

Kamal made some noise behind her. "No, you can't," he muttered.

Ebele turned back to him and gave him a warning look.

"Ebi, I'll win your heart back. I promise." Victor picked up his coat.

"Man, her heart ain't on the auction block," Kamal said.

Victor stared at him. Kamal returned his stare. Ebele had seen enough of the testosterone play.

"Okay, Victor …" She walked to the door, and he followed closely behind. When she got to the door, she opened it for him to leave. The look he gave her as he stepped out of the house was one of despair. She knew better though, so she ignored him. He kissed her on her cheek and left. Ebele locked the door and looked at Kamal. His eyes were blazing, and she found it amusing.

"Rude for no reason," Ebele said, walking toward her bedroom to get her things.

"Yeah, whatever. Come get in the car, so you can explain to me how I didn't know the person you had been talking about the whole time was a man." He folded his hand across his chest and leaned against the door. "Letting random people put their lips on you." He mumbled, but she heard him.

"I heard that."

"Good."

———

They'd been driving for ten minutes, and Kamal hadn't said a word. The car was silent, and she was tired of it. Ebele leaned her head to the side and studied him closely. He still had his jaw tight, and teeth clenched. She was surprised he hadn't shattered anything in his mouth with all that pressure.

"I don't understand why you're mad, though." she said, breaking the silence.

"You withheld information from me."

"Am I being punked? Where's the camera?" She looked

around the car. The fact that he was genuinely angry was amusing. She dared not laugh, though.

"I didn't withhold information. You assumed, and I didn't correct. There's a difference."

"Same thing."

"Says the guy who always seems to dodge the question when I ask if he's in a relationship." She crossed her arms over her chest.

Now she was getting upset. She waited, expecting him to say something about the relationship he never discussed. If there was an ideal time, it was now. "You don't have anything to say? You bust in my house and act all rude about a man from my past, but when I ask you about your relationship, you're silent? Really?"

When he didn't respond, she reached over and turned up the radio. Ironically, "I Try" by Macy Gray began to play. She listened to the lyrics as she saw her life going down the path it shouldn't. There was no way she was going to be caught up stumbling and choking like Macy Gray for someone who wasn't being forthright.

This was her final year. She had plans. She needed to concentrate on graduating and working toward her goal. No matter how he made her feel, she couldn't afford to be caught up in Kamal's confused drama. He was a multi-millionaire star soccer player whose family was well connected. She was just an ordinary girl trying to make a better life for herself and her mom. She had to put some distance between them for her sanity.

"Look, E, it's complicated. I like you a lot, and I know you like me too. But right now, my situation is complicated," Kamal said, softly. "I'm sorry about how I acted back there."

His words hurt, but he was being truthful, so she had to respect it. "Kam, until you uncomplicate it, you and I can only be friends. Meaning, I can date whomever I want. Your apology is accepted."

He probably thought she meant close friends as they'd been, but that wouldn't be the case. She was about to run for the hills.

Kamal didn't give her a response, so she continued. "For the record, Victor and I were high school sweethearts. We started this band together as I told you before. There were even plans for marriage. I mean we talked about it until I was injured. His celebrity shot up, and he left. Now he wants a second chance."

"Are you going to give him one?" Kamal's voice was almost inaudible.

"No, if I'm going to date, it'll be someone new. Oprah said when people show you who they are the first time, believe them. He's already shown me who he is. Why would I want to experience that again?"

Kamal grunted.

Ebele grinned. "Like you've shown me your crazy. Can I manage your entitled behavior? I don't know."

"Yes, you can. I have a manual that comes with instructions. Number one, don't let randoms put their lips on you." He smirked.

"Stop it. Put your foot on the gas. I have to get to Nse's. I have an online module to complete tonight."

"Got it. I did tell you I go on the road next week?"

"Yeah. I'd like to come to a football game."

"That would be a no. You can watch it from the comfort of your home."

"Why?"

"God forbid a favorite team here doesn't win the match. A stampede might break out. I don't want you anywhere near that."

"There you go being overbearing again."

"Call it what you like."

Ebele sighed, peering out the window. Her thoughts were all upside down. They both knew they had feelings for each other. She was so scared to admit that hers might now be love. How, she had no idea, but the grip on her heart confirmed it by the day. Things like this only happened in movies. She remembered scoffing in disbelief at the instant love between the hero and heroine in those romance movies.

She and Victor had dated for years, and it wasn't love at first sight. Neither was it for Nse and Tega. Now instant attraction was her reality. She turned and looked at Kamal. As good as he was, he was unavailable. How did she untangle her feelings when the one who was responsible for them couldn't even admit to his?

Chapter 13

"**M**an, where's your head?"

A toothpick landed on Kamal's hand. He looked down with disgust and shook it off.

"T, that's just nasty." He grimaced. "What?"

"I've been talking to you for a minute, and you're zoned out."

It was Saturday evening, and the team was on the club bus headed back to Essex from Lancaster, where they secured a 2:0 victory. Although it was a late evening game, they decided to make the one-hour journey back.

"He's been like that for a while," Freddie, another member of Turk West, chimed in. He turned around, kneeled over his seat, and faced the pair.

"If I didn't know better, I'd say he has women problems," Princeton added from the adjacent aisle.

Kamal glared at them, ending his stare at Tega. They'd all become close to some extent, but Tega knew not to blast him out there like that.

"Y'all need to get off my back." Kamal pointed at each of them.

The men held serious faces for some minutes before they busted out laughing. Kamal leaned back in his seat. He didn't find anything funny. They had no sense whatsoever, but the three men had made his adjustment in Essex, and play for Turk West, easier. Freddie was from South Africa, and Princeton was from Kentucky in the U.S. Both men were married and had been playing for Turk West for two seasons.

"We're playing good right now. You, my friend, are playing better than I saw last season. Averaging two goals and several assists each game," Freddie said to Kamal.

"So, what's really going on with you?" Princeton asked.

"For a while now, you've been acting like you're constipated," Freddie said, holding in his laughter.

"Constipated? Really?" Kamal asked. Freddie shrugged.

"Let me guess. Ebele is giving you the business?" Tega said.

"Who's Ebele?" Freddie and Princeton asked in unison.

Kamal remained silent. Tega gave him a knowing stare, waiting for him to fill the guys in.

Princeton snapped his fingers. "Oh, I think I know who that is."

Freddie glanced over at Princeton. His brows knit together in confusion waiting for him to continue.

"She's that fair-skinned chick, looks like she got bite and fine as h—"

"Don't get knocked out," Kamal growled, cutting Princeton off.

They all stared at him.

"You've got it bad," Freddie said.

Kamal had never had the feral need to pounce on anyone as he did right now. His burning stare remained fixed on Princeton, deciding whether to knock him in the mouth for trying to objectify the woman wreaking havoc on his mind.

He'd underestimated how bullheaded she could be. She'd

been avoiding him since that night in the car, and it was driving him insane. Since he was on the road on Valentine's Day, he'd sent her a dozen white, yellow, and red roses. It wasn't until the end of the day that she responded with a simple "thank you" via text. He hated being avoided just as much as being dismissed.

Princeton raised his hands in surrender. "Okay, man, be easy." He turned to Freddie. "She's the nice-looking lady that has come to see him at the facility. I think once or twice. Well, I've seen her there twice."

"Oh, man, is that you?" Freddie asked Kamal.

"No, it's not. He's being stubborn, and she isn't the one to mess with," Tega said.

"Can you guys stay out of my business?" Kamal looked between them. "And keep my girl's name out y'all's mouth."

The men laughed as the team bus driver turned into the Turk West facility and parked the bus. For the next several minutes, the players gathered their things, and everyone filed out of the bus. Freddie and Princeton made their way to their cars after saying goodbye. Tega and Kamal walked together to their cars.

"Your girl? How many do you have?" Tega questioned him.

"You know what I mean…"

"No, I don't, and neither do you. I told you that night; you gotta come correct or not at all." Tega paused. "She's been through a lot. Although late, she's back on track and has plans for her life. It's hard being with a celeb, but one that's confused is worse."

Kamal frowned. His chest expanded and retracted in rage. Where did Tega get off preaching to him about Ebele? Fine, Tega knew her first, and they had built a big brother/sister relationship, but right now, he was the only one who should be defending her.

"T, I love you like a brother but don't come at me like a sucker when it comes to Ebele. I know everything you're saying and more. I'm not trying to mess her life up. I lo—"

"You what?"

"I care for her a lot, and I'm trying to figure out how to go about what I need to do. But I can't do Brit like that over the phone. It's not right," Kamal explained. "I have to go to the US or get her to come here."

"That's fair. Oh, and I peeped your denial of your love for her." Tega nodded. "If it's any consolation, I think she shares the same sentiment from the one-sided conversations I hear from Nse."

Kamal opened the back door of his SUV and threw his bag in. Closing the door, he hopped on the bonnet of the truck.

"She did a complete one-eighty on me." Kamal tried to swallow the knot in his throat. He couldn't help the pang of regret and loss. He was in no way ready for marriage yet, but he wanted her. If he'd done what he was supposed to do before he left the US last year, this wouldn't have been a problem. He missed Ebele's laughter, her jokes, smile, smell, pouty face, all of it. He'd even refused to wash his red sweater because it had the strawberry, coconut scent of her hair when she'd rested her head on his shoulder.

"Yep, that's her. Self-preservation mode," Tega said and snickered. "Maybe this is a good thing. By March, you might be going back to America and Brittani."

Kamal gave him an incredulous look. "Are you for real right now? First, my going back hasn't even been finalized. Second, I don't care where I am; she'll be there too."

"But you need to tell her …"

"Man, her stubborn self isn't even talking to me now. Telling her of that remote possibility would be putting the nail in my own coffin." Kamal rubbed his forehead. "I need to get back in her good graces first."

"So, you actually busted in her flat like King Kong demanding when you haven't gotten your own situation together?"

Kamal smiled at how ridiculous his actions sounded. The thing, however, was that he'd do it again in a heartbeat. "Man, I almost made it to jail. All I could see was red."

Tega rubbed the back of his neck. "I heard about that Victor dude. He has some nerve."

"I know, right? Now that I think about it, if I weren't so mad, I would've laughed. You needed to see her midget self in the middle of us trying to regulate." Kamal grinned at the memory.

"You calling sis a midget? I'm telling."

"What's with these men and snitching?" He rubbed his hand over his face.

"Whatever, but on a serious note, I've never seen you act this way, ever. And after less than six-weeks. Kammy, if you've found the girl whose smile makes your soul stir, or presence gives you chills before she even opens her mouth ... *Hold am down o, sharp sharp, before story enter.* You know, before something else happens and another man sneaks up on you."

Kamal sighed. "Man, I need to get my girl back."

"She might be in church tomorrow," Tega informed him.

"And?"

"She can't dodge you there."

"Man, that's a Rasheed move. I can't go to church just to see a girl." Kamal furrowed his brows. He remembered the time he and Jabir picked on Rasheed when he dressed up to meet Ibiso in church.

"You don't have to. Come to church for you." Tega patted him on his back and picked up his bag from the ground. "The girl is the bonus ... seek ye first." He threw his bag over his shoulder as he made his way to his car.

Kamal watched him for a while, got in his car, and headed home.

AN HOUR LATER, KAMAL ENTERED HIS HOME AND THREW HIS travel bag in the corner. He was glad to be home after being gone for a week straight on away games. Adjusting his earpiece, he walked into the kitchen.

"Brit, I've been busy. You know how my schedule can be. Don't forget; I'm also in a different country. You have to bear with me a little." Kamal had been trying for the past thirty minutes to reason with his—he no longer knew what to call her. Girlfriend? That word left a bad taste in his mouth, especially since Ebele had been ducking and dodging him for the past two weeks. He was losing it. Confirmation of that was when he went off on his boys.

"I know, but this is different. You always take care of and have time for me. Even if it's a little," Brittani whined.

He opened the fridge to get a bottle of water. He unscrewed the cap and guzzled it down in one big gulp. He couldn't wait to stand under his showerhead for a long wash. He'd taken a quick shower at the stadium before getting on the bus, but it wasn't enough. He needed his therapeutic jets, and his bed was calling his name. Sleep, however, was another story. He hadn't been getting any lately.

"I have a couple of days off next week. Why don't you fly down? We can chill together, and I'll show you around. We need to talk about some stuff." After his talk with Tega, he needed to do something.

"Ugh, baby, why can't you come here? It's an eight-hour flight. I'd have loved to come see you, but I have auditions for a role I'm trying out for." She sighed.

Kamal let out an exaggerated breath. He didn't know what she wanted. She was always complaining when he didn't have time but had an excuse when he tried to fly her out. It was becoming clear that she wanted him but only as much as she needed him. Thinking about it, it was the same thing that he was doing. After enduring Ebele's one liner, annoyingly polite, and terribly distant texts, and calls, he knew he didn't want to live life like this.

"I thought you decided on modeling?" he asked. Every time they talked, she had a different career interest. Since they'd been together, she hadn't decided on one thing to do. It was between modeling, acting, or photography. Always something different.

"Yeah, silly, I'm trying both out." She giggled. "But I'll see what I can do to make it over there."

"Well, let me know. I have a game Tuesday; then I'm off for three days." Kamal made his way up the stairs to his bedroom. They talked a bit more and hung up with the usual parting pleasantries. If she didn't make it, he was going to fly to America soon. They needed to talk. This was no longer working. He tried to settle for mediocre to protect himself but failed.

Kamal was amused at how the sanity he was trying to guard was slowly slipping away. Tega's words ... *before story enter*, played in his head as he stepped into his bathroom for a shower. He and Jabir shared the same DNA, but there was no way he was letting Ebele live happily ever after without him. Now Kamal wondered how Jabir had let his wife, Damisi, get away from him for all those years before they got back together and got married. His sister-in-law must've dated other men during their hiatus. He shook his head; it couldn't be him. He wasn't the "I want you to be happy, even if it's not with me" kind of guy.

Ebele was ready. He saw it in her eyes and actions. He was the one who was playing safe. His muscles relaxed as the stream of hot water pounded his body. The timeline for getting his act together just got moved up. He never expected her to cut him off almost cold turkey. It wasn't a good feeling, so he was going to pull a Rasheed – go to church and call her on it.

Seek ye first. The same words Tega said to him floated through the air. He turned his head. He needed to sleep. Maybe that would clear his head. Because now he was hearing voices.

Chapter 14

Ebele rubbed her hands together. Pride shone through her eyes as she looked down at the robes her team of dancers was going to wear. She was glad that the pastor had asked her to lead a special number for service. She'd had a stressful couple of weeks. Between trying to pull away from Kamal, to traveling back and forth for clinicals, to papers and tests, she was glad to escape into another world through dance.

Christ the Good Shepherd Church was large with just under five-thousand members. It was a modern church with a pastor, who going by his preaching style, could be mistaken as being from an African country. Pastor Ricardo or Pretty Ricky, as some of the single ladies called him, was a gifted pastor who was off the market. First Lady Angelique and their three children had him on lock.

Ebele picked up the garments and walked into the dressing room at the back of the church. She handed out the clothes to her four ladies, one-man team.

"Please, put your clothes on quickly. They'll soon be done with the opening announcements," she told them.

Unlike other Sundays when Tega would've picked her and

Nse up, the ladies left early. They arrived about an hour before the beginning of service to make sure she had enough time. Nse whined about leaving her fiancé behind, but Ebele told her she'd be all right. Tega knew how to get to church. Besides, she was going to reserve a seat for him.

She grinned remembering Nse's reply, *"Bad belle. Just because your man is confused doesn't mean I should be affected. No, be only you waka?"*

She was being her usual playful self, but Nse's comment stung a little. She missed Kamal so much. In the short time, they'd become more than friends, but unfortunately, less than a couple. She shouldn't have been around him so much without knowing what the deal was. Now she was paying the price. She was almost 100 percent sure there was someone else.

"Ready?" The voice of the lead dancer interrupted Ebele's thoughts.

She was grateful for the interruption because it was time to push Kamal to the back of her mind and prepare for worship. Her daily routine consisted of worship and prayer, but at no time was she nearer to God than when she danced. She needed this.

"You all look fabulous. Join hands, let's pray." They joined hands, and Ebele looked at the team. "Blake, lead us in prayer."

"Lord, we come before you with a contrite heart, ready to worship, and open to receive Your Word. Let our movement communicate Your love. Receive it as our prayer and testimony and may it communicate Your love for mankind. In Jesus' name. Amen."

"Amen," the team responded.

They filed out with Ebele at the back of the line. Entering the sanctuary, the team took their positions. Ebele never looked out into the crowd when it was time for a performance. It was all about her and God.

"Brothers and sisters, today we have the honor of having one of our own grace us with her presence all the way from school in Newham. Enjoy in worship, Ms. Ebele, and her team," Brother Scott Pierce said.

The opening melody of "Background" by Lecrae featuring Andy Mineo began to fill the sanctuary. Blake started moving his body fluidly with the rap portion of the song. Once the chorus came on, Ebele and her girls joined in. Their bodies moved in unison to the song that was asking God to resume His first-place position in their lives. The song tugged at her heartstrings as the artist reminded Christians to be willing to play background to God's will. She was just as guilty as the musician for not always sticking to the script – the will that God had for her.

As she moved, a tear rolled down her cheek as she thought of the many times she got in the way due to her own selfish motives instead of totally surrendering, knowing once God led, and she followed, she could never go wrong.

As the rap portion of the song came back on and she and the ladies swayed from side to side, she heard God's voice; *I will be a lamp unto your feet* from Psalm119:105. An understanding she never had before came to her. He promised to be a lamp, not a floodlight. He wouldn't illuminate the whole path for her. God promised to guide her one step at a time, and that required trust and surrender.

It was as though Ebele was having an outer body experience. The melody and movement took over her body in worship until the song ended. She was brought back to earth by the thunderous applause from the congregation. Soon after, she and the praise team filed out of the sanctuary.

The team entered the back room with the adrenaline still high and pumping in their hearts. "Well done, guys. It's always a pleasure dancing with you."

"Thank you, Sister Ebele. That was great. I loved the song. The choreography was awesome too," one of the girls said.

"Yeah, we've always stayed away from rap because we didn't know how it would go," another chimed in.

"I agree, but I loved it," Blake said.

"Thank you, guys, so much. I'll see you after the service." Ebele smiled at them, picked up her small travel kit, and headed to the ladies' room. She changed as quickly as possible so she could make it back to the sanctuary for the sermon. When she opened the bathroom door, she ran into Nse.

"Babes, that was awesome. I told you to go back on the road. I'll be your manager," Nse said, excitedly.

"Thanks, girl. And you're not as interested in managing me as you are in getting a commission," Ebele quipped.

"You know me so well." The friends shared a laugh. "Come on, let's go. I'll show you where we're sitting."

They exited the bathroom, but before they entered the sanctuary, Nse leaned into her, and whispered, "Don't freak out. Kammy's here."

Ebele's face flushed, and she whispered back. "Why didn't you tell me before so that I could be prepared?" She could kill Nse right about now.

"Because I don't want you to be prepared. Suppose God brought him here for a reason bigger than you? Relax, it'll be fine. Besides, that you guys are beefing doesn't mean you don't like the man." Nse teased and quietly opened the door before Ebele could respond.

The congregation was still standing as the prayer leader was finishing up. Ebele followed Nse until they got to their seats somewhere in the middle of the sanctuary. Tega and Kamal made room for the ladies to enter the pew and take their seats. Tega was at the end, Nse sat beside him, Kamal was next, and Ebele sat beside him. She glimpsed up at him and smiled. He returned it.

Oh, God, I miss that smile. His cologne drifted past her nostrils, rendering her temporarily lightheaded. Ebele set her bags down and stole another glance at Kamal. The hair on his head and face had tell-tale signs of a recent barber visit. He was dressed like he stumbled out of the cover of a magazine. His eyes were covered with reflective shades. He was too suave for his own good.

They were still standing moments later when Pastor Ricardo took the stage. "Good morning, brethren."

After a thunderous response of "Good morning, pastor" from the congregation, Pastor Ricardo continued, "Let's remain standing for the reading of the Word." He looked out into the congregation. "Turn your Bibles to Mathew 6:33. I'm going to read from the Amplified version." He paused, as usual, giving people time to locate the passage.

Ebele didn't like toting her Bible around, so she used her app when she was away from home. She got out her iPad and went to YouVersion to pull up the passage. She felt Kamal fingers over hers as he took the device from her and held it for them to use.

"But first and most importantly seek (aim at, strive after) His kingdom and His righteousness [His way of doing and being right—the attitude and character of God], and all these things will be given to you also."

"Please, join hands, let us pray. Leave no one untouched."

She felt electricity shoot through her when Kamal took her hand. He intertwined their fingers as he bowed his head. She followed suit. After the short prayer, they were seated, but Kamal didn't let go of her hand.

"You look beautiful," he leaned into her and whispered. He'd taken off his shades.

"You clean up nice yourself." Her voice was shaky. Why was she nervous around him?

"Thanks, babe."

Babe? "May I have my hand back?"

"No," he said with a tone of finality. He turned and looked straight ahead.

She wasn't doing this here with this crazy man. In order

not to feel uncomfortable, she had to scoot closer to him. He glanced at her and gave a nod of approval. This was what he wanted all along. She took a deep breath and exhaled quietly.

Lord, please keep me focused on You.

"There was this man who decided to climb Mount Kilimanjaro," Pastor Ricardo started. "At the top of the mountain, there was a lot of fog. So the man got so far, but quit. Unbeknownst to him, he was almost at the top, but he couldn't see that because of the fog. The next day, the weather conditions were even worse, but he decided to try again. He did, and this time, he got all the way to the top. When he got down, reporters who marveled at his incredible feat asked what made him continue going up the mountain even though the weather was worse. He looked at them and said that the second day, his mindset changed. He decided to picture himself at the finish line despite what he saw. So, he put one foot in front of the other until he came to the end.

"Brothers and sisters, this world is like the fog. Some days are worse than others. If you try to make it on your own strength, your vision will be distorted. In the physical, we rely on feelings and emotions. But there's good news – we can navigate every day with confidence if we seek Jesus and His righteousness first. You'll no longer be controlled by what you can see with your natural eyes but the spiritual ones based upon God's rule."

Shouts of "Praise God" and "Amen" could be heard from the congregation.

"But how do you know the rule of God? How would you know what kind of picture to keep in your head as you navigate life?" the pastor asked and paused. "You'd only know that when you make a habit of actively seeking Him. Not only seeking Him but seeking Him first." The pastor walked from one end of the stage to the other, asking the congregation to repeat the word first.

Ebele glanced over at Kamal. He surprised her every day.

He was always the jokester, so she didn't think he'd be as attentive and participatory as he was. As though feeling her stare, he squeezed her hand.

"The fog symbolizes those things that go wrong in our everyday life. Relationships, family matters, business, school, work, you name it. But Jesus has promised, seek FIRST the kingdom and everything else will be added to you. Now listen, this is something Jesus said, seek Me, and I'll take care of you. Somebody hashtag this – #WhenISeekHimHeGotMe. Brothers and sisters, you must appeal to God's perspective before – not after – before anything else. Stop trying to do it on your own. Stop seeking the opinion of others and leaving God on the back burner. Seek Him. What?" Pastor Ricardo pointed his microphone to the congregation, and there were shouts of "First."

"Yes. Seek Him first. In closing, I'll say this, putting God before anything else addresses your anxiety. I never said everything would be sweet. You *will* have things that don't go right and have the tendency to worry but—everybody says but."

"But," they shouted.

"But you won't get anxious. The thing that goes wrong won't control you. You'll control it. You won't be shaken or worried because you have Him in the front of everything. 1 Corinthians 15:58 *Therefore, my dear brothers and sisters, stand firm. Let nothing move you. Always give yourselves fully to the work of the Lord, because you know that your labor in the Lord is not in vain.* Amen."

"Amen!"

"Bow your heads, and let's pray."

As they prayed, Ebele felt the atmosphere shift. Kamal loosened his grip on her hand. She held it tighter. The choir hummed Hillsong's version of "I Surrender." As he did every Sunday, Pastor Ricardo asked for those who wanted to give their lives to Christ to come to the front of the church. Next, he asked for those who wanted to rededicate their lives to Christ to also come forward.

Ebele tugged Kamal's hand. He leaned down to her. "You wanna go?"

"Nah, I've been baptized. Momsie made sure of it when we were kids," he responded. Something about his tone sent chills through her. He wasn't as jovial as he was when service began. She wasn't sure whether to push or let him be.

The atmosphere was permeated with screams, cries, moans of people praying, getting baptized, and being delivered.

"Being saved doesn't take away your cool factor. In fact, you'll be cooler because you're assured heaven. But what would you gain having everything on this earth and losing in eternity?" Pastor Ricardo asked.

Ebele eased her hand from Kamal's. She knelt and bowed her head. "Lord Jesus, thank you for this message. Thank you for bringing Kamal to this place. Lord, help Kamal to surrender completely to you. I love him, God. I can come to terms with that now, so I want everything good for him. Make everything right with You and him In Jesus name. A—"

Ebele felt a draft by her side. Kamal had moved. She mumbled "Amen," still on her knees, and looked up. Tega was walking with him down the aisle toward the altar. Words failed her, but emotion engulfed her as tears rolled down her cheeks. She felt Nse lift her up and hug her.

"Shh … this is a good thing," Nse whispered. "Stop crying."

"Tears of joy. God is so good."

"That He is."

Ebele looked on as Tega stood behind Kamal, who was now on his knees. Pastor Ricardo placed his hand over his head and prayed. She looked up to the ceiling and mouthed to God, "Thank you."

Chapter 15

In the men's restroom of the church, Kamal stared at his reflection in the mirror. He had to get away for a minute to recollect his thoughts. Since being in the UK, he'd visited the church twice. He even came here with Tega once for mid-week Bible study. Nothing compelled him to go in front of the congregation. So, what happened today?

This wasn't supposed to happen. He had no concrete reason for being resistant to God. Apart from his childhood, he'd enjoyed God's blessings, so he couldn't place what the problem was. Thinking about it, he just didn't want to give up how he was living. Suppose he failed at it? He already knew he might. That was the reason he declined when Ebele asked. They all had been baptized as kids, but he knew what she was really asking him. When he declined, he searched her face, but it held no disappointment. That was another reason he liked her. She didn't pressure him but took him the way he was. Really was, not the way the world looked at him.

Therefore, he couldn't explain how his feet began to move. All he knew was that as the song "I Surrender" continued to play, he felt a shift. Somehow the burden of inadequacy he'd dealt with for years, seemed too heavy to continue to bear. No one, except Coach Grams, knew of his struggles. He kept it hidden, after all, he was Kammy Danjuma.

He closed his eyes, took a deep breath, and exhaled. Recently, things had been happening that he couldn't explain. First, in a matter of two short months, he'd fallen in love with a woman he couldn't imagine himself without. He could admit it now. It took a lot of tossing and turning the night before to come to that conclusion. He couldn't tell her though because he was still in a situation.

He was playing better than he had played in the last year. Now, what was meant to be a simple church visit to get his girl, ended with him in front of the altar on full display. His brothers would have a field day. Something he read some days ago flashed before him. *But whoever denies me before men, I also will deny before my Father who is in heaven.*

"Come on, Jesus, ain't nobody denying you. I never have," he mumbled to himself. Figuring he'd been in the bathroom a little too long, he bent to wash his hands when the door opened, and Tega walked in.

"You okay in here?" he asked.

"Yeah, man, I had to step away for a minute." Kamal dried his hands. He turned to his friend. "I don't want her to think I did this just to get her …"

"She won't. Besides, the Lord searches the heart of man. As long as your motives are pure with Him, you're good."

"I feel lighter. But suppose I can't do it, man?"

"Bro, you got the Holy Spirit to help you. Just ask Him. Our flesh doesn't disappear. We now have the Holy Spirit to help us overcome. Besides, you got me, your brothers, and wifey. We're gonna help you."

"Wifey? Can you at least let me make her my woman first?" Kamal headed out of the bathroom. "Always trying to rush people."

Tega chuckled and patted him on his back. They both put on their shades but not in time to deter fans. They stopped in the hallway to sign autographs and take selfies with a few people. Kamal signed his last autograph as his eyes searched for Ebele. He saw her to his far left, standing next to Nse. While Nse looked through her phone, Ebele spoke to some guy. Kamal was cool until he saw the man put his hand on the small of her back and kiss her on the cheek. Tega must have noticed his jaw clench.

"Be easy, man. We at church, and that's the choir direc-tor," Tega said.

"So? I've told her about randoms."

"Huh?" Tega shook his head.

They began to walk toward the ladies, and his eyes connected with Ebele. Her face shone with glee. It disap-peared when she noted his expression. He saw the exact moment understanding of his mood came upon her. She rolled her eyes and stepped back from the choir director. He got to her, and she handed him his coat and scarf. He thanked her and put them on.

Kamal pulled her to him and bent to whisper in her ear, "What I tell you about randoms?"

"Duke, this is Kamal Danjuma. Kamal this is Duke, our choir director." Ebele made the introductions, ignoring him.

The man's grin widened as he stretched out his hand to Kamal. Kamal hesitated. Duke creased his forehead in confu-sion. Ebele elbowed Kamal.

Kamal took the guy's hand. "Nice to meet you. It would've been better if you didn't have your lips on my girl."

Tega snickered.

"Oh, Lord." Nse gasped. "We need to get out of God's house. Kammy will have us all turning to salt soon."

"Excuse me?" Duke asked.

Ebele shot Kamal a warning look. "Don't worry about it."

"Oh, okay. I'll see you next week, Ebi. See you, Nse. Gentlemen." Duke gave them a final glance and left.

Ebele turned toward Kamal and sucked her teeth. She

stomped toward the door. Nse looked at him with her hands on her hips.

"If I weren't so happy you've come to Christ, I'd be mad at you for upsetting my girl," she said. "I'm so proud of you."

Kamal drew her in for a hug. "Thanks, sis, now go see about my girl. She knows she's not too tall. All that stomping will have her in the ground. I can't lose her, man."

Tega shook his head and laughed.

"Oh, gosh. I'm telling," Nse said. She turned and headed for the exit.

"Sis, don't be a snitch. Your man's already one. Can't have both of y'all be snitches." Kamal joked as he and Tega walked behind her.

"Baby, get your friend," Nse said.

The three of them approached Nse's car. Ebele was in the front seat, scrolling through her phone.

"What's up, E? Is that how you welcome the brethren in the church? I need to tell Pastor Ricky," Kamal said, ignoring the frown on her face.

She ignored him. Nse and Tega exchanged glances, watching the pair.

"You not talking to me?" Kamal took the phone from her.

"Kamal, why can't you let me be mad without showing yourself?" Ebele asked.

"Oh, you can be mad. Just not with me."

"He has no sense at all." Nse giggled. She kissed Tega. "I'll call you later, baby. Let me get Ebele home."

"Nah, hold up. She's coming with me." Kamal put Ebele's phone in his pocket.

"Err, I'm right here," Ebele said.

Kamal bent and kissed her forehead. "I know, babe. I'm telling you too."

"I'm still mad at you. You had no right to intimidate that man," Ebele said.

"Yeah, I figured that. Tell me more about it on our way." He reached for her hand.

"Sis, just go with the man because we'll be here all day," Tega said.

Kamal waggled his silky brows at her. She put her hand in his, and he helped her out of the car. Kamal drew her closer and hugged her. He missed her so much.

When they broke their embrace, she looked up at him. "I need to change out of these clothes," she said, softly.

"We'll follow behind Nse so you can get your stuff." He cupped her face with both hands.

"My stuff?"

"Yeah, E, we need to talk. I'll drop you off at the rehabilitation center in the morning. Trust me," he pleaded.

Ebele nodded, and Kamal let go of the breath he was holding. The couples said their goodbyes. Kamal grabbed Ebele's hand and led her to his car.

———

SEVERAL MINUTES LATER, KAMAL GOT THE FIREPLACE GOING IN his living room. When he left that morning, having Ebele here wasn't the plan, but here they were. While he waited for her to get her stuff at Nse's, her friend gave him a lecture about hurting Ebele, and something about taking him out if he did. He just laughed at her but didn't argue. Ebele was his heart, and that wasn't his intention.

She was in one of the guest bedrooms changing. He walked into the kitchen and opened the fridge. His housekeeper had stocked up when she knew he was returning the previous day. He wasn't sure what to cook for her, so he brought out steaks and some vegetables, and headed upstairs to change.

On his way, he felt buzzing in his pocket. He reached in and removed Ebele's phone. It was her mother calling. He knew how service got in Nigeria and didn't want her worrying or wasting her phone credit. On the other hand, he wasn't going anywhere near the room Ebele was in. His manhood was being tested enough. He didn't want to accidentally run into her undressing. So he did the only logical thing.

"Hello?" he answered the phone and continued up the stairs.

"Oh, I'm sorry. I thought I dialed my daughter's phone," Ebele's mother said. Her raspy voice sounded just like her daughter's. Fear was evident in her tone.

"Yes, you did, ma'am. Ebele isn't available now."

"Oh, then, young man, who are you?"

"I'm her future husband—"

"Her what?"

"Her future husband, Ma. Although she doesn't know it yet."

"Do you have a name?"

"Yes, Ma. Apologies, that was rude of me. My name is Kamal Danjuma."

"*Onye* Hausa? *Ha Chineke Na.*"

Kamal suppressed his laughter over the woman's panic that he was Hausa. It never failed. Immediately people heard his last name, they assumed he was Muslim.

"Yes, I'm Hausa, Ma. My mom is Igbo from Enugu, and I'm a Christian." He sat on his bed.

"Okay *o*, young man. Since my daughter doesn't know your intentions, I won't take you seriously until she tells me to. Just don't distract her."

"Ma, I'm very serious, but I understand. Distracting her isn't my plan. Putting a smile on her face, loving, and providing her heart's desires is all I want to do," he insisted.

"You know we don't do *obodo oyibo* marriage. You have to come home and know her people."

Kamal chuckled at her insinuation that he'd marry Ebele abroad without seeing her family back home. Although he knew off the bat, those *Naija* wedding shenanigans weren't for him. His mother would have to be satisfied with the *gele* she's already tied at Rasheed and Jabir's weddings. "I know, Ma. My mom would kill me if I did that."

His nostrils picked up the aroma of cooking meat. He shot up from the bed. He wanted to cook for Ebele and not the other way around. These Ashiedu women always tended to get his head gone.

"Tell my daughter to call me as soon as possible."

"Okay, Ma. It was nice talking to you. I hope to see you soon." Kamal hung up, changed into more comfortable clothes, and headed downstairs.

He sauntered through the living room to the open kitchen. Ebele was in there with her back toward him. She belonged here. Well, not in the kitchen, but in his house. He walked up behind her and wrapped his arms around her waist. He nuzzled her neck. She relaxed her back into him.

"Whatchu doing, short stuff?" he asked.

"I was hungry, and you were taking forever. So I started on the steaks." She turned off the faucet and dried her hands with a kitchen towel.

He watched her, looking her over from the top of her wild, curly hair that called out for his fingers, to her well-manicured toes against his heated floors. She'd changed into gray sweatpants and a long-sleeved, V-cut top with an inscription "My God Stays Awesome." Cute. He kissed her forehead, picked her up, and sat her on the island. He handed her the remote to his state-of-the-art satellite radio system.

"I keep it on old school, but you can change it if you want." He made sure she was safe from the burner but close enough to satisfy his craving for her presence.

"No, I like old school." She placed the remote to the side. "What are you making?"

"Woman, this is my show; let me run it." He quickly

washed his hands and turned the steaks she'd started searing in the pan.

"Make sure you can cook *o*, or I'm subtracting points," she warned.

"Oh, so I got some points already? Good to know."

"You're in the red. Nothing to be happy about."

"What I tell you about lying, E? We just got back from church."

"Whatever. Speaking of church, I'm so proud of you." She beamed, and his heart expanded. "How do you feel?"

"I don't know, really. I guess it hasn't sunk in, but I do feel a sense of freedom."

"You *are* free in Christ. He has asked us to cast our burdens upon Him," she encouraged.

"I always give my brothers a hard time, but I can feel what they probably felt." He brought out coconut milk, rice, and spices from the pantry. "Living like how the pastor described sounds like a tall order. But my soul is too fly to be hanging out in hell."

"You can never be serious, can you?"

"E, I'm being serious." His brow shot up. "Jesus and I were cool; now we're cooler. But for real though, I'm afraid to fail."

"It's a tall order, but the Holy Spirit is there to help. If Paul, who was the biggest prosecutor of Christ followers, can become one of His greatest apostles, then know Jesus provides help to the willing. You just have to open your heart to him. John 14:26 says, the *Holy Spirit is our Helper, Teacher and will help us remember what He has said*. But you must read the Bible to know what He has said," she finished.

"Cool, I hear you, E. How much we get for participation, though?" He turned on the oven.

"Huh?"

"All that standing up, shouting. Then the pastor tells us to repeat after him. That's participation. How much we get? Kamal asked, opening the bag of mixed vegetables to steam.

Ebele laughed so hard that Kamal feared she'd roll off the island. "Why are you like this?" She wiped the tears that formed from laughter. "Even though you have no chill at all, I'm still proud of you."

"Don't try to butter me up. You still in trouble, but we'll talk after lunch."

"I have no idea what you're talking about, but since you're feeding me, I'll pretend to listen." She shrugged.

"Keep testing me." He washed some rice and put it on the stove to boil.

"Yay, goody, you remembered my coconut rice."

Kamal opened the heated oven and put the seared steaks in to bake. "Yes, greedy, I remember everything that comes from your mouth." He walked over to kiss her lips.

"Move. I'm not greedy, just a healthy eater."

"You are perfect."

"Including my height, you make fun of?" She pouted.

"Especially your height. Your head makes the perfect armrest."

"You know what …" Ebele jumped down from the island, leaving the kitchen.

Kamal laughed and followed her. "Hey, where are you going?"

"Leave me alone, Kam." She kept walking toward the living room, and he followed her.

"My bad. This is why I love your height …" He slung her over his shoulder and carried her back to the kitchen. He placed her back where she was sitting. "Stop that pouting. I was just playing. Everything about you is perfect for me."

He walked over to the fridge and got out a bottle of Heineken and Malt. He turned around, and she shook her head at his choice of drink. He sighed, returned both drinks, and brought out a bottle of sparkling wine. She smiled, and he chuckled. He had to remember to get rid of the alcohol in the fridge. He opened the wine and poured them both a glass. He felt buzzing in his pocket. How could he forget?

"Here, Momsie called. Tell her my bad, and I'll make it up to her," Kamal handed Ebele her ringing phone.

Confusion etched on her face. She took her phone and answered it. "Mummy, *Oliwe* ma."

Kamal continued to put their meal together as he half listened to her one-sided conversation. She spoke a mix of her native tongue and English. She was so sexy to him. Especially when she became nervous and bit her lip. When she did that, he could tell they were talking about him. After promising to call back tomorrow, Ebele hung up.

"*Oliwe?* What's that?" he asked, curious about the greeting.

"In my mom's hometown, each village has a greeting. My mom is from the royal lineage of *Ishe Kpe*. That's her village, and her greeting is *Oliwe*."

"Nice." He began to set the table.

"Kam, err … why is my mother calling you "my son"?"

"Oh, we rapped earlier, and I guess she just loves me. Not all Ashiedu women give me a hard time."

"I don't even want to know." She got down from the island and helped him carry the food to the table.

"I wasn't telling no way."

They sat at the table, said grace, and enjoyed their meal. Kamal waited for her expression when she took the first taste of her food. He saw bliss, pleasure, satisfaction, and his mind travelled to where it shouldn't. *Holy Spirit, help me.*

They talked about her classes, and he shared what had been happening in the weeks they were apart. AnkFeets, a Nigerian based footwear company that specialized in Ankara shoes, had contacted his agent, wanting him to be their spokesperson. They sent over some samples. He smiled when he saw they had put his initials on them along with their logo. It gave him an idea then.

They finished eating. He took her hand and walked her to the living room.

"I'll be right back." He took the stairs two at a time to his room. He got there and retrieved an AnkFeets bag. When he got back, she had her laptop on her lap with the TV on. He sat next to her and took her laptop from her.

"I got something for you." Kamal handed her the bag.

"Kam, what is it?" She looked closely at the bag. "Are these the shoes you were telling me about?"

He studied her as she pulled out a pair of women's wedge sandals. She nodded in appreciation until she got to the initials. She looked up at him. He took one sandal from her and lifted her feet. He put it on her.

"Perfect."

"Kam, no, no …"

Chapter 16

Ebele didn't know whether to laugh, cry, or run. She was engulfed with emotion as she read the initials E.V.D. It didn't take a genius to figure out it stood for Ebele Vanessa Danjuma. Tears won the day as she took off the sandal and placed it on the floor.

"Kam, no, no, no …" Her voice croaked. She continued to shake her head.

"E, look at me." He used his hand to bring her face up to his. "I'm not saying now or tomorrow, but please don't say you won't consider the possibility."

"Kam. I can't do that. We're back to where we started before I pulled back." She loved this man but refused to be stuck in transition with him. "You haven't been straight with me. You told me to trust you, but you can't or won't even tell me the real deal."

Kamal leaned back in the chair. She glanced at him and anger rose in her. How dare he come at her, and he hasn't even gotten himself together? She stood to leave. He grabbed her hand, pulling her down.

"Hold on. Listen. I don't want to disrespect you by talking

about someone that's still part of my present with you. I wanted to do what I had to do about the situation."

"I don't read minds, Kamal. Can you tell me what's up or leave me alone?" She huffed.

"The second choice is *not* an option."

"Then speak," she demanded.

"I met Brittani when I moved to LA. We've been exclusive for about two years, but over the last couple of months, it fizzled."

He was right. It did hurt to hear. Jealousy crept into her veins when he mentioned being exclusive with someone else.

"Did I have anything to do with that?" she asked.

"No, but you did make me recognize it faster than I would've," he confessed.

"So what do you want with me? You're still in a relationship."

He lowered his head in his hands. "I'm being totally selfish, but I'll be that with you. I want you to wait for me."

"Let me get this right. You want to have a girlfriend, have my emotions running awry while I sit and wait for you?" Her blood boiled, and she was sure her cheeks changed color.

The audacity. This was on her. In her subconscious, she knew Kamal wasn't single. That knowledge didn't keep her heart from breaking. She tried to stay away, but her mind gave way to her heart, and she didn't. The past couple of weeks were pure torture, but she survived. Not knowing might have been bliss. Now she had confirmation that he had someone. She wasn't that special; she was just convenient.

"Ebele, I can't break up with her over the phone. I just can't do her like that." He rubbed his hand over his face.

"That's actually honorable. I would've thought of you as a coward if you did." She could feel the stress roll off his body. She could actually feel it. The atmosphere was clogged with emotion.

"E, I never saw you coming. You've broken down my

defenses and challenged me in ways no one else has. All others see is the star, so quite frankly, I get away with anything. With you, I begin to wonder whether I'm enough because fame means nothing to you. You're like a book; I want to keep reading to uncover what's next. You see, I'm using book analogies when I don't read. Audio is more my thing."

She giggled. It was so hard to keep her hard exterior when it came to him.

"I never did anything about Brittani because she was comfortable. She allowed as much as I gave. I'm not going to bash her because she was okay for what I needed. You made me see that there's so much more. Your laughter gives me joy; in your eyes, I see hope. Your touch makes me feel safe. You can break me and cause me pain, but not being with you is unimaginable."

Kamal thumbed away the tears rolling down her cheeks. He was always so playful that hearing these words and the intensity with which he said them, sent her into a downward spiral of emotion.

"I'll never be an intentional source of your pain, but ..." she started, knowing that regardless of her feelings, God would never give her someone that belonged to another person. Despite his words, she had to stand firm.

"No, babe, just listen. I asked her to come for my off days," he said. "That's the end of the week."

Her eyes turned to slits. Was she supposed to twiddle her thumbs while he and his girlfriend played house?

"Don't look at me like that. It's either she comes here, or I go to America, but I need to talk to her face to face."

She decided to be petty. "Let me know when, so I can have some dates lined up too."

"Don't test me. I'm serious, E." Kamal's jaw clenched, and he stood. He walked to the kitchen. "Holy Spirit, I'm gonna need some immediate assistance with this woman."

She huffed and watched Kamal get two small packs of *Kuli*

Kuli and two bottles of water. He had some nerve being territorial. He got back to the living room and tossed her a pack.

"Just rude," she mumbled, catching it.

"Well, you're getting on my nerves talking about dates. I just opened up to you," he hissed.

"Kam, think about what you're asking me."

"And? I didn't say indefinitely. I'll see her next week and let her know what's up." He picked up the remote and started changing the channels on the TV.

How was he getting mad at her? She sighed. She did love him, but she'd keep that to herself for now. One thing was for sure – she wasn't waiting around for him. She was just going to let him believe that. She didn't have time to date anyway, but if someone came knocking, she'd go out with them. Kamal or not.

After a few minutes of silence, Ebele threw a piece of her snack at him. He ignored her. She repeated it. When he ignored her again, she scowled. "I can't believe you're mad at me." She threw another piece at him.

"Stop, E, I don't speak to enablers." He continued to stare at the TV. East Enders was on, so she knew there was no way he was concentrating on that.

"How am I an enabler?"

He looked at her. "You're enabling me to commit ungodly acts."

"Huh? What are you talking about now?"

"The Holy Book says thou shall not hurt another man. You, on dates, will enable me to do just that," His expression held no emotion. "Jesus and I just got real cool; now you're trying to spoil it."

She laughed and picked up her laptop. "First, the Bible doesn't say it that way. Second …, never mind, I simply have no words."

She needed to check her grades and some emails. Since it was her last year, she'd sent some re-introduction emails to her top choices for employment. She'd done placement assignments with those places over the years and hoped for a favorable response.

He glanced at her laptop. "What are you doing? Do we have an understanding?"

"I thought you weren't talking to me." She put her laptop on the floor.

Kamal pulled the leg she had on the couch and slid her down until she was next to him. He stared at her. His gaze became intense as his silence grew. He lifted her to his lap. She tried to wiggle away. This was dangerous territory.

"E, relax. I promised to be good, and I have been."

"Yeah, but we shouldn't invite temptation."

"Chill. Do you know how much self-control I've had to learn in the two months I've known you?"

"Trust me, I know."

"Besides, I respect you too much." A beat of silence passed between them. "I know I'm asking for a lot, but you did say I was spoiled, so you knew that."

She remained silent.

"Promise me, no dates." His eyes held hers captive.

"Promise me, one week."

"Deal."

"Okay, deal."

"Give me a kiss to seal the agreement," he said.

She leaned into him and brushed her lips against his cheek.

"Good." He tapped her, and she slid from his lap back onto the chair. He stood. "Now go study while I check some emails. Can't have no half-baked physiotherapist on my team."

Ebele picked up a paper from the table, balled it up, and threw it at him. He dodged it and winked at her. The last time she checked, she already had a daddy. At least in some kind of capacity. The thought reminded her that their monthly lunch was coming up. She looked at her new sandals. Her heart thumped against her chest. She let out a dreamy sigh. "Not my will but Yours, Lord."

———

EBELE SET HER BOWL OF *BANGA* RICE DOWN ON THE SIDE TABLE and tossed her Kindle on the couch. She walked back into her small kitchen and got out a bottle of chilled water from the fridge. She'd been out all day, and the cold seemed to seep into her bones. She knew that no amount of tea or cocoa would help her, so she whipped up a small batch of the extra spicy dish.

She went back to the couch, got comfortable, and changed the channel to Sky Sports. She was finally going to catch one of Kamal's prime time games. It wasn't for another two hours, but she'd just keep it on the station, and delve into the fiction world. That way, she wouldn't get so lost in her reading and forget when it was time.

Her time was so limited that she was happy for the early night. It had been two days since she last saw Kamal, and she missed him terribly. Every morning since Sunday, she got "Good morning. Have you eaten? How was your day?" routine texts from Kamal. Texts that led to full blown discussions until she or he had to get off the phone.

Ebele covered her socked legs with her blanket, picked up her food, and turned her Kindle to her designated location. For several minutes, she read and ate while the TV played in the background. She looked up when she heard the presenter mention Kamal's name. She set down her empty bowl and drank some water while listening to the presenter praising Kamal for his performance since joining the club. The presenter's guest gave a couple of statistics and gushed his excitement about seeing Kamal play soon. They showed pictures of him about London. Her heart constricted at all the female fans hanging on to him at various team events.

"I don't even know what's wrong with me. He has a whole girlfriend." She picked up her device to resume reading after the segment. Changing her mind, she picked up her phone. Opening her iMessages, she found his name and typed a quick message.

U ready?

A few seconds later, she beamed as she read his response.

Always Baby. U home now? He was always so concerned about her.

Yes, watching you.

You pray for me?

Always.

That's my girl. I wanna hear your voice but can't call. It's too noisy here.

I'll call you tonight.

You better. A'ight short stuff I gotta go.

Ebele sent him numerous hug emojis, for which he responded by sending her a kissy face emoji and a heart. She couldn't wipe the grin off her face even if she tried. She set her phone aside and continued reading.

An hour later, the game started. She got on the phone with Nse, and the two of them chatted about Nse's wedding while idly watching the game. Suddenly the commentator went wild; the stadium looked electrified. Kamal had the ball and was headed over to the opposite side of the field. Tega was running after another guy on the opposing team. From what Kamal had explained to her, Tega and the other member of their team were trying to protect him to ensure he got to the goal post free and clear.

Ebele jumped up from her seat. "Babe, go, go, go!" she yelled.

"*No commot my ear drum o.* Ha! See our men *o*," Nse screamed on the other end of the line.

Kamal used his leg to steady the ball, looking for who to pass it to. When the other guy outran Tega, Kamal started to move with the ball again. To get the ball away from him, Kamal extended his right leg. The man couldn't stop himself in time. Ebele watched in horror as the men collided. She knew the impact wouldn't be good, and the commentator agreed with her. Ebele screamed and sank to the floor as Kamal flew up into the air and came crashing down.

"Oh, my God. Oh, my God. No." Her heart raced. She crawled closer to the screen. This couldn't be good. Kamal's leg was facing the wrong way. She dropped the phone. She put one hand over her mouth and the other over her heart. Her lungs struggled to fill up with air. Flashbacks of her injury sent her into a panic. She couldn't control her breathing.

"Ebele!"

She heard Nse yell her name but couldn't coordinate her mind to respond. She tried to maintain some calmness. Raising her knees to her chest, she put her head between her legs. Moments later, her breathing returned to normal. She looked up at the screen, and Kamal was writhing around. The team medical personnel continued to work on him just as the camera got a close-up of his face. Ebele saw and felt his pain. She picked up her phone.

"Why is he not standing?" she said more to herself, holding her blanket. She was a physiotherapist and knew all about sports injuries but watching it happen to him – her Kamal – tore her heart in two.

"Ebele, calm down. He'll soon stand. You know how these things go," Nse said.

"I do but not to him," she whispered.

"Aww, someone's in love. If I ask you, you'll deny it like how the embassy denies people Visa."

"Nse, not now," Ebele absently responded as she watched them strap Kamal to a stretcher and carry him off the field.

She threw off her blanket and headed to the room. "I have to see him."

"Ebele. Hold on. Think. There's no way for you to see him now. I know you're worried, but it'll be all right."

Ebele sat on her bed and put her hand in her hair. She knew she couldn't call him.

"See, they'll take him to the locker room and evaluate him. If he's good, he'll come back out. If not, he'll be sent home or to the doctor. Hang up. Let me call you back. I have the number to one of the medics."

"How?"

"My dear, Tega wasn't going to send me to an early grave." Nse hung up the call.

Ebele walked back into the living room. She stood in front of the television with her arms crossed over her chest. She sucked her teeth when the commentator said it was a knee injury. Anybody could see that. She needed to hear his voice. She remembered what she should've done instead of unraveling at the seams. She got on her knees and prayed for the man that came from nowhere and took her heart away.

Chapter 17

From the examination table in the sterile corner of the locker room, Kamal watched his team celebrate a 3:2 victory. Pain shot through his swollen knee as the medics pushed, pulled, and tapped on it trying to figure how extensive the damage was. His heart beat at a rapid pace dreading what their conclusion would be.

As he came down from his adrenaline high, a lone tear rolled from his closed eyes. The implication of what this injury might mean settled in. The pain medication was working on the ache in his knee, but his heart was another story. God wouldn't allow this to happen to him, would He? He'd turned over a new leaf since that day at church. Doing what he was supposed to do – praying, reading the Bible. Something he found challenging until Ebele agreed to do it with him every night. Kamal shook his head to rid it of his negative thoughts. He was now saved. God wouldn't cut short his dreams just like that.

"Danjuma," the lead medical professional spoke.

"What's up?" His monotone answer mirrored his mood.

"I have it wrapped up in a compression bandage, and this ice pack should help you out tonight." He walked to the other side of the room and came back with some Naprosyn tablets. "Here, take these tonight for the pain. Looks like you have a torn ligament, but you need an MRI for us to know the extent of the damage."

The man helped Kamal sit up and elevated his injured right knee. Kamal stared at the swelling and sighed, hopeful that the next day, the doctor would bring better news.

"Okay, thanks—"

"Kammy, how you feeling, bro?" Tega walked into the room followed by Freddie and Princeton. The team's coach wasn't too far behind them.

Kamal gave them a rundown of what the medic told him. The coach pulled the medic to the side, and they began to talk, looking over at him at intervals. Kamal wondered if there was something the medic was telling the coach but didn't tell him.

"You ready to head out?" Tega asked.

"Yeah."

Freddie and Princeton helped stabilize him on the crutches they'd given him. Kamal hobbled on one leg until they made it to the team bus. Soon, everyone was on the bus for the short ride from the London stadium to the Turk West facility. There, the players would get into their cars and head to their various homes. The plan was for Kamal to leave his car there and ride to Essex with Tega.

"Aye, you see my sports bag? I need my phone," Kamal asked, once they got off the bus. Still balanced on his crutches, he put his weight on his left side.

"Yeah, here you go." Tega handed him the bag.

Kamal retrieved his phone from the side pocket and slung the bag over his shoulder. The second he turned it on, his phone lit up with notifications from social media and texts. He leaned against Tega's car and went directly to his messages. He needed to get to Ebele. She must be terrified. The one time she could catch his whole game, he got injured.

His jaw clenched at the thought of her being worried about him.

He had since changed her name in his phone to **My Everything**. Just like he imagined, she'd sent him a text almost every ten minutes from the time he was injured until about a short while ago. Reading them confirmed his thoughts – she was terrified. The realization of that worried and gave him a warm feeling inside. They might not have their situation fully sorted out, but he knew she loved him, no matter what she said. Good thing was, he loved her right back. He sent Brittani a quick text because he knew she'd see the news story in the morning. She was supposed to arrive in two days, and he wanted to make sure she was still going to be on that plane.

Ebele's last text read for him to call her no matter how late. It was now a quarter to midnight. Tega came over and helped him into the back of the car. He sat with his back against the window and his leg stretched out on the seat.

"Call your woman, man. Nse says she was about to come to the stadium when you fell." Tega chuckled and got into the driver's seat.

"That's my girl." Kamal dialed her number. She answered on the first ring.

"Hey, baby—Kam. Is that you?" she stuttered.

"So I gotta get injured for me to be your baby?" He imagined her rolling her eyes. "You could've told me that. I would've injured myself a long time ago."

"Good to know your mouth wasn't affected."

"No, it wasn't, baby. How would I get those kisses if anything happened to my lips? Don't speak that into existence." His aim was to brighten her somber mood.

"Kam, stop joking. Where are you?"

"Tega is taking me home."

"How are you going to manage tonight? When do you see the doctor? Did they say anything now? How bad is it?"

"Breathe, woman. Breathe, your man is good." He

paused. She remained silent. He heard her take a deep breath and exhale. "I won't lie, I'm high on these meds right now. The pain is lethal, but I'm good, babe," Kamal reassured her.

"Kam, come get me. You need help tonight. At least until you see the doctor in the morning."

He grinned at her, ignoring his reference to him being her man. "E, it's past midnight. You have class in the morning and need to be rested." His eye caught Tega's smirk in the rearview mirror.

"Kam, if you don't come, I'm taking a taxi. If anything happens to me while I'm out by myself, it's on you."

"Guilt trips, E? Really?"

"Hmmm."

"Stay home, please." She didn't respond, and he knew her; she'd do what she wanted to do anyway. "You better not come out this late, E. I'm not playing with you."

"Give Tega the phone," she said, completely ignoring him.

"Why?"

"Kamal Emeka Danjuma, give Tega the phone!"

"Here, she's on something tonight, calling my full government name." Kamal put the phone in Tega's outstretched hand.

After a few "ah ha's … I hear you … Ok, Ebi," Tega returned the phone to Kamal. He put the phone to his ear, but she was gone. He felt Tega turn the car around.

"What did she say? Where are we going?" Kamal asked.

"We gonna get her."

"Huh? No, she has a seven a.m. class," Kamal scolded. Her flat wasn't far from the Turk West facility, about a twenty-minute drive, but he still didn't want her up.

"Man, y'all figure that out. I have a happy home. I don't need Nse's wrath, and sis threatened to tell her," Tega said.

"Her short self always trying to threaten people," Kamal said.

"Well, that's your woman."

Kamal leaned his head against the window and closed his eyes. "That she is," he mumbled to himself.

———

KAMAL WATCHED EBELE SET DOWN A CUP OF CHAMOMILE TEA on the nightstand. She fluffed his pillow and ensured the one under his leg was steady, again.

"E, stop fussing, and go to bed," he said.

She'd been hovering over him ever since Tega picked her up. When she sighted him, she hugged his neck so tight, sweaty and all, that he thought he'd pass out for a minute. She rained kisses on his forehead, thanking God in between that he was all right. She did all this even before she got in the front seat of the car. He was happy when she dozed off because it was late, and he could tell she was tired. But they'd been back to his house for a while now, and she was back to moving around like the Energizer Bunny.

"Okay, I'm sorry. I don't mean to smother you." She stepped back with one hand wrapped around her stomach and the other rubbing her neck.

"Come here." He reached for her. She walked over to him. He patted the space next to him for her to sit. She did but didn't look at him.

"I'm sorry I worried you," he said.

"That wasn't your fault." She looked at him with scrunched eyebrows. "Kam, I was so scared for you. I know I should be used to this considering my profession, but …"

Emotions took over, and she looked away.

"I know, seeing it was me. I know how you feel because if the reverse were the case, I'd go crazy, too," he confessed.

"What time is your appointment tomorrow?"

"I think they put it for ten in the morning."

"Okay, I'll go to school then come back to go with you."

"E, you can't do all that running around. Go to school. I'll call you when it's over to let you know."

"I don't recall asking for permission. I'm going with you," she said with finality. Her brows shot up daring him to argue.

"You're lucky I'm in pain." He snickered. He'd definitely rubbed off on her, but he needed to remind her who was still the boss.

"Yeah, yeah. Whatever."

"Okay, you can drive, right?" He knew she didn't have a car. Being a student and having everything she needed in Newham, she didn't need one. He didn't know if she could drive, though.

She nodded.

"I don't want you traveling by train only to turn around again. Use my car to go to school. When you come back, we'll go to the doctor together."

"Kam, your plates are personalized." She frowned.

"That's your only option." He shrugged.

"Fine. Give me your hands. Let's pray."

Kamal put his hands in hers, and she said a prayer for him, her, their families, and for God's will to be done the next day at the doctor's. She placed a kiss on his forehead and rubbed his cheek with her palm.

"Drink your tea, baby. It'll calm you. Use your cell phone if you need me."

"Thank you, babe. Good night."

Kamal watched her leave, ensuring to keep the door slightly ajar. He had to have her. Other than his mother, nobody had ever worried about him or taken care of him the way she did tonight. She didn't even care that it was now two in the morning, and she had to be up early.

When they'd arrived, she made up the spare room downstairs so that he wouldn't have to climb the steps. He chuckled when he remembered the horror on Ebele's face when he said he wanted to take a shower. He called her a scaredy cat, and she pouted but still helped him with the water temperature and retrieved his stuff from the bathroom upstairs. To his surprise, when he was done, he saw Ebele had also laid out his sleepwear.

He drank his tea, and she was right, it did have a soothing effect. Kamal logged in to his Twitter account to see numerous "get well" messages in response to the update he gave his fans earlier. He didn't do social media all the time, but when he did, he stayed on Twitter or Instagram only. After responding to some fans and retweeting others, he closed the Twitter app.

He took a picture of his elevated knee and posted it on Instagram. He captioned it *Down, but E makes sure I stay Up.* He so badly wanted to tag Ebele but knew he couldn't until the cloud over his head had been cleared up. Before he could log off, his DM's, and notifications lit up. He ignored them and signed off. The next thing he did was send Jabir a text. Finishing up his tea, he leaned back and waited for sleep to take him away.

———

Ebele had returned from school and was now driving him to Broomfield Medical. While she was gone, he spoke with Jabir, Rasheed, and Brittani. His brothers wanted to hop on planes and come down. He was amused by their over-protectiveness. He told them to hold on until he got back from the hospital. By that time, he'd have a clearer picture of what he was dealing with. Brittani, however, was on her way to London.

He glanced over at Ebele. He loved the way she looked maneuvering his SUV. She was in her own world, concentrating on the road while humming to a song by a Nigerian artist called Ada. Kamal picked up the CD case and looked at the back of it for the track currently playing. It was "Testimony." She looked so happy and reserved but knew that underneath that exterior was a lioness who'd tear him to pieces when Brittani arrived. She promised him a week, and he prayed she kept her word.

Two hours later, the representative from the UK office of his sports agency, Warren Edwards, and the head coach of Turk West stood at the other end of the room, waiting for the doctor and the results of his numerous tests. Kamal lay on the examining table. Ebele stood next to him. His arm was snaked around her waist. She used her hand to hold it in place while she absently caressed the old scar over his brow with the other.

He'd had an MRI, been poked, stretched, and prodded. Despite the ice pack, the swelling didn't seem to go down. Although he knew there was nothing wrong with his head, when the doctor suggested a CT scan, Ebele insisted he take one because of the way he fell.

Dr. Mathews swung the door open and strode to the exam table. "Okay, Kammy. I have some good and bad news for you." Coach and Edwards walked closer.

"Give me the bad news." Kamal sat up.

"You've completely torn your ACL, and you have a tiny bone fracture around the area. I'm afraid you're out for the season."

Kamal's worst nightmare had been confirmed. He put his head in his hand. A tear of the anterior crucial ligament was no small injury for an athlete. It took a long time to get back to full play. His eyes misted. He wouldn't be able to play in the Regions International Championship in May. That was his last shot. Ebele rubbed his back, giving him the comfort he desperately needed.

"Doctor, what's the good news?" Kamal asked, softly. His focus was no longer on the doctor but on the Coach who he knew was avoiding eye contact with him. This wasn't good at all.

"Warren, when does Pete get here?" Kamal asked before

the doctor could continue. He needed his real agent and not the representative. Things looked like they were going to get bad.

"He should land later tonight," Edwards answered.

Kamal nodded and looked at the doctor, giving him permission to continue.

"Because of your strength and fitness, your range of motion isn't that bad. The stability of the knee isn't tip top but with full reconstructive knee surgery, and aggressive physical therapy, we can get you back to full play in about six to nine months."

Kamal stared at him. How was that good news? Either way, he was messed up.

"We won't be able to do anything now until the swelling goes down. But for the best results, if you start physical therapy now, healing will be much quicker," Dr. Mathews said.

Kamal ran his fingers over his head. This couldn't be happening. He had had a meniscus tear earlier in his career in his left knee. It took a while to gain confidence in it. Now, he was being told that his right knee was shot. Ebele continued to rub his back but remained silent.

"Kamal?" Dr. Mathews called him. Kamal looked up at him.

"Do you want to set up an appointment so that we can discuss your options?" Dr. Mathew asked. "By then, the swelling would've gone down."

"No," Kamal said. He started to get up. He motioned for Ebele to hand him his crutches.

Ebele didn't move. He glanced at her. She had a frown on her face.

Coach walked over to Kamal, patted him on his back, and signaled for the doctor. "Doc, let me see you for a minute." The doctor and Coach left the room.

Edward walked closer to him. "Kamal, you should give this some thought. You have some more years left in you. Let's just get you home so that you can rest that knee. Pete will be here soon, and we can all connect." Edward turned to leave the room, "Call me. I have my phone on."

"What do you mean by no?" Ebele asked when it was just the two of them.

"N.O. Let's go." He hopped off the table on one foot. He leaned over and got his crutches. Without looking back, he wobbled out of the room.

Kamal heard Ebele call him but kept going. At this point, he just wanted to be left alone. His life was over. What was the point?

Chapter 18

E bele wanted to take Kamal's crutches and beat him over the head. The drive back to his house was silent. Kamal hadn't spoken to her since they'd left the hospital. She tried to get him to open up to her, but he barked her away. She pulled into his garage and got out of the car. She went around to the other side to help him out.

"I got it." His response was curt as he pushed himself up to stabilize on his crutches.

Gone was her panic of the day before. Now, even if he didn't want her to be, she was going to help him through this like a professional. She knew there were emotional and psychological effects of being on the sidelines while you watched your teammates play. There was more at stake here than just his feelings. Her heart couldn't see him sink into an abyss of depression because of his stubbornness.

She opened the door to the house. He wobbled inside and went straight to the room he slept in the night before. She'd give him space to sulk while she made him something to eat. She'd called Jenny, her manager at the studio, to inform her she wouldn't be coming in later. Contrary to what Kamal thought, her class in the morning wasn't her only class, so she had to study and make up for what she missed.

Entering the kitchen, she pulled open the fridge to see what she could whip up for them. She got out tomatoes, pepper, onions, and eggs to make egg sauce that she'd serve with yam chips. She worked in silence, letting her mind wander.

How could, in just a short time, her life gets turned upside down? She wasn't complaining but could do without the uncertainty. As much as she wanted to be here for Kamal, she knew there were still boundaries to maintain. In the back of her mind, she knew his girlfriend would be here any day now. So she'd help him as much as she could until his family got here.

Several minutes later, she finished cutting up the yam, pre-boiled it a little, spiced it with seasoned salt and put it in the oven to bake. In that time, Tega and Nse had called, separately, both saying that they tried Kamal's phone, but he wasn't answering. She told them she'd get him to return their calls later. She lowered the heat on the egg sauce and walked into his room. She tried the handle, but the door was locked.

"Kam, are you okay?" she asked but didn't get a response. She knocked again and waited a few more seconds.

"Ebele, I need a minute, okay?"

Ebele? He never called her that. Right now, she'd give anything to hear one of his short people jokes.

"Okay, but I've made lunch, and I need to give you another ice pack soon. You also need to exercise the knee, Kam."

"I said give me a minute!"

She thought she heard him curse under his breath. "Okay, I get it. I'll leave you alone for now, but I'll be back."

Ebele turned around and went back to the kitchen to finish up. When done, she wrapped his food up and put it in the microwave. She quickly ate, cleaned up the kitchen, and pulled out her laptop. She looked online for the knee machine that would help with stretching and bending the knee within the limits he could endure. It would help give him more range of motion, and he could exercise with or without her, in preparation for surgery. After searching a couple of options, she settled on two she'd show him.

She glanced at the clock. It was time for that ice pack. She set the laptop aside, got some fresh ice, and made her way down the hall. The door was unlocked, so she entered. Kamal glanced at her and turned his attention back to the XBOX ONE he was playing. The smile that made her heart beat was gone. The gleam in his eyes, absent. It was replaced by a darkness that she tried to decode. In a matter of hours, the funny, playful man had vanished. This wasn't good.

"What's up?" Kamal asked, not taking his eyes off the screen.

"You need to eat, Kam," she said, softly. Ebele wrapped the ice in a towel and placed it on the side table. She helped him stretch and bend the knee for about ten minutes. He winced in pain, but she didn't stop until she'd done the amount of exercises required. He still hadn't said anything to her. She checked the black compression bandage to make sure it wasn't too tight, so his blood could circulate. She put the new ice pack on his knee and walked into the bathroom to empty the water in the old one. He didn't even acknowledge her, but she pushed past her hurt. She stood away from him and stared at him.

"Really, Kam? Is this how you're going to be?"

"Can I have a day? Can you just give me one miserable day?" he asked, clearly irritated.

She was not in the mood to argue with him. "Fine."

"Thank you!"

"You have to eat and take your meds. After that, you can have your miserable day." She walked out of the room.

Leaning against the closed door, she let out a frustrated

breath. She gathered herself and walked into the kitchen. Ebele prepared a bed tray with his lunch. She turned to go back to the lion's den, tickled at the inference. She set everything down, and he mumbled his thanks. He was so pigheaded and stubborn. She rolled her eyes, watched him eat some of the food, and take the pills. Once she was satisfied, she left the room. She had homework to complete. He should be good for now.

Ebele went to the garage to bring in her backpack from the car. She'd packed an extra set of clothes because she didn't know how the day would turn out. As she closed the door, she heard a ringtone. She bobbed her head to the AfroBeat sound. She knew the song all too well. It was "Standing Ovation" by Tiwa Savage featuring Olamide. Kamal must have changed it recently.

She found the phone in the backseat's cup holder. The missed call notification on the screen indicated it was his brother, Jabir. She took the phone inside, and it started ringing again. She knew he was in America and was probably worried, so she rushed to Kamal's room. She found him knocked out with the plate almost falling off his lap. The phone stopped ringing. Conflicted, she didn't want to wake him because he needed rest. Removing the tray, she walked back out of the room and shut the door.

Ebele had only said hello to Jabir once, but from the way Kamal talked about him, she felt like she knew him. She went into the guest bedroom and changed into something more comfortable. Returning to the living room, she flopped down on the couch with a throw blanket. The phone started to ring again just as she was getting into the Nigerian film, *Muna* on Roc Sky TV. It was Jabir again, so she answered the call.

Immediately, Jabir went off. "Kammy, what is wrong with you? I see your crazy has started. Why aren't you answering the phone? You have everybody worried. Rasheed is blowing up my phone asking me if I feel any twin vibe because you didn't answer him earlier!" Jabir yelled. "Don't let me come over there and put my hands on you."

Ebele struggled to hold in her giggle. She now knew who to call for backup when Kamal bullied her. She hadn't seen or talked to Rasheed yet, but he seemed like a no nonsense kinda guy.

"Kamal!" Jabir yelled.

"Hi, Jabir. It's not Kam. It's me, Ebele," she said, in a low tone, her nerves taking over.

"Oh, hey. Where's Kammy?"

"He's sleeping. I answered because I didn't want you worrying, being so far away."

"At least someone has sense. My bad, I didn't mean for you to get that side of me. I thought it was my brother." He huffed. "He's so hard headed sometimes."

"Tell me about it."

"That bad, huh?"

"Yes, and everything you said, I wish I could say it to him." She giggled.

"Don't worry. I'll hold him down while you do. Deal?"

"Deal."

"How is he?"

"Moody and won't talk to me. The news isn't good, though. He'll need surgery, but I'll let him give you specifics." She wanted to give him the "Kamal refused the surgery" conversation but decided not to over the phone. Besides, she'd love to be there when Jabir got on him about it.

"All right, I appreciate it. Thanks for looking out for him. Let me call Rasheed before he goes crazy. One or some of us should see you in a couple of days," Jabir said. After thanking her a couple more times, he hung up.

She envied their big and loving family. She was having lunch with her dad the next day. Her disappointment rose at this moment. She wanted to know her siblings. They may not like her or even know about her. Some part of her wanted not to care, but another part of her did. How could they build a relationship when her father was keeping some parts of his life away? Could she truly forgive him even though he was only partially sorry?

———

Ebele woke up to pounding on the door. She squinted her eyes to gauge her surroundings. The credits to a film were rolling on the television. The pounding came again. She opened her eyes and stretched to her full length. The blanket fell off her as she made her way to the door. She stopped midway and wondered if she should be answering Kamal's door. As she stood there, she was happy to see him come hopping down the hall on his crutches.

She walked to him. "Are you okay?"

"Yeah, I'm good, thanks." His monotone voice was still present. "Let me get the door."

She shrugged. "No, hang tight, I got it."

He stood back and leaned against the sofa. Ebele walked to the door. The knock came again. She stood on her tiptoes to reach the peephole but couldn't. Kamal snickered. She gave him a warning stare then opened the door. With the speed of lightning, a figure flew past her straight into Kamal's arms.

Ebele turned around and saw a tall, white woman with blonde hair drape herself over him. "Oh, Kam, baby. Oh, my poor baby. I was so worried."

Ebele hadn't had a chance to see her face, but the scent of her perfume screamed money. She stood stoic, watching the display before her. The shattering of her heart must've deafened her because she blinked, and the woman had been trying to get her attention.

"Hi, you must be the nurse. I'm Kam's girlfriend, Brittani." She extended her hand.

Ebele looked over at Kamal. She shook hands with Brittani, noticing how pretty she was. The two of them couldn't be more different – Ebele with her olive skin and wild, curly hair, no makeup, and short stature. Brittani was tall and lithe, with too much makeup on and long, straight blonde hair. Something about her face looked strangely familiar.

"Thank you for taking care of my baby."

The woman whom she'd heard of, but never wanted to meet, was now standing in front of her. Her smile was so big that Ebele's hurt and pain was swallowed by the guilt taking its place. How could she steal someone else's joy?

"No problem, it was nothing. Well, since you're here now, I can leave Kamal in good hands." Ebele scrambled to put her things together. She was so thankful for the foresight of not leaving anything in the upstairs bedroom earlier. She would've died if she had to go upstairs to pack anything.

"Baby, just relax. Let me get some juice. I'm parched." She set what Ebele recognized as a Birkin handbag to the side and walked to the kitchen.

That bag can pay my tuition. Look at me trying to compete with her for her man. Ha, Chukwu aju. God forbid. I need to get out of here. Away from these rich people. Who am I?

"Ebele," Kam whispered.

She refused to look at him or acknowledge his call. She couldn't be mad at him, though. He'd never lied to her. She refused to let him see her cry. She put her backpack on her shoulders and headed to the door.

"Ebele," he called out with a little more force.

She held on to the doorknob. She looked everywhere but at him. "Kamal, it's okay. Take care of yourself. I'll check on you in a couple of days. Rest, keep ice on your knee. Make sure it's elevated and take your meds." She spoke with a steady voice.

Brittani walked back in the room with a glass of juice. "Baby, you hear what the nurse said?" She looked at Ebele. "I'll make sure he follows instructions."

Ebele felt Kamal's eyes boring a hole in the side of her face. She knew he was looking for reassurance of their deal. She couldn't give him that. Not when she'd seen the woman and saw how happy she was with him. She opened the door and walked out, closing the door gently.

She called an Uber and texted Nse.

I'm coming over.

She included a shattered heart and a crying emoji. The Uber pulled up soon after. Ebele pulled open the back door and tossed her bag in. She got in and looked at the house one last time. Ebele couldn't help but wonder if she was being her mother. The cycle was repeating all over again. Why did their hearts attach themselves to those who were attached to others?

Chapter 19

Brittani had been in London three days, and Ebele hadn't talked to him since. It was official – Kamal was slowly losing his mind. He gritted his teeth, something that had become a habit in the last couple of days. He growled his frustration as he looked at his phone for the umpteenth time in the last thirty minutes. He shifted on his bed to lean his back against the headboard.

"Kam, elevate your leg." He heard Ebele's voice in his head. He'd never missed anyone as much as he missed her. Even when she had avoided him in those previous two weeks, the pain wasn't this bad. It could've been because he knew it was just the two of them, and he'd get her back even if he had to carry her here himself.

This time the look of disappointment and hurt in her eyes before she left, haunted his every waking moment. Him not being able to get up and go talk to her made it worse. His anger rumbled in his belly. He was angry at himself for not handling this earlier and at her for reneging on her word. They had talked about it.

She promised me a week and bailed on me after a day. His nose flared, and he picked up his phone again to call her. After a couple of rings, it went to voicemail.

He didn't want to leave a voicemail because he didn't want to sound too harsh and drive her further away. He sent a text.

You promised me a week. So, you're just gonna leave me like that?

He hit the SEND button and waited for her response. He waited for a few moments and the three dots indicating she was typing a response came up. His chest tightened with anticipation.

I did, things have changed. I'll come check on you in a few days.

Her response wasn't what he wanted, but she was talking to him. He read it again. He was about to toss the phone on the bed when another reply came through.

Follow the doctor's instructions, Kamal.

He grinned. That was better than nothing. He'd sent numerous texts since the night she left, and she'd responded to none. Not only was his leg injured, but his heart was hurting as well. If only he'd been nicer to her before Brittani appeared. He looked at his phone again. These responses gave him hope. Her insistence on him following the doctor's instructions meant she still cared. When she got here, they'd talk. He was okay with that for now.

Kamal picked up the remote and settled down to watch TV when a loud piercing sound moved through the house. The smoke alarm – again. He reached for his crutches and with care made it to the direction of the noise. He saw Brittani in the kitchen coughing. He shook his head and made his way over to her.

"Brit, this is the third time. Whatchu doing, man?" He picked up a hand towel and fanned away the smoke to stop the alarm. He looked over at the stove; there was a burnt frying pan, and the kitchen looked like a tornado had passed through. He didn't want to be mad because she was trying.

"Baby, I was trying to make breakfast for you," she whined.

Breakfast? Kamal looked over at the clock on the wall. It was noon. If he had to wait on her, he would've starved, and not taken his medicine. He'd woken up earlier and made breakfast for himself. She never ate breakfast, just granola, and smoothies; so the day after she arrived, he asked his housekeeper to stock up on what she needed.

"Thank you, but I've already eaten." She'd never tried to cook for him before. Never. But when she saw the leftovers Ebele packed for him the day she arrived; she tried to cook something. Each time, the alarm went off. Seeing the pout on her face made him feel bad.

"Brit, come here," he said.

She walked with him to the living room, helped him get comfortable, and sat down next to him.

"What's going on? You don't cook," he said.

"I'm trying to do what I can to make you strong enough to play again." She lifted her hand to his cheek.

Kamal furrowed his brows. She never asked how he was doing but was concerned about when he'd get back to playing.

"You do know there's a possibility I won't play again." Saying the words aloud left a bitter taste in his mouth. Jabir would arrive in a couple of hours, and they had an appointment with the doctor tomorrow. Kamal knew he had been unreasonable the first day. The shock of him missing his one last shot to play in the Regions International Championships messed with his head. He was now ready to get his knee fixed and salvage what was left of his career.

"Stop saying that, Kam. A lot of players get injured, and they go back on the field."

"Yeah, but everyone's case is different."

She stood and began to pace. "Well, you *will* play. I wish you hadn't come here. This wouldn't have happened." She ran her hands up and down her arms. "I can't stand London."

He frowned. "I didn't know that. Why?"

Brittani shrugged but remained silent. She had grown up in London but left not too long after her mother died five years ago. She loved living in the States, but he thought it was just because she was enjoying life there – not because she hated her hometown.

She put her head down for a few minutes. He studied her for the first time in days. Her blonde hair with black highlights was long and straight, her face was carefully made up, and her body clad in Adidas sportswear.

"Come, sit down. Let me talk to you," he said.

She walked over and sat in front of him on the coffee table. He took her hand in his, remaining silent; he waited for it. The *it* that made his heart run a thousand miles in seconds. The *it* that made him lose all sensibility. The *it* that made him want to go to the moon if that's what her heart desired. The *it* that made him want to put a permanent smile on her face. The *it* that wanted them to breathe in unison, communicating without words. Their hearts so entangled that they couldn't tell which heart belonged to the other.

The *it* wasn't there. In fact, at this moment, he acknowledged that it was never there. He'd never experienced what he had with Ebele since he and Brittani had been together. His settling had not only wasted his time, but hers, and for that, he felt remorse.

"Where do you see us going next? Our relationship?" he asked.

"Why so serious? Err … I guess where all relationships go at some point." She seductively ran her hand over his thigh. He was still a man, so he did feel a stirring but not one that made him want to run for the hills like with Ebele.

He placed his hand over hers to stop her. "Come on, Brit, we're trying to talk here."

"I'm sorry. It's just that I want you, Kammy. It's been soooo long."

He chuckled. "I'm injured, Brit, in case you didn't notice. And things have changed."

"Okay, okay. I know." She caressed his face. "But when you go to the doctor tomorrow, let's ask if we can engage in physical activity. I leave next week." She leaned in to kiss him.

He leaned back. She frowned and rubbed her hand on his shoulder. "I'll do all the work, baby." Her voice was laced with seduction.

Nothing she said registered except the tidbit about leaving. He couldn't let her go without breaking things off. He had been in too much pain and was too worried about his future to take care of it. But now he realized how important it was that he broke things off. What threw him though, was the fact that she'd leave without knowing how he'd manage or what his future would be. That was just messed up.

"Brit, stop. I'm not the same man." He exhaled and looked her in the eye. "I've given my life to Christ. I can no longer have sex outside of marriage." His faith wavered some days because of his condition, but that didn't mean he intentionally wanted to sin.

"First, you come here, get injured and might not play again. Now you can't satisfy a woman anymore because you're a Christian?" Brittani seethed.

"Don't play yourself, Brit. I didn't say nothing about 'can't satisfy.' I said I can't have sex outside of marriage," he clarified. He could satisfy just fine. He wanted to make sure she got that straight. Although the woman he wanted to please was on the run.

"Then we can get married," she blurted out.

"For sex?" He'd started looking at sex differently when he and Ebele had a conversation about it some time ago. A smug grin appeared on his face when he remembered her showing him a quote that said, "When sex becomes easy to view, love becomes difficult to find."

"Ugh ... I don't know. All I know is you've changed, and I don't like it."

"Brit ..."

"No, let's drop it for now, baby. Jay will be here soon, and I have to change." She brushed her lips against his cheek.

Jay? Jabir hated being called that. He and Brittani had a cordial relationship, but he'd get nasty in a minute if she called him that. Especially since he'd told her not to. Kamal watched her leave and prayed for strength to do this right. He didn't want to hurt her. At this point, he didn't know if she'd even be hurt, but he still wanted to be careful. What he did know was, he wanted Ebele, and he couldn't have both. He wasn't sure about his future but knew he needed Ebele to survive it.

———

THE NEXT DAY, KAMAL LAY ON THE EXAMINATION TABLE AT Broomfield Medical while Jabir stood by his side. Pete, his agent, and Brittani were seated in the corner as they waited on Dr. Mathew. Jabir put his hand over Kamal's knee again and examined it.

"Man, what are you doing? Can you just be my brother?" Kamal asked. This is what he'd had to put up with in the last twenty-four hours since Jabir's arrival. He was worse than Ebele, and Kamal was tired of him doing too much already.

"Keep quiet. I'm your brother. The big one at that, but I'm also a doctor."

"But you ain't *my* doctor. Now chill." Kamal shook his head. "And you're not that much older than me."

Pete laughed at them. "Brothers – must be nice. You know, I've never seen both of you in the same room before."

"Man, what's that supposed to mean? We're twins, not a circus act." Kamal furrowed his eyebrows. He looked over at Brittani. She was lost in her own world, taking selfies.

Jabir swatted him on the arm.

"Ouch, I'm injured. Cut it out," Kamal said. A moment passed between them as Jabir shot his brow up, daring him to retaliate. "I wonder how Dami deals with your aggravating self."

"She deals just fine."

"Yeah, keep telling yourself that. She's just buying time." Kamal knew the best way to get under Jabir's skin was to hint that Damisi was trying to run away from him again. Considering their past, nothing got on his brother's nerves more.

"Watch it. I'll break the other knee," Jabir warned with a grin. "Then I wonder how you'd catch your runaway train."

Kamal's face grew tight as he understood Jabir's inferred meaning. Ebele was still on the run. She told him that she'd be by but never showed up. He wanted to respond when Dr. Mathews entered.

"Gentlemen, apologies for keeping you," Dr. Mathews said. He did a double take when he saw Jabir.

Kamal made the introductions. Brittani had finally gotten off her phone and made her way over.

"Okay, Kamal, as I told you before, your knee needs reconstruction. The first thing is, you'd have to see an orthopedist that specialized in sports medicine." Dr. Mathew paused. "I have a few recommendations. They're the best."

"Am I guaranteed to play again?" Kamal asked. His tone somber. Why would he set himself up for failure? He had so many fears he hadn't voiced. He tried talking to God, but the words failed him. He didn't feel it fair that the one thing he wanted so much in the world was taken from him. Granted, he couldn't play forever, but he thought there was still time.

"Nothing is guaranteed, but like I said, your health is good. It's a good thing you've started your physical therapy program. It'll speed up the healing process after the procedure."

Kamal shut his eyes and ran his hand down his face.

Dr. Mathews continued, "Delaying it any further isn't in your best interest, regardless of football."

Over the next several minutes, the doctor described the process – what to expect before and after, the healing process, and the different surgery options. Kamal's head was spinning.

He looked over at Pete, who was texting on his phone. The scowl he wore on his face didn't look good. They were still waiting on Turk West to decide on his extension. Some members of the team had come to see him, including the coach. His guys – Tega, Princeton, and Freddie, called every other day. They were on the road and here he was with his career hanging in the balance. This was so unfair.

Kamal allowed Jabir and the doctor to spar about the details. He trusted his brother and knew that any question he'd ask would be in his best interest. Brittani held on to his hand. He looked up at her and saw fear in her eyes. Was she frightened for him, Kamal, or Kammy? He figured he'd get his answer soon enough. He glanced over at Pete assaulting the keys on his phone. Anger rolled off him. Kamal hoped it wasn't about him.

"I need to step outside to take this," Pete said.

Kamal had been with Pete as a client for close to seven years now. They had a good relationship that went beyond the ten percent commission, to a genuine respect. Being one of his highest paid clients didn't hurt either. With endorsements and modeling contracts, Kamal wasn't at risk of being broke by a long shot. He not only had stocks and was the silent owner of some businesses, but he'd also recently inherited a large sum from his late father. At the end of the day though, soccer held a deeper meaning for him. It was more than money.

Minutes later, Pete reentered the room just as they finished up with the doctor. Jabir held on to all the informational pamphlets they'd been given.

Pete let out a frustrated breath. "We done here?"

"Yeah, we're heading back home. We need to go over this

information," Jabir said. The hunger pangs he was experiencing kept his lips sealed.

"Okay, I'll come by later. I need to check on some stuff," Pete said over his shoulder, walking away from them.

"Everything straight?" Kamal yelled behind him.

Pete nodded and waved his hand over his head. As Kamal watched him walk away, he sent up a prayer that things were indeed good.

Later that evening, Kamal's fragile faith took another blow when Pete stopped by. Turk West FC management had decided to terminate his loan contract. His club back in LA was sending a team for assessment in a week. Kamal interlocked his fingers and placed his hands over his head.

Jabir leaned against the wall. "Kammy, I know this isn't what you expected, but God always has a way of making things work out."

Kamal remained silent. He didn't want to blaspheme. At least that's what his mother called it when they spoke in a bad manner about God.

"There's still hope. Get the surgery done and go back to LA. You're still signed with the Sun Sides," Pete said.

Kamal's gaze stayed fixed on the ceiling. The fact he still had a job should have made him feel better, but the feeling of relief eluded him. He felt empty. His soul desperately needed rest, but he had the sneaking suspicion things were about to get a whole lot worse.

Chapter 20

Thursday evening, Ebele steadied her books in her hand as she unlocked the door to Nse's flat. The melancholy of the last week hadn't dissipated, and she had a whole playlist to prove it. She paused "Airbrush" by Seyi Shey. The song talked about trying to cover up the reality of a tumultuous relationship for outsiders. It wasn't exactly her and Kamal's case, but the similarities were there. They lived in their own world, airbrushing the reality of their fragile situation until it came crashing down.

"Ebi, is that you?" Nse yelled from the back room.

"*Yes o. How far now?*" Ebele set her books down and walked into the kitchen to put the kettle on. She needed something hot.

"*I dey o.* How was school?" Nse came out of the laundry room with a pile of clothes.

Ebele pulled off her shoes and picked them up. It was early March, and she was so ready to wear open-toe shoes.

"Same thing, different day. I'll be back. Let me take a quick shower." Ebele headed in the opposite direction. "*Abeg* when the water boils, turn it off for me."

Minutes later, refreshed from her warm shower, Ebele

entered the kitchen and made herself a cup of tea. Nse didn't drink tea. Coffee was more her thing.

She re-entered the living room and sat with her legs under her. "What are you doing?" Ebele noticed swatches of fabrics scattered on the center table.

"I'm trying to come up with a color scheme for this fiftieth birthday party I was contracted to plan." Nse scratched her hair in confusion as she put the pieces together. "You know *Naija* people like to party, and their taste is never cheap."

"Are you telling me? And you better come correct. Someone will be there that'll like the decorations and ask for the planner. Contract you to plan their event only to—"

"Outshine the other," both ladies said, in unison and chuckled.

"*Chai*, she laughs o," Nse said with a hand over her chest in mock surprise.

Ebele sipped her tea. "Stop exaggerating."

"Are you kidding me? When you got here, you know, after what's her name arrived, I nearly threw your phone away."

"Ah? Why?"

"You were walking around here with your phone, listening to, and singing all those heartbreak songs. You had me thinking hard if Tega had done anything to me recently so that I could join your pitiful self in solidarity," Nse said, with a straight face.

Ebele let her head back in laughter. "Between you and Kam, you have no sense at all."

"Speaking of …"

"Oh, Lord, here we go. Let me save you the stress. No, I haven't seen him. We texted once. I was going to see him, but I can't do that to his girlfriend. And before you ask, yes, I do miss him terribly. But he's not available." Ebele finished and picked up her cup to drink her tea.

Nse stared at her. "I guess you think you just told me,

right?" She rolled her eyes. "Well, you didn't. I was going to ask if you knew he was let out of his contract."

"Oh, my God! Really? When?" Ebele set her cup down and stood. Kamal loved soccer. Granted he couldn't play now, but to be fired when he was down was terrible.

"Is it me you're asking?" Nse scrunched her nose as though there was a foul odor. "I thought you had everything covered." She turned back to her swatches.

Ebele knelt next to her and pouted. Nse never could resist her pout and pleading eyes. "*Ndo, biko nu gwam.*"

"You know I'm Efik, so if you're begging, you need to do it in my language and not yours. This crime you committed is beyond begging in English," Nse said.

"Really?"

Nse shrugged and continued what she was doing. Ebele quickly pulled up Google on her phone. In seconds, she found what she was looking for. "Okay, *Mbok.*"

Nse looked at her, then eyed her phone. "Cheat."

"Yeah, whatever. Cough up the info, lady," Ebele said.

In minutes, Nse gave her the rundown of events. Ebele's stomach tightened with guilt. How could she leave him at a time like this? She berated herself until Nse talked about him going back to the US. She'd been so wrapped up in him that she didn't understand that part of his loner. In fact, she was sure he omitted it. She didn't expect him to eventually go home. Then what had they been doing? She wanted to go over there and smack him. But then, she didn't know if she had the right.

"I thought you guys were friends before feelings got involved?"

"We aren't involved." She gazed at the TV. "I honestly don't know what we are or were. Now I know what Janet Jackson meant by like a moth to a flame."

"I won't pretend to understand. You know Tega had to chase me *tire*. It wasn't love at first sight. But I've seen the two of you together. I have also seen you apart. You guys are meant to be." She raised her hand when Ebele opened her mouth to talk. "Let me finish. I know it's not the right time. I know nothing about the girl; he never mentions her. But he can't keep *your* name out of his mouth." She paused. "If nothing else, check how's he's doing. If it's meant to be …" Nse opened her arms to the possibilities.

Everything Nse said was true. She remembered the pain that rumbled through her when she came face to face with their reality. It was so gut wrenching she didn't think she'd be able to focus. In the last week, she'd thrown herself into her school, work, and church, but it lingered. Its intensity dimmed only because she'd cut off contact. Could she expose herself to that again? For all she knew, his girlfriend could still be there.

———

ON THE OTHER SIDE OF TOWN, KAMAL LOOKED AWAY FROM Jabir as they sat around his kitchen island.

"It makes sense, Kammy. Why are you stalling?" Jabir asked him. "The sooner you do it, the faster you'll begin to heal."

"I'm scared, bro," Kamal confessed.

"What are you scared of?"

"Suppose I lose the desire to play? And Turk already cut me. Who's to say things will be the same in LA?"

"But you've had a knee injury before."

"I was younger, and it was minor compared to this." Kamal rubbed the back of his neck. He stood on one foot and hopped the short distance to the chair. The swelling had gone down. The pain was minimal, but the knee was unstable. It couldn't take any weight. "What if I'm never the same?"

"Suppose you are? Why would you worry about the possibility of something you have no control over?" Jabir walked over. "Hope, bro."

Kamal remained silent. He'd told his brother about his new status as a believer, and unlike what he'd expected, Jabir didn't clown him but congratulated him.

"The mind is a battleground. And you know because you're new in the faith, the enemy will try to attack you. Look at Jesus. The minute He got baptized, the Holy Spirit led Him into the wilderness, and there the devil was ready." Jabir waited for his response, but Kamal didn't have any. "Whatever you think about all the time will grow. If you keep being afraid, it'll eventually keep you a prisoner. We as Christians, should keep our thoughts on good, pure things."

"Is that in the Bible?" Kamal was far from a Bible scholar. He was just trying to get himself to stay in order.

"Yes, Philippians 4:8. There was this time the twins were sick. I, a doctor that helped others, felt so helpless. I panicked, thinking the worst since they were preemies. My wife gave me that Scripture, and I've kept it close."

"Ok, I'll check it out." Kamal picked up the remote. They were giving highlights of the game.

"Speaking of wife, you still haven't heard from Ebele?" Jabir asked, softly looking around. Kamal knew he was making sure Brittani wasn't within earshot.

"Nope."

Jabir frowned. "You mad?"

"I'm furious, but forget her." He waved his hand in a dismissive motion. "She's just like the rest. They come a dime a dozen." Kamal's feelings swung from anger to longing, depending on the day. He never thought Ebele would abandon him at a time like this. He didn't expect her to hang out with him but not even a text, or call to see how he was doing? He thought they were more than that. He knew she had the ability to hurt him, but he never expected the pain to cut this deep.

"I know you're feeling bad about it, but look at it from her point of view. It's wrong timing, bro. You still have to get yourself right."

"Whatever. If nothing else, our friendship should've superseded all that. She should've cared enough."

"I agree with you there. But the girl I talked to does care. Seeing Brit was probably too much," Jabir whispered. "Tega told me how you acted crazy in her flat over her ex. How do you think she feels about your present?"

Kamal wanted to absorb what Jabir was saying, but he couldn't. They had a deal. And Brittani was harder to talk to than he thought. She claimed she hated London so much but spent most of the day shopping.

"Give it time," Jabir said. "So are you going to schedule the surgery? It's an outpatient thing."

Kamal was glad he changed the topic. "I guess so. I'll go with the specialist you say is best. All it should take is to call and set it up."

"Cool! The surgeon says he can fit you in any time. Call them. Let me go call my wife and kids before they go to bed." Jabir stood and walked over to him. He placed his hand on Kamal's shoulder. "You know the team from LA will be here in a couple of days. This is a good way to show you're making steps towards your recovery, and they have nothing to worry about."

"'Preciate it, bro." Kamal picked up his cell to call the doctor's office. If he still had a team, they would've done it for him. But he was now basically on his own. He needed to get with Pete about hiring a new assistant when he got back to the States. He didn't anticipate going back so soon, but that seemed to be the hand he was dealt.

A few minutes later, the appointment was set up for two days' time. He wanted to text Ebele but changed his mind. Last weekend, she should've had lunch with her dad. He knew those always made her emotional. Although he was angry, he still wanted to make sure she was okay. But Jabir was right. He needed to let her be until he became unattached.

———

THREE DAYS LATER, KAMAL SAT IN HIS RECLINER WITH HIS NEW knee elevated. He doodled on his sketchpad, something he was doing more of. The day of the procedure, he went in about seven a.m. and was back by six in the evening. The process was seamless. It wasn't as invasive as he'd thought. He was on mandatory rest for the first two weeks; however, the doctor ordered one to two hours therapy every day. He kept the physical therapist he used prior to surgery. Tina came highly recommended from the Turk's management.

Once the initial two weeks were over, he'd start an aggressive PT program. Since he no longer had access to the Turk West facility, Kamal set it up with Coach Gram. He wasn't sure if he'd keep Tina or get Coach Gram to get him another therapist. Tina was easy on the eyes, but he really didn't look at her as anything other than a therapist.

The first day they met, she fawned over him. She knew all his stats and was a fan. He appreciated it. Because of her interest in his career, she had an enthusiasm that motivated him. Kamal's lips turned up into a grin as his thoughts went to Ebele. She might kick his behind if she found out he'd hired a female therapist. Well, as things were, she wouldn't have wanted the job anyway.

Tina had just left, and he was done for the day. She'd replaced his ice pack and put his knee in its brace. Kamal was committed to doing everything in his power to get back to full play. Jabir's advice, before he left some hours ago, rang in his ear. *Do your part so LA would know you're trying.*

He was still signed with the Sun Sides, and his aim was to get back there and play. Prior to leaving, Jabir wrote down some Scriptures for him to meditate on.

"Hey, Brit, can you get me some water, please?"

She was to his right, engrossed in the movie, *Grease*. He knew for a fact she had watched the movie a zillion times. She loved it.

"Yeah, sure," she said, absently. She stood, eyes still focused on the TV. They hadn't revisited the conversation of the other day. He still had to talk to her but was no longer in a rush since he hadn't heard from Ebele. Ebele or not though, their current situation wasn't fair to either of them.

A few seconds later, Brittani returned with the water and helped him with his medication. Kamal leaned his head back. He closed his eyes as he fought back the pain that had begun to take over his body. He tried to keep his thoughts trained on good, but they switched to doom every time.

His phone rang. It was Pete.

"Hey, man," he answered.

"Hey, Kam, how are you feeling?"

"Can't move, but other than that, I'm fine." Kamal chuckled.

"I'll be over in a few."

Before he could agree or protest, Pete hung up. The next several minutes were filled with anticipation until Pete arrived. A few minutes later, Brittani answered the door. Kamal heard her and Pete exchange pleasantries as they made their way over to him.

"Hey, Pete. What's up?" Kamal looked up at him.

Pete stood to the side of him with his hands in his pockets. Kamal felt bile rise to his throat. Pete paced, and Kamal knew that whatever was making him hesitant wasn't anything he wanted to hear.

"I'm just gonna come out and say it, Kam." He swallowed, winced, and frowned. "Instead of sending their medical experts, the Sun Sides sent lawyers."

"What does that mean?" Kamal growled.

"It means they came over to let you out of your contract."

Pete looked down. His discomfort in delivering the news was evident.

"So they're cutting me?" Tears misted at the corner of Kamal's eyes. He closed his eyes and leaned back. Although seated, he felt like the rug had been pulled from under him. After all this, they still cut him. He was out of a job. He struggled to breathe. What was he going to do? Soccer was his life. He reached for the empty can of soda he'd finished earlier. The rage in him moved through his hands. He squeezed it and threw it clear across the room. God had let him down.

Chapter 21

"Kammy, hold on. It's not that bad." Pete walked closer to him. Brittani tried to touch him, but his eyes told her not now.

"Do I have a team to play for?" Kamal asked, with his brow up.

"Err ... not now—"

"Then, it's that bad." Kamal cursed under his breath." Don't try and sugarcoat the stuff, Pete."

"I know that's what you think now, but you're Kammy Danjuma. We'll be able to spin this." Pete looked over at Brittani, then continued. "Look, I'll be in London for another week before going back to the States. We'll figure this out."

Pete had a policy of discussing money with only the client present or their lawyer. Kamal's jaw tightened and fists clenched. He felt like hitting something, but his immobility kept him in place. He needed to get his lawyer on the phone. He trusted Pete, but he had to make extra sure that Sun Sides didn't try to cheat him.

Pete sat and made small talk. Kamal wasn't listening to anything he said. Brittani made up for it by keeping him company. He knew Pete was trying to get a feel for where he was emotionally, but that would be impossible because he didn't even know where his head was. He wanted to be alone.

After a few more minutes, Pete left. He heard the locks on the front door engage, and he stood. Balancing himself on his crutches, he went to his room. Nothing mattered to him anymore. He heard footsteps behind him and prayed Brittani would go straight to her room. He didn't want to talk. He sat on the bed, and closed his eyes, trying to chase away a headache.

"Kam," Brittani whispered.

He ignored her and lay on the bed with his head turned away from her. She called out to him again. He remained silent. When he heard the door close, he allowed the floodgates to open. He turned into the six-year-old boy whose father left. The only thing that made him significant was gone. He didn't even have a say. It wasn't supposed to be this way. The gut-wrenching loneliness of the months to come tore at him. The will to fight left with his contract. The tears he'd been holding back for three weeks flowed until he finally fell asleep.

The next couple of days went by in a blur. Kamal had no desire to know when one day ended and another started. He'd done the bare minimum – shower, eat, take his meds, and get back into the bed.

Pete did come back as promised and explained the details of the cut. What he'd assumed was right. The club felt that he was getting old, and an ACL injury would be hard to come back from. They also cited his bad publicity of the last season. Kamal figured the main reason had to do with the almighty dollar. They wanted to free up their international slot since the MLS only offered a limited amount to its clubs in a season.

Kamal got to keep his ten million dollars signing bonus, which was guaranteed. He also got to keep all his performance bonuses, and the team would be responsible for his medical treatment for the time recommended by the physician, which was eight months. What good would that do him? By then, it would be October, which was the middle of the season in Europe, and the beginning of the off-season for the teams that didn't make the play-offs in the US.

There was a knock on the door.

"Go away, Tina!" he yelled.

He'd dismissed Tina for the day. Some days he let her do her job, others he didn't. He hadn't done any structured therapy in the last couple of days, so why did she think he'd want any now? It was one of those days; he didn't feel like being bothered. He raised his hand to his head.

"Kam, it's me," Brittani's voice came through the door.

He remained silent, but she came in anyway. The day after he got the news, she ranted about how him being called an ex-soccer player by the media and how the team would be sorry when he got back into shape. He couldn't tell if she was angry for him or at him. Whatever the case, he tuned her out completely.

"Not a good time, Brit," he said.

"It's never a good time, Kam." She sashayed over to him and sat on the bed. "Look at you. You look terrible."

"Gee, thanks, not like I care," he said, irritated. He hadn't shaved since Pete gave him the news.

"You're really turning into a mean person. I don't know you anymore."

"Only a couple of rough days and already you don't know me?" He folded his arms across his chest and cocked his head to the side. "Did you ever?"

"That's not fair."

"Neither is the world." He watched her lower lip quiver. He suddenly felt bad. "Look Brit ..."

"No, Kam, it's okay." She lowered her eyes for a few seconds. "Look, I came in here to talk to you. I got the role I auditioned for right before I came. I just got the call." She stared at him waiting for a reaction.

He didn't have one. Everyone left eventually, so he didn't have anything to say.

"We start shooting next week, and I have to go so I can be prepared."

"When do you leave?"

"Tomorrow."

He blinked. He thought she said the shooting started next week. They were still in the beginning of this week. "Tomorrow? Okay."

The atmosphere shifted, tension filled the air. The only noise was coming from the theme song from the game on his Xbox.

"Kammy, I don't know what the future holds for us, but I know that you're in a bad place now."

He tried to figure out where this was going. Was this a "Dear John" speech? He was the one that was supposed to break up with her and not the other way around. "Brit—"

"Let me finish. This is hard to say, please. I know you need me, but my new career is important right now. I finally found something I enjoy. While I concentrate on that, you get better. Sometime apart would do both of us some good."

Kamal shook his head. If they were gonna break up, it had to be permanent. He wasn't trying to hold on to something that was dead.

"I'm proud of you for sticking to something. You hopped around more than a rabbit," he joked.

Brittani giggled. "Thank you. I really like this." She nodded, and her blonde hair fell out of its bun.

"That's good. But Brit, I think we should call it quits. Do your thing, and I wish you all the best. Really."

Her expression showed her disappointment. Her lips parted like she had something to say. He shook his head. He wasn't going down that route with her. All she wanted was to put him on a leash in case he was restored to his former glory.

He wasn't trying to hurt her, but he wasn't trying to live in limbo and hurt himself either.

They both remained silent. There was nothing left to say. This was it. Would he miss her? Of course, she'd been there for two years, but there was nothing left to fight for. Ebele had opened his eyes to what love meant. Although, right now, he often questioned whether he'd even found it with her.

———

IT WAS NOW A WEEK SINCE HIS SURGERY, AND KAMAL'S MENTAL state hadn't improved. He knew what he was doing wasn't healthy, but he remained in this state of depression. His faith wasn't strong enough to sustain his present situation. He stopped praying altogether and shut everyone out. His family was worried. Rasheed threatened him, and so did his sisters-in-law, but he couldn't find the energy to fight. Jabir empathized more, but he couldn't help him either.

All Kamal did was drink shakes, bathe, and lay around. The darkness became his comfort. His mother's tears were the only thing that caused him to let Tina do her job. But he no longer felt like being bothered. She was presently standing in front of him and setting up her mat.

"Aye, Tina, I don't think I can do this today," he said.

Tina let out an exaggerated breath. "Kamal, the first four weeks after surgery is critical and shapes how the next six to eight months would go. You either cut the sessions short or don't do them at all. It's not a good thing."

"Didn't you hear? I don't play football anymore. So, no need for all this extra."

"I understand that psychologically and emotionally you're in a bad place from the cut and the surgery, but you have to find a reason to fight." Tina sat down on her heels in front of him.

He bowed his head, putting his hands over it. He wanted

to get better but didn't have it in him. He felt Tina's hands wrap around his arm. He lifted his eyes to meet hers. They were hooded with lust. He knew the look well as he'd seen his fair share over the years.

"Tina," Kamal said, in a low tone. He'd no idea what she was doing, but this wasn't the move.

"Shhh." She placed her index finger over his lips.

He stayed frozen in place.

"I have admired you from afar, and now I get to help you heal. Please, let me take care of you."

Kamal tried to respond to what he assumed she was implying, but she continued, "Will you help me to help you? Who knows what would happen?"

"Yeah, Kam, who knows what would happen? Help her to help you."

Tina jerked back, and he straightened up as he heard the voice he hadn't heard in almost a month. Ebele stood at his entryway with her wild hair up in a messy bun. His eyes roamed over her body. His perusal returned to the angry scowl on her face. If he weren't so angry, he would've felt bad. He was going to ask how she got in, but he remembered she never returned his key.

"Man, you need to leave," Kamal said to Tina.

Chapter 22

Nse was right. This physical therapist had a thing for Kamal which went far beyond helping him get back into shape. The previous night, Nse called telling her she'd gone to see Kamal. Nse said he'd been acting like a brat about his rehabilitation, so Ebele went to talk some sense into him. Nse's main reason for calling was to tell Ebele that the way his physical therapist was looking at him when she thought no one was watching, didn't sit well with her.

Ebele crossed her hands over her chest as Tina packed up. She stood in place and rolled her eyes. She'd stepped back from Kamal for him to get his situation with his girlfriend together but not to be replaced by another woman.

"I apologize, Kammy. I'll see you tomorrow for our next session," Tina said, walking to the door.

Ebele gave her a glance over. "Thank you. We'll let you know about tomorrow."

Once Tina left, Ebele walked into the living room, tossed her bag on the couch, and went into the kitchen to wash her hands. Her stomach bubbled with nerves. Kamal, who still hadn't said anything, looked like he'd been run over by a bus. Despite that fact, he was still sexy to her.

They had a lot to talk about, but she was stalling. She knew that he knew it too. But first, she needed to finish his session. She knew from Nse that he was past the first full week so he could go for only one or two hours. Because she also heard he wasn't doing well with it, she'd make it two hours.

Ebele walked back into the living room, and he was watching TV. Or rather he was ignoring her. She looked at him for a few moments, then walked closer to him.

"You no longer have the right to come in here regulating anything." He seethed, with his eyes still on the screen.

"The right never belonged to me in the first place." She walked into his room and brought out a blanket. She laid the blanket on the floor, removed her boots, and got a pillow. "Now lay down."

He simply stared at her. She met his eyes and didn't back down. "I have all day. But I won't leave you alone until you get your two hours in."

"You left me," Kamal said. His tone was accusatory.

"I had to," she whispered. Why couldn't anyone understand that her sanity depended on her cutting ties with him? She'd seen her mother love a man who was married to another. Ebele acknowledged she'd set herself up for that and took the necessary step to fix it.

"I needed you."

"You weren't free to have me," she countered. "What you needed was to get your house in order." She patted the makeshift mat. "We'll talk later, but for now, get down. Let's do this."

After a few moments of silence, Kamal took the position. Ebele saw uncertainty and hurt dance around in his eyes. It upset her to know that it was directed at her. Kamal being who he was, she knew that coming back wouldn't be easy. True, she did give her word to bear with him for a week. She shouldn't have agreed to that. She had to cut him off completely, and she had no regrets.

For the next hour, there was total silence from the pair. At least from him. She hadn't met a man, who could keep a grudge as well as this man right here. She tried to make small talk by asking about his family and telling him about school. She'd kept up with his life a little bit from Nse. That was how she found out that Brittani had left, and they'd called it quits. She didn't know the specifics, though.

After a bunch of hisses, muttering under his breath, and grunts of frustration, Ebele removed her hand from his calf. She'd been doing stretches for his hamstring. She leaned on her heels and put her hand on her lap. She'd since changed out of her sweater and was wearing one of his T-shirts.

"Kamal, I know you're hurting, but you have to work with me," she tried to assure him. "It's going to take some time."

"Yeah, it's easy for you to say." He sat up. "Why am I even doing this? Why are you still here?" His frustration was getting the better of him.

"You're doing this because you need to get better, and I'm still here because even though you've barely talked to me, I want to help you."

"In case you didn't know, I no longer play soccer. I was fired," he gritted his teeth. "So you can leave now like the rest."

Ebele remained silent. She knew he was fired, but what was he talking about, he no longer played soccer? Wasn't he supposed to be going back to the US to play for LA?

"You don't play *now*, but you need to get yourself together for when you go back to the States." She stood and went into the kitchen to get them bottles of water. She had to get away from him, or she would've thumbed his forehead.

"Speaking of … when were you going to tell me the grand plan was to go back to the US at the end of this month?" She handed him the water. He snatched it, and she thumbed his head.

"Go and verify your facts from who you've been getting

them from. That wasn't the grand plan because I was trying to get an extension to remain here." He drank his water. "What difference does it make? Even that team fired me so …"

Soccer was everything to him, but she had to make him see that it wasn't the totality of who he was. He played the sport, but that wasn't what he was created to do. There was a bigger purpose for him. She knew now wasn't the time to preach to him. He could barely look at her. But she was going to help him see that just because this season had ended, didn't mean his life had to. With Kamal, though, he was so stubborn. To get to him, she couldn't be soft about it. She'd display her femininity but give him the aggression he needed.

"I'm sorry about you not having a job. But you can still get one, and you do want to walk well again, right?"

He eyed her and didn't say a word. He struggled to get up. She saw him wince in pain and went to help him, but he shooed her away. He walked to the room without saying a word to her.

Where was her Kamal? He wasn't only injured physically, but his ego was hurting. She sighed.

After a few moments, she followed him to the room and heard the shower going. She helped him change his sheets, which smelled like sweaty socks. She tidied up as well. There were cans of soda, pizza cartons, and cookie packets tossed everywhere. She wondered what the housekeeper or his Brittani were doing. Then again, knowing him, he probably barked them away from the room.

Ebele went into the kitchen and saw some leftover pasta. She heated it for him and took it to his room with his medication, which she saw lying on the floor. He was still in the shower, so she set it down and left.

"Kam, I'm leaving," she yelled. It wasn't the weekend, and she had one class she couldn't miss in the morning. For the remainder of the week, she had online course study and preparation for her final project. There was no response, but he came out of the bathroom a few moments later with basketball shorts and a T-shirt on.

"That seems to be what you're good at," he said.

"You know what? I'm not going to argue with you tonight. You're acting childish, and I need to get back to school."

"Thanks for the food, but I'm not hungry." His eyes darted to the clock in his room. Her eyes followed him. It was five thirty p.m. She knew exactly what he was going to say next. "It's late. Take the car."

With the train, she'd be at school in an hour, with his car, only forty minutes. It was a no brainer, and she wasn't trying to stay on his bad side.

"Okay, I'll see you tomorrow."

"Hmm, sure." He dismissed her and got in his bed.

Ebele shook her head and walked to the door. She paused, remembering to make sure he was comfortable. She turned and walked back to him. She inclined his injured leg. Then she picked up the plate of food and twisted some spaghetti on the fork. All the while, he ignored her and selected the game to play on the gaming console. She put the fork up to his mouth.

"Ebele, move, man. I told you, I'm not hungry." On cue, his stomach growled.

"Yes, you are. You're just mad at me."

He patted his stomach and looked down. "You can't count on anything to be loyal anymore."

"Why should your stomach be loyal to pettiness?" She moved the fork closer to his mouth.

He leaned back. "Move. I can feed myself." He took the fork from her and put it back on the plate. "If you're gonna leave, you better leave now. When it gets dark, you aren't driving either."

"Aww, he still cares."

"Barely."

"The lies we tell." She walked to the door. He tried to

move, and she caught the grimace on his face. "Stop chasing the pain, Kam. Take the medicine at the required time and not when the pain hits."

"I'm not trying to be dependent on those things."

"Then we'll talk to the doctor about an alternative. But you'll still feel pain for a bit, so you need to take them."

He eyed her. "If you were on your job like you were supposed to be, you would've let me know that a long time ago." Kamal took a bite of his meatball.

She chuckled. "My job?"

"Yep. Then you gonna try and be mad when Tina was trying to do it for you." He furrowed his brows and inclined his head toward her.

Ebele looked at him. The things that came out of his mouth surprised her more each day. "Okay, I'm gonna let you think that."

"Let me? By the way, Tina will be here bright and early tomorrow. We've got exercises to complete," he said, with a smug grin.

"Oh, really? Don't let us be on the news *o*." She winked at him and left. She heard him chuckle and was satisfied. Picking up his keys, she prepared to make the ride back to school.

———

YOU CAN'T TEXT AND LET ME KNOW YOU MADE IT?

Ebele read Kamal's text and rolled her eyes. She walked in barely fifteen minutes ago. Her first goal was a shower, then some food. She knew that a lot of his aggression was caused by his bruised ego. On the drive back to school, she thought of the perfect way to get him out of his funk and possibly get them back on track. There was no way they could talk with so much animosity.

I'm back, Kam. Stop being mean.

You made me mean.

How?

By leaving me.

I had to, but I'm sorry.

Nah, that ain't enough. You on punishment.

How am I going to help you while on punishment?

What does that have to do with anything?

His response came with a confused emoji. Before she could clarify, another response came.

A Naija mom raised you just like one raised me. Hasn't she ever knocked you out one minute then gave you a chore the next?

She laughed because her mother had done that more than once. She remembered something else.

Or told you to clean the beans while sitting in the corner on punishment?

Her mother loved that one as she was forever cooking moi moi.

He sent back a laughing emoji.

So you already know the drill. You can be on punishment but still do what you need to do.

Say the words ... Help. Me.

She had no intention of taking over Kamal's rehabilitation full time. She'd leave that to experienced professionals, but she was going to be a part of every step. She wanted to make sure what was right for him was what was being done. She didn't need people rushing the process just to get a buck. Or being too slow to milk his dime. He told her about Coach Gram, so she was comfortable that the best team would be put together for him. She'd be there for him spiritually, emotionally, and psychologically.

Help YOU. Me getting better reflects you. I don't know how you trying to look out here. But how can you be a PT and I'm like this? It's a bad look, E.

Ebele threw her head back in laughter.

Okay, so you forgive me.

I ain't say that. I just said you can do your job. Hold on.

Ebele tossed her phone and brought up Google on her laptop. She typed Monica in the search box and hit enter. The song she was looking for came up first. She allowed the opening verse to play. She swayed to the beat and got lost in the rhythm. When it was time for the chorus, she positioned her phone and FaceTimed Kamal. His frown came on the screen a few seconds later, but she didn't let that deter her.

She watched his frown disappear as she crooned the chorus to Monica's "U Should've Known Better." Despite his bruised ego, he should've known she cared for him. She looped the chorus a second time and sang it using her pen as a microphone for dramatic effect. She smiled when she heard him laughing at her. She stopped the music and waited for him to say something.

"I missed you, big head," he said, his tone was soft. Vulnerability shone through his eyes.

"I missed you too, Kam." The extent and intensity couldn't be put into words. "More than you'd believe."

"I'll let you convince me. You got time," he said.

"Good night, Kam."

"Good night." He hung up the phone.

Ebele looked at her books spread across the bed. There was no way to come off that high and still get some studying in. She did the next best thing – said her prayers and went to sleep with a smile that had been missing for a while.

Chapter 23

"You're almost there, Kam."

Ebele's soft voice knocked down his anger some but not a lot. He was tired of his knee not feeling like it was a part of him. The day before, after about three weeks of the same routine with her, he fell. Ebele came from school every other day and helped him with extra therapy. If he couldn't even hobble around without falling after all this time, what hope did he have of ever playing again?

They were in his gym behind his house, which he turned into a mini rehabilitation center. The team Coach Gram had recommended for him came in the mornings, and Ebele was there in the evenings. Some days she stayed over, some days she didn't, but she hadn't left his side since she came back to him.

He grunted his dissatisfaction at the pain that accompanied her massaging around the incision.

"You want to try walking without the crutch again?"

"No." His response was harsher than he intended.

"What about swimming? Let me get your trunks, and you can get in the pool." She stood and walked away. She returned shortly with his trunks and a towel. He snatched them from her. His anger at her, God, and himself increased with his inability to do the things he should at almost six weeks post-op.

"Enough, Kamal. I have been here helping you for almost a month. You throw tantrums and scare off the professionals that are supposed to be helping you. On the days you don't let them do their jobs, I pick up their slack to make sure you're on schedule. I have no idea which Kammy I'll meet when I get here."

Kamal watched her go off.

"Is it happy Kam, mean Kam, woe is me Kam or spoiled brat Kam?" She counted off on her fingers and started to pace. "The world does not revolve around Kamal Danjuma, you know. I'm still in school, and I must graduate; but dealing with you, I'm all over the place. Yet you have the nerve to get angry at me. You can't play now, so what?"

"Just because you gave up on your dreams doesn't mean I have to give up on mine," he barked.

"The way you're going, you won't have any dreams."

He remained silent and stood. He hovered over her. They were at an impasse.

"God has a plan for you Kammy, but don't drown in self-pity before you're able to figure it out." Her voice was softer and her tone soothing.

He sucked his teeth. "God?"

"Yes. He loves you."

Kamal shook his head and carefully wobbled out of the room. He had been at it for about two hours because Ebele felt he needed to be punished for sending the regular therapist away. He craved the hot pounding water from his shower head.

A few minutes later, he was out of the shower, refreshed, and famished. As she always did, even when he told her not to, Ebele made him something to eat. Now it was pounded yam and okra soup. He thanked her and scarfed down the food while she stared at him.

"What? I'm hungry, and I'm tired of you fussing at me," he said.

"Then don't give me anything to fuss about," she sassed.

He was tired of this house and needed to get out. Starting the next day, he'd take walks around the neighborhood.

He entered the living room. It smelled different. There were aromatherapy candles lit in strategic places. The scent was like apples and cinnamon. He grinned at Ebele's little touches in his home. She never slept over unless she had to, but she left small items here and there that one would instantly know there was a woman nearby. He still thought about that night she sang Monica's song for him. It was something he never expected.

Kamal picked up his sketchpad and started to draw a dress. He started out with nothing particular in mind, but as he continued to draw, he saw it was a wedding dress. It was a long-sleeved, body hugging, lace dress with Ankara patches on the sides. He heard Ebele walk in and put the pad away. He wanted to keep it to himself for now. He saw a serious expression on her face. He wanted them to chill without talking about his present state. He was tired of arguing with her.

"Kam, do you still believe in God?"

"What kind of question is that?" He scratched his head.

"One that needs an answer."

"Of course, I believe there's a God." He looked at her like she was losing it.

"I didn't ask whether you believe there's a God. I asked do you believe in Him? Do you have faith in His word and that He loves you?"

"He can't love me too much if He took away my ability to do what I love."

"God didn't make this happen to you." She paused, and he challenged her with his eyes. "Bad things happen for a reason. Draw from His strength to get through and get the lesson."

"I could have done without the lesson."

Ebele didn't respond. She put her book bag over her shoulder and panic took over him. She wasn't supposed to leave now. Had he pushed her beyond her limits?

"Where are you going?" he asked.

"This person you've become sucks. I want my Kam back. When you find him, tell him to call me."

Kamal watched her turn to the door. He owed her some background. He couldn't expect her to continue sticking with his moods without knowing why. "Soccer is my life. I'm nobody without it!" he yelled.

She turned to face him. She put down her bag and walked to him. She stood in front of him. He reached for her. Pulling her close, he rested his head on her stomach and wrapped his arms around her waist. She lifted her hand and caressed his head.

"I knew the day would come. I knew I couldn't play forever. That's why I got my degree. Well, that and Rasheed's constant harassment. But I wanted to have time to prepare." He decided to tell her everything, so she could understand what was really happening to him.

"My father and I were the closest. I went everywhere with him for the six years he was with me. I was even closer to him than my mother. Anytime he was around, we'd kick the ball around together. Do you know that the first ball he bought me, I still carry around 'til this day? It's flat, but it goes with me to every city I play. After all that, all we shared and how much he knew I'd hurt, he left. He still left. Was it something I did or didn't do?

"The day before he left, my team lost our little league game. It was pre-K, so it wasn't much, but we lost, and he left. I know it's ridiculous now, but I thought his disappointment in me drove him away. Everyone took their place in his absence, trying to make my mom happy. Rasheed, the oldest, stepped up to hold us together. Jabir is the smart one. My mom was always going to one award ceremony or the other. And I, on the other hand, flunked at everything. I wasn't stupid, but what was the use of applying myself? I got into so much trouble that my mom enrolled me in the camp run by Coach." Kamal sighed and held on to Ebele tighter. She hadn't said anything, but the reassuring caresses on his scalp encouraged him to go on.

"It was Coach that revived my love of the sport. After a while, I figured that if I played well, my dad would come back. He never did. When he came back when I was sixteen, I couldn't go against my brothers and talk to him. They had done so much for me. Keeping my mother's hand off my behind was chief among them." He gave a faint laugh at constantly being at the crux of his mother's anger growing up.

"So I never got to ask him questions I wanted to. Over the years, soccer became my crutch. As long as I played well, people didn't leave me. As a star, people are all around me. It's who I am. Now it's gone ..." Kamal let out a deep, pained breath.

"It's hard, E. It's hard not knowing who you are because the only thing that made you who you are, has been taken away. Ball is all I know."

A beat of silence passed between them. Ebele removed his arms from her waist. She knelt in front of him. They were both sobbing. He tried to wipe her tears, but she wouldn't let him. Instead, she cupped his face in her small hands. She looked him directly in his eyes. He held her gaze. It was as though they both had the key to each other's soul.

"You're more than ball. Far more. I would say I can't relate, but unfortunately, I can, and my dad is still alive. I also struggled with who I am. I'm mixed. People see us, and the first thing they notice is our beauty or curly hair.

"But that's all they see. The exterior. They don't understand the struggles people like me face if their parents don't handle the interracial thing properly. I'm black and white, but I can't identify with either of them fully. At home, they call me *oyinbo* when they wanna tease or gossip about me. Or give my mother and I nasty looks like she stole me. They look at me like I can't compare because my skin is lighter. I can cook, clean, dance, speak my language, and pidgin, and do just about anything *Naija*. But my mixed race still sets me apart.

"Here? Don't get me started. I get these pointed looks of curiosity. The first question I get is, 'Where are you from?' If I say the UK because technically, I am, the next question is, 'No I mean, where are you really from?' Like they want me to justify the color of my skin. If I say Nigeria, some turn their nose up like how dare I contaminate their color.

"Dance was all I knew. It was what kept me from all the extra. Nobody saw color. On the dance floor, my talent was what shone through. But that was taken away. I was in hell, sinking just like you. I had to accept help from my mom and pastor to know that there was purpose in my pain. But there was no way I would've found it without leaning on God. Trust Him in the season. Kam, you may not be playing soccer now, but that doesn't mean your life doesn't have purpose. When you walked up to the altar that day, you were no longer a soccer player, who is Christian. You're now a Christian, who is or was a soccer player. That's your identity. Not what you do or don't do. I had to learn that if our identity is in anything based on our own efforts, we set ourselves up for insecurity. Our only anchor should be in who we are in Christ Jesus."

She stood. "Scoot up." He did as she instructed. She sat down, and he rested his head in her lap. The feel of her fingers in his scalp nearly sent him straight to sleep.

After searching her phone for a few seconds, a man's voice came through.

"Who's that?" he asked, with his eyes closed, enjoying the melody.

"Marvin Sapp. Now listen to the lyrics." She held on to him, providing the comfort he craved. Before her, he didn't even know he needed that.

"What's the name of the song?"

"It's "He Has His Hands on You." Now will you listen to the song?" she fussed. "Ughh, now I got to start it over."

"Next time, introduce the whole song before playing it. Then I won't have to ask questions, Meanie," he said.

"I learned from the best."

They played the song twice. She pulled up her Bible app and went to Psalm 51:10, *Create in me a pure heart, O God, and renew a steadfast spirit within me.*

They prayed together for his change of heart, his healing, and surrendering the future to God. He shed a few more tears, but this time it was in deep regret for not trusting God as he should. He and Ebele talked a few more minutes until they fell asleep.

Waking up some time later, he eased out of her arms and positioned her correctly on the couch. He covered her with a blanket. He limped to his car and got her things out of it. He wasn't allowing her to drive back this late.

Entering the kitchen, he picked up the menu to *Naija Small & Big Chops.* This was why he loved London. There was no shortage of places to cure his periodic craving for Nigerian cuisine.

Kamal ordered their grilled Tilapia with extra spice in his. Ebele loved spice, but he didn't want her turning red, so he ordered a milder version for her. It would come with Jollof rice and fried plantain. They had Zobo, so he ordered that as well.

He looked at Ebele, sleeping soundly on the couch. She was it for him. No one had ever stood up to or intrigued him like she did. He knew there was a reason he was attracted to her at first sight. Their stories mirrored each other. As she had helped him, he'd help her get back on track with her dad. She might not think so, but she needed that. One thing though, he wouldn't let anyone hurt her.

He picked up his phone and personalized her ringtone with "Last Bus Stop" by Dr. Sid. That expressed his sentiments exactly. Replacing his phone, he was happy that all that was left was to talk to her when she woke up. To make sure she was on board, and they were on the same page about their future. On second thought, they had to settle this now.

Kamal shook Ebele gently. She didn't even stir. When she was going off earlier, she did say that he made her run around ragged. His poor baby. He'd set up a spa day for her.

"E, wake up, baby. I need to talk to you."

She whined but didn't open her eyes.

He smiled at his thought and braced himself for her attack.

"Aye, E, let me get this spider real quick." Kamal hit the couch.

"Huh? What? Where?" She jumped up and nearly stumbled with the blanket entangled around her head. He watched with belly aching laughter as she struggled to break free. When she was successful, her hair was all over the place. He was bent over the side of the couch holding his stomach that was now hurting. Kamal looked up and could see imaginary smoke coming out of her ears. Ebele stomped over to him, and he put his hands up to block her.

"E, remember, I'm injured."

"Kam, that wasn't funny." She hit him on his shoulder repeatedly.

"Chill, man, your blows are hard."

"What if I fell and knocked my teeth out?" She huffed with her hands on her hips.

He pulled her down to him. "I'd love you regardless."

She was about to speak until she realized his confession. "You love me?"

"I have loved you since I saw you at Nse's party. I only

admitted it to myself when you left me the first time – after I acted out at your apartment." He removed her hair from her face.

"I love you, too, Kam. It killed me to leave you here with your girlfriend, but it was only right," she said.

"Ex-girlfriend unless …" He put his index finger under his lower lip in contemplation. She frowned. "Unless you are saying I can still have girlfriends while you're wifey."

She looked at him like he'd lost his mind. "Are you okay?"

"Yep. It's your world, baby. Let me know how we're going to do this. All options end with you being my wife, though." He decided to mess with her a little more. "You do know I'm entitled to four wives, but I'll only marry you."

She tried to get up from the couch they were sitting on, but he stopped her. He wasn't ready to stop playing with her yet. "The rest will be concubines. I promise."

"Kamal, let me go. See how you ruined a perfect moment." She struggled against him.

He kissed her forehead and held her tighter. "Come on, baby, don't be that way. You know I'm just playing with you."

"Keep playing, and we'll end up on the evening news. I've told you before."

"Stop trying to leave me. So, you gonna marry me?"

"Is this your proposal?"

"No, but I want to know."

"You'll know then."

He cupped her face and kissed her lips with passion. "I love you, E. You can't leave me again."

"I didn't leave you. I was just giving you space to do what you needed to do. I love you too, baby. But don't make me hurt you because of that mouth of yours."

"You know you only got licks in because I'm sitting, with your short self."

"Okay, keep playing." She got up and walked in the direction of the kitchen. "What are you cooking? I'm hungry. I need to eat and head back to school."

"Nothing. I ordered, and it's already late."

"Kam, I have to go. I have class in the morning. I need to be prepared."

"Prepare here and drive in the morning. I don't know why you're bringing that up. You already know the answer."

"I think you intentionally try to keep me here."

"I don't know how it took you this long to figure it out." He grinned. "But I've told you before, trust me."

The doorbell rang. She answered the door and paid for the food before he could make it there. He frowned at her putting her change in her back pocket. He scolded her about paying for things when they were together. She ignored him the whole time he ranted.

They finally settled down to enjoy their meal. He filled her in on the details of his contracts. She told him she'd be done with clinicals next month, and there wouldn't be a need for her to stay in Essex. That's what she thought, though. He had his lifeline back and was going to do everything within his power to make sure they stayed connected.

Chapter 24

The leaves on the trees swayed from the movement of the early May breeze. Their whistling woke Ebele from her slumber. Her eyes opened, and her mouth offered thanksgiving for another morning. As a matter of fact, another year. It was her birthday, and for the last couple of days, Kamal wouldn't stop talking about it. He told her to free up her schedule for the day, not to call him and ask no questions.

She was proud of her man. In the last two months, he'd shown so much improvement that even the doctors were impressed. He pushed himself well beyond his limits and took the whole healing program seriously. Physically, he was jogging, swimming, and driving short distances. His range of motion was good, and she was so happy. Spiritually, he was praying and meditating more. They covered each other with prayer every morning. He sent her a "good morning" text accompanied by a blessing and a declaration of his love. She, in turn, sent him a verse for the day.

The theme she focused on was hope. To her surprise, he let her hire a yoga instructor for him, and he was enjoying it. He no longer needed crutches or knee braces. He still had a limp because he wasn't treating both knees equally, but they were working through that together.

She rose from her bed and slipped on her robe. She picked up her Bible and made her way to the kitchen. The barrage of birthday phone calls would soon start, but before then, she wanted some time for herself and God. She set her Bible down on the small dinette and heated the water for her tea. She was reading the book of Ruth again but wanted to see if God had another word for her.

She pulled up a search engine on her phone and typed in the words "birthday" and "Bible verse." A knowing smile spread across her face when Ephesians 2:10 came up. She went to her Bible and read it. *For we are his workmanship, created in Christ Jesus for good works, which God prepared beforehand, that we should walk in them.* Her mother harped on this verse when Ebele was in her, "I have no worth, so why should I celebrate my birthday?" phase.

The kettle whistled. Ebele quickly prepared some mint tea and went back to her study. She clicked on the link that was right below that Bible verse. It took her to a series titled **Dear Woman**. According to the website, it was a five-week series in the form of letters aimed at empowering women. Intrigued, Ebele clicked on the first week and began to read.

Dear Woman,

Let's break Ephesians 2:10 down. Webster defines "workmanship as the skill of the workman." A skill, as we know, is something that it takes time to develop. So, in Christ, we are His workmanship, "predestined to do good works so we can walk in them." Key words predestined and good works.

Dear Woman, fear and doubt should not hold you back from doing the good works that God had predestined you to do. While you were being formed, He already knew what you were going to do. Not what your neighbor or friend was going to do but YOU. There's an African Proverb that says, "If you think you're too small to make a difference, you haven't met the mosquito." As we know, the mosquito, though small, does mighty damage.

Dear Woman, you are fearfully and wonderfully made. You will feel fear but what makes you crested in Christ is your ability to rise above it and push forward anyway. Don't allow the opinions of others or the negative thoughts to stop you. You don't have to have it all together. All you have to do is start where you are. Why? Because you are the skilled product of the Almighty and through Jesus, He has predestined us to do good works and walk in them.

Dear Woman, I pray for you as I pray for myself that you recognize the potential in you always. Let the scars you incur along the way be your way of saying you showed up for the task He set before us. Amen.

When Ebele was done, her mouth was ajar, and her tea lukewarm. She saved the link, as she intended to complete all five weeks of the study. She quickly repented for the error of her ways. If her dad didn't want her, she had a God who was unchanging who did. A God who gave her a man who adored her. She'd let her feeling of worthlessness put her on a road with Victor she shouldn't have been on. However, she regretted nothing as everything worked together for the good.

Ebele rinsed her cup and headed to her room. As expected, at six a.m. sharp, her phone started going off. The first caller was her mother, as usual. Ebele answered her the phone and a sheepish grin formed on her face at her mother's "Happy Birthday" rendition. Her mother prayed for her, and they chatted. She hung up promising to call her at the end of the day to tell her how her day went. Without fail, Mummy asked of Kamal and Ebele supplied an update on his injury.

Any time her mother called when she was with Kamal, he insisted on talking to her. He'd even begun calling her *Momsie*. On the reverse side, Ebele was apprehensive about speaking to Mrs. Danjuma and had done so only once. At the back of her mind, Ebele feared she'd think she was after her son's money.

Next came messages from the few friends from school that

she kept up with. Nse and Tega, as they did every year when they could, called and sang to her. They always had a gift for her too. She'd always treated it like a normal day, but this year, Kamal had her expectant, and she wasn't sure why she hadn't heard from him.

She took a shower and dressed. Soon after, her phone buzzed. She hurried to it; sure it was Kamal. The excitement disappeared when she saw who the message was from. A frown appeared upon her face when she opened her iMessage.

To the woman I love, Ebi, baby. Happy birthday. May the Lord give you all your heart's desires and more. Have a great day.

It was from Victor. She deleted it as soon as she read it. She didn't need to get Kamal worked up unnecessarily.

One day last month, Victor had tagged her as his Woman Crush Wednesday on Instagram, and Kamal almost had a stroke. He didn't even think when he posted for Victor to take the picture down. She'd been in class when Nse left her a voicemail to get her man. At first, she was confused until she went to IG and saw his exchange with Victor. Sometimes Kamal forgot he had more to lose, being a celebrity. Victor's fame was no comparison to Kamal's. She wasn't going to allow him to go toe-to-toe with Victor on IG. So when she finally got to him, she took his phone and deleted the comments. Luckily, the hungry bloggers hadn't taken notice. Victor backed off after that, although he still sent her these flirtatious messages occasionally.

Her and Kamal's relationship wasn't public yet. She'd been photographed with him a few times, but her face had been hidden or covered. Since they weren't in a compromising position, and she had on her scrubs, the press had pretty much left her alone. She knew a time would come when their relationship would be exposed. For now, she'd relish in the quiet.

Her thoughts were interrupted by a knock on her door.

She answered and was met by a flower arrangement of yellow lilies. He remembered.

"Ms. Ashhhhh—" the delivery man tried to pronounce her name.

Not trying to give an enunciation lesson, she cut him off. "Ashiedu, yes, that's me."

"We have a delivery for you. A lot of them in fact." The man grinned and handed the first vase over. She took it and stepped aside as two men offloaded a total of five vases of different colors of lily arrangements. She signed the delivery papers and ran to her phone. As she began to type her thanks to Kamal, there was another knock on the door. Thinking the delivery man forgot one of her flower arrangements, she didn't bother checking the door. She flung it open, and a man dressed like a chauffeur stood there.

"Err. Hi," she said, with her nose scrunched up in confusion.

"Good morning, Miss. I was sent to pick you up, and I also have a message from Mr. Danjuma." He handed her a note.

E, baby,

The day God created you, He was really looking out for me. Happy birthday, my love, and I'll see you later. You got the flowers? Five vases, one for each month since you intercepted my world.

I know you have your nose scrunched up at the chauffeur. Go with him. He has instructions. I hope it's the old guy they sent. The one that looks more like a grandpa than a date. As a matter of fact, take a picture and send it to me.

PS: I know you have on that smile that centers my world, but I ain't playing, E. Send me a picture of the dude.

I love you.

Kam

Ebele chuckled and shook her head. How was she supposed to tell the man to pose so she could take a picture for her not-wrapped-too-tight boyfriend? She folded the note, placed it on her chest, and let out a dreamy sigh. His crazy was consistent. But he belonged to her, and that was okay. Besides, underneath his two-hundred-twenty-five pounds, he was a cuddly bear.

"I'll be right back." Ebele closed the door and ran to her room. She wondered what Kamal had in store for her this early. It wasn't even nine a.m. yet. Minutes later, she'd changed into an off-the-shoulder, multicolored dress.

"I'm ready." She locked up and entered the back of a sleek, black Mercedes Benz S class. She sank into the leather seats and was enveloped by their warmth. Sometimes she marveled at how well Kamal knew her. She'd shy away from an actual limousine, so he sent this over instead. It was perfect.

Before closing the door, the older man tipped his hat. "Miss, you'll find breakfast and beverages to your satisfaction. Enjoy the ride."

She acknowledged him with a nod and pulled out her phone to call Kamal. The phone rang twice, and she was sent to voicemail. She wanted to be angry, but he did tell her not to call him. She agreed, thinking he'd call her.

She put the phone on her lap and got lost in the scenery. Her stomach was in knots from anticipation, so she dared not put anything in her mouth. Her phone chirped again, and again, she was disappointed when she saw it was her dad. She contemplated answering it. The last time they had lunch together, it was more of the same. Idle chatter. She and Kamal were on the outs then, so she had no shoulder to cry on. She was tired of crying on Nse's. She answered the ring before it went to voicemail. She might as well get it over with.

"Hello, Father," she answered, dryly.

"Happy Birthday, Vanessa."

"Thank you. How are you?" Ebele asked, for lack of anything else to say.

"I'm fine. Any big plans? I'd love to take you to lunch."

They'd already had lunch once this month. That was enough. Not like it was even an option today.

"Yes, I do have plans. I'm not sure what they are, but I have a date." She hadn't really gotten to the point of sharing personal things about herself with him. Not like he was sharing himself with her.

"I didn't know you were seeing someone. I hope he's treating you right," her father said.

Ebele rolled her eyes. Was he serious right now? Because of him, she'd learned the hard way how not to let someone treat her. Not wanting to spoil her day, she gave him a dry affirmation and switched to a safer topic. The call ended with him saying he put some money into her account. That's what it always came down to with him – money.

She hung up and was about to question God on why He couldn't give her a father who loved her. Then she heard a whisper. *Father of the fatherless and protector of the widows is God in the holy habitation.* She remembered the verse from Psalm 68:5. It's been one of her go-to verses over the last few years.

"We're here, Miss." The driver alighted the vehicle and came around to open the door for her.

Ebele had been so engrossed in her thoughts that she didn't know when the car came to a halt. She got out of the car and muttered her thanks as she read the sign on the building she stood in front of. The Body Temple. It was *the* day spa. She'd only heard of this place on TV. The commercial was filled with wives, or girlfriends of top politicians or celebrities, as their clientele. Kamal was blowing her mind.

She walked in the door. Before she could introduce herself, she was met by a pretty woman with jet-black hair. "Welcome to Body Temple. You must be Ebele. Mr. Danjuma had the timing of your arrival so precise. My name is Lin. Please, follow me."

Too stunned for words, Ebele did as she was told. They walked down a long hallway with rooms on each side. The walls were decorated with ancient oriental art. Ebele had never had a massage before. From her tight school schedule to traveling back to Nigeria as often as she could to see her mom, to her meager, part-time paycheck, she didn't have the time or frankly, the extra money. Her and Nse got regular mani/pedis, but she never went with her when she went to the spa.

"Right here." The woman opened a door, and Ebele walked in. It was dark, lit with only aromatherapy candles – the same apple and cinnamon scent she put all over Kamal's house.

Oh, gosh, had he paid that much attention to detail that he remembered that?

"Your masseuse will be with you shortly." Lin closed the door behind her.

"Thank you." Ebele looked around, taking in the ambiance of the room. She put down her purse and read some of the quotes on the wall. Soon after, a woman came in, instructed her to strip to her panties, and lay on the table. She was covered with a sarong, and the woman went to work. Using a combination of hot stones and her hands and elbows, she worked all Ebele's muscles until they were almost tender. Ebele felt like a noodle when they were done an hour later.

After she was dressed, Ebele was taken to the back of the building where she was given a facial, manicure, and pedicure. She felt like a princess and couldn't wait to see Kamal later. He made all this possible. He sent a text some time during her massage asking her how her day was going.

After getting the works, she walked to the front of the building where another woman was waiting for her. She introduced herself as Pamela, personal stylist to the stars. Ebele didn't know Kamal had a stylist. Well, in the last five months, he hadn't had any contractual appearances that he had to get dressed up for, so it was never a topic of discussion. Pamela accompanied Ebele to the car and told the driver to head to Harrods. She told Ebele she'd meet her there.

Pamela took her on the shopping expedition of a lifetime. After two hours, Ebele had called Kamal so many times for him to rescue her. Not getting an answer, she texted him. He responded that his queen deserved the best, but he did call Pamela off. They'd bought so many clothes and shoes that Ebele believed she could probably wear some in the next world to come.

It was now mid-afternoon; she was exhausted and famished. They got back in the car, and the driver headed back to her flat. She was about to tell him to stop at her favorite restaurant when he handed her a bag. The aroma of spicy snails and coconut rice permeated the air. She smiled as she took the food and began to dig in. *Kamal.*

It was five minutes after three in the afternoon by the time she got home. She was full and sleepy. The driver helped her carry her things in and gave her one last note.

Hey, beautiful, I hope you enjoyed your day. It's not over yet. The main course is still ahead. We have plans at six. Some people will be by to help you get ready by 4:30. See you soon.

I love you.

Kam

Ebele was so overjoyed that an outward reaction eluded her. She left the bags in the living room and went to her bedroom. She showered and slipped into bed. A quick power nap was duly needed.

Light banging woke her up. She peered at the time and flew out of bed. It was 4:45 p.m. She'd overslept. She picked up her phone and rushed to the door. There were ten missed calls from Kamal. He must be worried. She quickly sent him a text that she overslept and went to open the door. Pamela was back, with a man in tow.

"Hi, Ebele, I'm back," she said, with a faint smile.

"Sorry to keep you waiting." There was an awkward silence between them as Ebele eyed the black box the man had with him, and the garment bag Pamela was holding.

"Not a problem. Kamal got himself a winner in you. The other lady I—"

Ebele cleared her throat to cut her off. She didn't need to hear about Kamal and any other lady. She knew they existed in the past, and that was where they should stay.

Pamela's expression gave away her understanding of her error. "Oh, I'm so sorry. Please, don't say anything to Mr. Danjuma. I didn't mean any harm."

Ebele ignored her. Her eyes turned toward the man that Pamela should've been introducing instead of trying to resurrect old things.

"Oh, this is Tray. He'll be doing your hair and makeup while I get you dressed for your date." She held the garment bag close to her chest. "Mr. Danjuma picked this out himself."

Ebele and the man exchanged greetings, and they quickly got to work. About an hour later, they were done. As they packed up to leave, Ebele looked at herself in the mirror. She could barely recognize the reflection that looked back at her. Her makeup was minimalist and done to perfection. Her simple, knee-length, lace black dress made her feel sexy. Elegant, flirty yet classy. On her feet were a new pair of nude Louboutin. Her hair was in a chignon with tendrils left hanging at the sides. The duo left, and she continued admiring herself when her doorbell rang. When she opened the door, there stood her Nigerian protector and the one who made her soul sing.

Ebele's beamed, and her heart leaped as she took him in. He was clad in an all-black ensemble. The first two buttons of his shirt were undone, leaving the simple but expensive gold cross chain he always wore, visible. He finished his look with nude-colored patterned Ankara loafers and a Fedora made of the same fabric. Once again, she blessed God for putting her on that British Airways flight.

"Hey, baby, you ready to go?" Kamal asked, his eyes roaming her body. His satisfied grin told her he liked what he saw.

"With you? Always."

Chapter 25

K amal took the keys from Ebele and locked her door. He looked at her again, and his heart thumped. She was all his, and he was grateful. God gave him his piece of peace in human form. They walked the short distance to the car service, and he opened the door for her. Once she was seated, he walked around and got in.

"You look amazing," he said.

"Thank you. So do you."

"So how was your day?"

"Oh, gosh, Kam, it was beautiful. Thank you, thank you!" she gushed, and it made him happy and satisfied to be able to put that smile on her face.

"You're welcome, baby. It's my job to always make you happy." He took her hand.

Her expression turned somber. "You do know that I'm happy with just you … without those things."

"I know Miss 'I want to know Kamal and not Kammy.'" He mocked what she'd told him months ago. Her face flushed in embarrassment. "Those things, however, come with who I am. So, by default, my queen gets to share it with me."

While they drove to their destination, she told him about

her day. When she mentioned her father, his jaw tightened when her larger-than-life presence shrank.

"E, you're going to have to make up your mind on that relationship. You can't keep letting it get to you." He caressed her hand. He didn't want to seem insensitive, but after talking with her father, she always felt sad.

"I don't know," she said, her tone low.

"Maybe he doesn't have the capacity to give more than he's giving you. Either you accept it for what it's worth and love him unconditionally, or you get off the merry-go-round and keep it moving. I have never met someone as beautiful, in and out, a fighter, fierce protector, and intelligent as you are. If he can't see that and embrace you, then it's his loss. But you need to get off the emotional hamster wheel, baby," he said.

She leaned her head on his shoulder. He wanted to tell her that everything would work out the way she wanted, but he was the last person to make that kind of promise.

A few minutes later, they reached their destination. He helped her out of the car, and she took in her surroundings. When she saw the private plane, she squealed, almost bursting his eardrum.

"Come on, baby. Let's go." He grabbed her hand and made the short walk through the airstrip to the plane.

He helped her on and stood at the door admiring her as she inspected the aircraft. They were on a six-seater, private jet with a small bedroom, and adjourning restroom at the back.

"E, we'll soon take off." He stretched his hand out to her. She walked up to him and put hers in it. He kissed the back of her hand and led her to their seats. Remembering their first flight together, he opened his hand, and she grabbed it like her life depended on it. She looked at him nervously.

"When I barely knew you, I had you. Now that you're mine, you'll always be safe with me." He reassured her. She gave him a nod and a faint smile as the plane began to taxi.

When they were at cruising altitude, they were served a bottle of sparkling wine. Lifting the drink to her lips, she said, "Kam, please, tell me where we're going."

"No. I know I've said no before. Do I need to draw it, so you know what it means?" he joked.

"Go *jor* …" she pouted.

"That's not working, young lady. Relax, we'll be there soon."

Two hours later, they were being seated by the maître d' at the Chef's Table of the prestigious Kinveles restaurant in Amsterdam. The Chef's Table was a nice, intimate setting that had a behind-the-scenes look at how the meal was prepared. Ebele hadn't said much since they alighted from the plane a while ago. When the pilot said, "Welcome to The Netherlands," she looked at Kamal stunned. He'd never in his life had so much satisfaction pleasing a woman. The Chef came over to welcome them, and they chatted for a few minutes.

When their drink orders were in, she leaned in to him. Her eyes glazed over. "I can't believe you remembered. I just can't believe it."

He reached over and wiped the corner of her eye. "E, I can't do the tears. Please, don't cry, baby."

"I'm being a baby—"

"You're my baby, so it's okay. And I listen to everything you say. I might be stubborn about it, but I listen."

During one of their numerous talks, they talked about their favorite movies. Her favorite was Ocean's Eleven. She told him it was set in Amsterdam and expressed her desire to go there some day because of the places she'd seen in the movie. He'd been planning for months to make her dream come true.

"How did you know about this place?" Ebele beamed.

"Early in my career, I tried out for teams in Hague and here in Amsterdam." He looked up at the waiter, who arrived with their drinks. The couple placed their orders. When the man left, Kamal continued. "I didn't get selected, but I did check out the city. Also, I've come back numerous times to play."

She nodded. "How did it go with Coach today?"

"Nope, today is about you. I hope you're having fun?" He placed his hand over hers.

She sighed. "It's been the best day I've ever had." She looked around. "Thank you, Kam. I'm in awe."

"This is just the beginning."

"Ok, so I want to know. Tell me about how it went with Coach and that Chris boy?"

"He's almost twenty, baby, hardly a boy, but it was cool. Today, he actually let me talk to him."

Over the last months, Kamal's routine was pretty much the same. In the morning, he had breakfast then went over to Coach's rehabilitation center, where he was involved in rigorous workout routines. He'd gained more confidence in his knee. He could now run, hop and his height of step had gotten better. He'd then go home and sleep or draw. But his life felt empty. He wasn't hurting for money, but something was missing. He wanted to get back to playing ball, but there had to be something more. For the first time in his life, he longed for something more.

He met Chris one of the days when he went to the center. He was this young chap that reminded Kamal of himself at that age. Headstrong, and focused on only one thing – playing ball. However, he'd gotten injured and was taking it bad emotionally. After shunning him a few times, he allowed Kamal to talk to him. And a new mentee/mentor relationship was born.

"Kam, Kamal ..."

Ebele's soft voice brought him to the present. "Yes, baby, sorry I zoned out for a second."

"Yeah, you did. You okay?"

"Yeah, I was thinking about Chris. It did feel good to talk to him and see him become motivated. Like it was something I was doing for someone else."

"You sound confused or worried about it."

"Is this what I'm supposed to do?"

"Only God can help you with that. Whatever you're passionate about can lead to the calling God has for you. But you have to seek Him in prayer for Him to tell you who He's calling you to be in this season."

"I guess, but how will I know?"

"When you are aligned with Him, there'll be joy in the depths of your soul doing it. Will there be hard times? Yes, but it'll be worth it." She squeezed his hand.

"I have always been so centered on me that I never took time to think about it," he said, more to himself.

Shortly after, they were served their five-course meal. Kamal and Ebele had the same thing, Dutch Suckling lamb. The Chef had explained it was from the top-grade, Texel sheep. When they tasted it, he and Ebele laughed because it tasted no different than regular lamb, but they wouldn't tell the Chef that.

The evening was filled with laughter and talk of the present and future. Ebele's final exams would be in late August, and she'd complete her degree requirements in September. October would be a big month for them. She'd have her graduation ceremony, and he'd be able to try out for a new team.

Kamal checked the time and signaled the waiter. A few seconds later, they rolled out a small birthday cake with Ebele's favorite flavor, red velvet. He observed his woman; she shied under the attention but glowed under the light of the lone candle. He couldn't stop her from crying to save his life, and he wasn't done for the night. Soon after, they were back in the car. She laid her head on his shoulder. They savored the moment as they rode in comfortable silence to their next destination. When they pulled up to the lot, Ebele nearly jumped out of her skin. They were at the Amsterdam Performing Arts Theater. They were just in time for the ten p.m. show.

They got out of the car, and he grabbed her hand. They had been lucky in the restaurant but here, not so much. Despite his Fedora, Kamal was recognized by one man. And from there, he was accosted for autographs and pictures from about six more people. He tried to keep Ebele by his side, but she eased away from him. He frowned at her, and she gave him a knowing shrug.

"Hey, folks, I'd love to stay, but I'm out with my lady tonight. Enjoy your evening," Kamal said to the crowd that was forming. He walked over to Ebele, reclaimed her hand, and they were escorted to their skybox seats.

"Don't do that again, E," Kamal scolded once they were seated.

"Do what?"

"Move away from my side like that." He'd panicked in the second he couldn't feel her next to him.

"I didn't want to get trampled by your following," she joked.

He looked over at her. "I have never needed security, but you're going to make me get some."

"Were you worried about me, baby?" She pouted.

He ignored her. This woman had the potential to send him to the psych ward. She began kissing the back of his hand.

"Don't be mad." She stood and tried to cup his face.

"Okaaay, E, move. I wasn't mad, just worried. You know you barely come up from the ground. Can't have someone putting you in their pocket." He chuckled.

She twisted her lips in a frown and hit him with her purse. "I can't stand you."

"Yeah, you can. Give me a kiss."

"No." She sat with her arms crossed.

"I bet you forgive me when they announce what we're watching." He'd hidden everything from her. He had called ahead and used the back entrance, but his surprise was almost ruined when the man recognized him.

"Yeah, whatever. Let's see how much you're laughing when I actually disappear on you."

"Why do you like threatening folks?"

She was about to respond when the lights dimmed, and they announced the *Remake of Sarafina the Musical* accompanied by the Soweto Choir.

"Oh, my God, Kam. Oh, my God!" she said, in a loud whisper. "Thank you. Thank you. I remember watching this growing up, and I love the Soweto Choir."

He pulled her close. "You're welcome, baby. I'm glad you like it."

The show lasted about seventy-five minutes, and soon after, they were back on the jet headed to London.

"E, you gotta stop crying, man." Kamal covered her with a blanket. She was still emotional about the Apartheid-themed play. She couldn't understand how people came to another person's homeland and treated them that way. He tried to compare it to the Israelites and Egyptians. She explained that it wasn't the same because the Egyptians did them wrong in Egypt. This, however, was white people doing wrong to South Africans in their own homeland.

"I'm sorry. The musical was so beautiful and brought back memories. I loved when the woman that played the girl in the film came out and said a few words. Oh, the interpretive dance, and the choir, I loved everything. Thank you, Kam." Her voice was low and drifting. She was falling asleep. It had been a long day and would be about one a. m. before they landed back in London.

"E, baby, stop thanking me. But don't go to sleep yet." He pulled out a long velvet black box and handed it to her.

"No, Kam, you've done so much already." She put her hand on her heart.

"If I didn't have you, I'd have sunk so deep that I don't know if I would've recovered ..."

"I love you, Kam, and I'm sure you'd do the same for me."

"I'd bring down the sun or die trying if you wanted it."

"You know that was so corny." She giggled.

"That's what you make me do. Here, open it."

Ebele teared up when she saw the necklace. It was tri-colored with an E & K encrusted in little diamonds.

"E, if you cry, I'm locking you up in the back."

"Shut up. This is beautiful."

"Turn around. Let me put it on you."

Ebele turned around and lifted her hair. She'd since taken it out of its bun. He put it on her and kissed the nape of her neck.

"Don't take it off, E. If you're mad at me, that's fine, but don't take it off."

"You put it so eloquently, but since I know what you really mean, okay."

"One more thing, then I'll let you sleep."

"What?" she slurred.

"Will you go home with me next month?" He knew it was a long shot. For some reason, she dodged his mom. How she thought she'd continue dodging her mother-in-law was funny to him. He knew her reservation, but his mother loved her already when he told her how she went off on him.

"Huh? Why?" She was visibly frazzled.

"Calm down. It's my mom's birthday, and everyone is going."

"Everyone? As in your whole family?" she asked, her eyes bugged out.

"Yeah ..."

"I don't know, Kam." Ebele rubbed her hand across her forehead.

"Okay, when I come back and have to use crutches again, you gonna be mad. Who's going to help with my therapy when I'm there? And do you really want my sisters-in-law introducing me to their friends?" He raised his eyebrow. "You know I'm a catch."

"So am I, and?" she challenged him.

"Let me quote you. Don't let us be in the news *o*."

She laughed. "See, you can dish it, but you can't take it." She paused. "But really, blackmail?"

"Is it working?" he asked, hopeful.

"I guess. I can't be gone more than a week."

"That's all I need."

"Okay."

"Thank you, baby, and *I love you scatter*."

"Oh, Lord, he's speaking pidgin." She laid her head back on his shoulder and drifted off.

"All for you." Kamal leaned his head on hers and covered them with the blanket. Right before he drifted off, he said a prayer for them and their future, whatever that held. Kamal also said a prayer that what he was about to do didn't backfire.

———

Two days later, he woke up with one mission on his mind. He said his prayers and sent Ebele the usual morning text. Since she was tied up in school, he hadn't seen her since they got back from Amsterdam. They did make sure to check in each day. He took a shower and headed out.

He pulled up to the Law Offices of Zacchaeus & Watson, parked his car, and went in. A while ago, Ebele told him that her dad had since left the company where he met her mom. He now owned a law firm. With that information, he wasn't difficult to trace. Kamal walked up to the receptionist.

"Hi, I'm here to see Mr. Watson."

"Hello, do you have an appointment?" the middle-aged woman asked.

"No, I don't, but I'm sure he'll see me." Kamal took off his sunshades, and the woman smiled.

"Of course, Kammy. My son and husband are big fans. I'll get Mr. Watson," she said, with glee. "Please, can you sign an autograph for me?"

"Sure." If it would get him what he wanted, why not?

Minutes later, Kamal was done signing and headed back to Ebele's father's office. The first thing he noticed when he entered the office was that it was very impersonal. No pictures. When Mr. Watson came around the corner of his desk, Kamal immediately knew Ebele must've gotten her height from her mother. The man was tall. Another thing was his eyes. They were a dead giveaway.

"Hello, sir, I'm Ka—"

"I know who you are." The man beamed. "What can I do for you?"

He must be a fan. *I'm about to lose him or keep him. Either way, it doesn't affect my salvation or bank account.*

"I'll make this quick, sir, as I have to get to physical therapy."

"Yes, yes. I was bummed about the knee. You were really an asset to Turk West." Mr. Watson showed him a chair. "Please, sit."

Kamal sat, and the older man sat right next to him.

"I'm here about Ebele," Kamal said.

"Who?" Her father looked confused. "Oh, Vanessa, is she okay?"

Kamal gave him an incredulous look. He didn't even call the girl by the name she preferred. That angered him.

"She'll always be as long as I have the honor of having her in my life. I'm in love with your daughter, sir. And I plan to marry her. But I came to you about your relationship with her," Kamal explained.

The man's face bore a frown.

Kamal couldn't care less. He continued, "She's strong and resilient, but any time you guys talk, she shrinks into this little girl that's no longer sure of herself. That bothers me. With all due respect sir, quite frankly, I'm tired of it. I know she is too."

"What gives you the right to come in here and talk about a situation you know nothing about?" Her father stood.

Kamal glanced at him, unbothered by his aggression. He expected it. People never liked to be told about their short-comings. Even him. Kamal sat back in his chair and crossed his legs.

"I know a lot more than you know because my father did the same thing. I know the effects. She's still living through it because unlike my father, you're alive, but won't accept her fully." Kamal paused.

The older man's chest was puffed out, but he remained silent.

"As for my right? I'm the protector of her heart. It's my job to make sure it's not tampered with. When she gets off the phone with you, it's bruised. Three things I hate, being dismissed, avoided, and my *Ebele's* heart being bruised." His calm tone surprised even him. He did make sure he stressed her name – the one she liked.

"The relationship between my daughter and I is fine."

"No, it's not. It's what she makes you believe. She feels obligated because you pay her fees." Kamal kept his stare on him, almost challenging him to deny it. "If it's only about the money, I can pay you back every penny. So neither you nor she would feel obligated to each other."

"Look, young man, it's complicated, but it's not all about money." The older man looked defeated.

"Oh, it's not? You either accept her, or you don't. Stringing her along isn't helping. I'm not here to judge you on whatever happened. I'm just here to tell you, step up or step down, but the half stepping isn't working anymore. It's doing more harm than good." Kamal stood, not willing to go back and forth with him anymore. He'd said what he had to say. He'd no longer take Ebele being hurt.

He left the office, got in his car, and headed to therapy.

Chapter 26

Music blasting, horns blaring, and the three-wheeled vehicles popularly called *keke* weaving back and forth across the road were all the familiar sights and sounds of her beloved town Asaba in Delta State. Ebele and her mother moved from Benin City when she was about to finish secondary school. Her mother had struggled to bring her up on her own but later decided to be closer to her family, so they moved. Her mom and grandma were her world.

After a six-hour flight from London to Lagos and another flight from Lagos to Asaba, she was exhausted. Ebele looked over to her left, and Kamal was on the phone talking to who she assumed was his mom to let her know he was in the country.

If she thought he was something in the UK, nothing prepared her for what happened at Lagos airport. His fans couldn't get enough. She knew this time not to leave his side. After signing numerous autographs and taking selfies, Kamal begged the crowd to let him go.

His sister, Halima, was out of the country so his big brother, Rasheed, sent someone to meet them at the airport. The man had helped them get their luggage and driven them to the local airport to catch their second flight. Kamal didn't have the patience to wait for the family jet.

"Ok, Mama, hold on."

When Ebele heard that, alarm bells went off in her head. She shook her head no. She knew she was going to have to face Mrs. Danjuma sooner or later, but she preferred it to be later. She was seriously unprepared. Not only was she delirious from travel, but she was also hungry. Kamal shrugged at her.

"Mama, she said no. I don't know why," he said.

Ebele eyes bugged. This man was really crazy sometimes. She snatched the phone from him and gave him a warning look.

"Hello, Ma," she said, nervously.

"Hello, Ebele, how are you?"

"I'm fine, Ma. How are you, Ma?"

"I'm doing well, my dear. I hope you had a good flight?"

"Yes, Ma."

"Okay, my dear, I'll see you in a couple of days, right?"

"Yes, Ma. I'll be there. Happy Birthday in advance, Ma."

"Thank you, my dear. Say hello to your mom."

"I will, Ma. Bye, Ma."

Ebele handed Kamal the phone. He told his mom that he'd be in Abuja the next day on the evening flight. They had agreed that Ebele would stay with her mom and fly into Abuja two days before the celebration.

"Why would you tell her that?" she asked him.

"I always tell the truth. You said no, I told her no." Kamal looked out the window. She saw the smirk on his face. He joked too much.

"When I say I can't stand you, you wonder why," she muttered.

"You know you love me. But what I tell you about saying that?"

"I always tell the truth," she mocked him.

"Okay, I'll let you have that." Kamal pulled her to him.

She lay her head on his shoulder. "Aye, driver, you know where you're going? You've been driving forever."

"*Oga e remain small. We go soon reach.*" The driver beamed and looked at Kamal with admiration through the rearview mirror. He was also sent by Rasheed to transport them while in Asaba. Ebele hadn't met or spoken to Rasheed yet, but the way he babied Kamal was so sweet. From the little she'd seen, he took that big brother thing seriously. He was the protector of that family. Suddenly, the car swerved a little. Ebele sat up straight.

Kamal stopped scrolling through his phone. "What happened?"

"Ah, nothing. *Oga,* sorry. *I been wan take my phone so I go take picture with you when we come down.*"

Kamal gave him an incredulous look. "Are you serious? You're trying to drive and get your phone so we can take a picture? Guy, I'll sign anything for you and all your village people. But if anything happens to this woman, they won't be able to hide you from me. Wait 'til I tell your *Oga.*"

"Ah, *Oga, sorry no tell Oga* Rasheed *o.* I'm sorry, sir."

Ebele looked at Kamal with a smile in her eyes. "Stop threatening the man."

"He threatened my life."

"Stop exaggerating. He's enamored." She giggled.

"Whatever, man. We ain't got to your village, yet?" Kamal looked out the window.

"It's not a village; it's a town. Driver, it's the next turn."

Minutes later, they stopped in front of her mother's compound. "All right, baby, so you'll go to the hotel, freshen up, and be right back?"

"Yeah, how far is Best Western from here?" Kamal asked the driver.

"About ten minutes, *Oga.*"

Kamal opened the door and came around to open hers. He helped her out and told the driver to bring down her luggage. He hugged her and kissed the top of her head. "I'll be right back. Tell Momsie I'm coming to see about her skills in the kitchen."

"Love you. See you soon." Ebele walked up to the black gate and pressed the bell. Soon after, the young girl that helped her mom, Kachi, came to open the gate. She waved to Kamal again and entered the compound.

"Aunty Ebele, welcome *o*," the twelve-year-old girl greeted.

"Kachi, my baby. How are you?" Ebele walked toward the three-bedroom bungalow that her mom inherited from her grandad. Her mother was an only child and female at that. This was the only house her father's brothers would allow her to keep. Ebele would never forget the stories of how the elders degraded her grandma. They claimed she had only a female child, so she wasn't entitled to their late brother's property. They took all her grandfather's property and left her with only this house. Over the years, with the help of her cousins, her mother renovated the house.

"I'm fine, Aunty. Ha, Aunty, that man I saw, is he not the one that plays ball?"

Ebele stopped. "How do you know that?"

"Uncle Ezi always watches him when he comes to see Mama and Mummy."

Ebele's grandma lived in the detached quarters at the back of the house. She loved having her own space and kitchen. Growing up, when she needed to avoid a spanking, Ebele's grandmother's house was the perfect hiding spot. By the time her mother got to her, her grandmother would've calmed her down. Uncle Ezi was her mother's protector. Ebele loved that man. He was her mother's maternal senior cousin. He and his family resided in Benin City. He didn't allow the other family members to treat his mother any way they felt like.

"Where's Uncle Ezi?" Ebele asked.

"He travelled to Lagos."

"Yes, he's the one that plays ball," Ebele answered, pulling her luggage along. She caught Kachi's smile and knew her family was about to sell her out.

"*Nnem o. Nnem o!*" Ebele yelled as she entered the house. "My mother, where are you *o*?" Ebele turned to Kachi, "Where is Mummy?"

"She's in the backyard. Aunty Ebele, we didn't know you would arrive this early."

Ebele frowned. If they didn't know, would there be food, cold drinks? Ha, what if there was no light? They would need fuel for the generator. Kamal would be here soon, and she wanted him comfortable. She'd told her mom she wouldn't stay overnight in Lagos. She'd be in Asaba the same day. Ebele left her luggage in the living room and ran out back. She smiled when she saw her mom, sitting between her grandmother's legs, and her grandmother parting her hair and scratching it for her.

"Ha, you this woman. You love enjoyment o," Ebele said, sneaking up on them.

"Ha! *Nwa m a nuwa ga o*. My child is back." Ebele's mother hopped up and danced over to her. This was the routine every single time Ebele visited for the last four years. Ebele hugged her mother, went to her grandmother, and kneeled before her in greeting. Her grandmother placed her hand on her head as she did every time and prayed. Ebele stood up and hugged her grandmother.

"Mummy, I told you I was coming now," Ebele said, dragging her mother into their house. "Mama, we're coming back *o*." She would've chatted with her grandmother longer, but she needed to get things ready for her man. The back entrance led right into the kitchen.

"I know now. What happened? Don't break my hand." Her mother reclaimed her hand from Ebele's grasp and leaned against the gas cooker.

"Kachi said you didn't know I'd be coming early."

"Don't mind Kachi. Is it my in-law you are worried about?" her mother teased.

"Mummy, he's not your in-law. He's only my boyfriend. And yes, I want to make sure everything is ready. He'll soon be here."

"Ebelechukwu, relax. I have Egusi soup, Ogbonna, Oha, or Onugbu. There's pounded yam and fried rice. Whatever he eats, I'm ready. Go and take your shower. If NEPA takes light, there's fuel for the generator."

"*Mummy de Mummy*. I was panicking for a minute."

"Trust me. That young man sounds pleasant on the phone, so I can't wait to meet him. But money or no money, if he *yeyes* my daughter, he'll feel my fire," her mother proclaimed.

She placed her hand on her mother's shoulders "Calm down, fighter. I love him, and he loves me. We're good, Mummy. Let me go and take a shower." Ebele walked toward her room.

"Okay, let me go and dress up for our in-law."

"He's not your in-law, Mummy," Ebele spoke over her shoulder. She was convinced her family was about to sell her out. Good thing Uncle Ezi wasn't here. He would've packaged her and handed her to Kamal on a platter.

"*Chai*, Momsie, you put your foot in that soup." Kamal scooted his chair back.

"My leg? *Mba o*. Noooo ..." Ebele's mother replied from the living room.

"Mummy don't mind him. He means the soup was delicious." Ebele gathered up their dirty dishes and took them into the kitchen. Kamal had opted to eat pounded yam and *Onugbu* soup.

Everyone laughed, and her mother responded, "Oh, thank you, my son. I'm glad you enjoyed the food."

Kamal used his clean hand to rub his stomach and winked at Ebele. She blew him a kiss. His eyelids were drooping, so she knew he was tired; but in the usual Kamal fashion, he came in, and commanded the place. Everyone laughed at his antics and jokes. He handed out gifts like it was Christmas. Her mother beamed, and her grandmother was mesmerized by his charisma. Ebele knew his house in Abuja was probably ten times the size of hers, but he didn't even blink an eye in discomfort when he came in. His humility showed. It was a long way from when she first met him.

Ebele brought water in a clean bowl and some liquid soap. Kamal looked at her confused. "Who's that for?"

"For you to wash your hands. Didn't you use them to eat?" she asked.

"Nah, baby, my legs work fine. I'll follow you to the kitchen to wash my hands." Kamal stood up from the table and followed her into the kitchen. Ebele emptied the water and turned on the faucet for him. She poured the washing liquid in his hands as he scrubbed the sticky pounded yam off. She gave him a paper towel to dry them. He pulled her close.

"Thank you, though, for trying to serve your king the traditional way. You want me to help you with the dishes?"

Ebele blushed. "No, go sit. I saw you in pain earlier. You're overexerting." She'd worried about him when she saw him wince in pain and knew he needed to ice his knee or rest it. Before their flight, they'd done an hour of therapy; on the plane, she'd gotten him an ice pack.

"Yes, ma'am. I need to holla with Momsie about something."

"About what?" Ebele asked.

"It's an A and B conversation baby. Mind ya business."

"Ugh, go *jor.*"

"I'm gone. But don't get an attitude, or I'll dirty my hands again and make you bring the water back out. You know grandmomsie will tell you to kneel while I wash my hand. Don't play." He took out a toothpick from the canister on the counter and picked his teeth.

"Get out of my kitchen, Kam!"

"For yelling, come give me a kiss first."

"No, this is my mother's house."

"And? I'm not your brother, so I know she knows you've kissed me before."

"Jesus, help me."

"Don't be calling the name of the Lord in vain."

Ebele let out an exaggerated breath. She should have allowed him to leave earlier, and he wouldn't be aggravating her now.

"Aye, I'm about to go dirty my hands ..."

Ebele knew her grandma was old school. She'd have her kneel while Kamal washed his hands like wives did for their husbands in the old days. Kamal would never let her hear the end of it if that happened. She stomped over to him. He leaned down, and she pecked his lips.

"That was an attitudinal kiss. I wanted a real one."

"Don't push it. Go!"

Kamal raised his hands in surrender. "All right, my queen. I know when to back away. I still love you, though. I don't care what anybody says."

Ebele rolled her eyes and turned to wash the dishes.

———

Friday afternoon, Ebele got out of bed and walked up to the mirror. She examined her face to make sure there were no tell-tale signs from her nap. She looked around, finally being able to admire the décor of the room she was occupying in the Danjuma home. The soft tones of the room gave it a feminine feel. It came complete with a vanity, a spacious closet, and a full adjourning bath. The fact that Mrs. Danjuma had only sons and Halima lived in Lagos, made her feel the room was decorated for her.

She walked into the bathroom, turned on the faucet, and splashed water on her face. After spending two more days in Asaba with her family, Ebele had arrived in Abuja earlier in the day. Kamal was waiting for her as promised. After almost squeezing the life out of her in a hug, he brought her to his mother's house. Not before they had a disagreement about her sleeping arrangements. When she suggested putting up in a hotel or her friend's house, he looked at her like she'd sprouted two heads and quickly shut it down. Finally, she conceded. He knew she was nervous about being with his mom alone, so he reassured her that Jabir and his family would be staying there also.

Ebele went down the long hallway, then the stairs. She grinned when she heard Mrs. Danjuma's voice. "Damisi, please, hand me that suya."

The older woman was gorgeous and so graceful. Her smooth complexion was a shade or two darker than Kamal's. Her black, wavy hair was sprinkled with patches of gray and in a low cut. When she smiled, her high dimples came on full display. The woman wanted to suffocate her with love. She had shooed Kamal away and made sure Ebele ate; then she suggested the nap Ebele just woke up from. She even asked to speak to Ebele's mother to reassure her that her daughter was okay.

Ebele listened to see if Kamal was back. He'd left to meet with his brothers at the site of Jabir and Damisi's new home. The home was under construction for when they returned home to Nigeria. His brothers and Ibiso were the only people she hadn't met yet. Ebele was star struck when she met Damisi earlier. She, like so many others, had watched Damisi on TV for years. She was more demure than her on-screen personality. Her twin girls were beautiful.

Ebele walked into the living room with a faint smile on her face. Mrs. Danjuma was reclining in her chair, and Damisi sat by her side. The twins were in their own world, playing with their dolls in the corner.

"Ah, she's up. Hope you rested well, my dear?" Mrs. Danjuma asked.

"You look refreshed. Let me know if you need anything." Damisi scooted to the front of the chair and returned the plate of suya she'd given Mrs. Danjuma earlier back to the coffee table.

"Yes, Ma, I didn't know how much I needed that nap. I'm good, Damisi. Thank you." Ebele took her seat on the other couch. One of the twins stood and wobbled over to her. She picked her up and put her in her lap.

"Please, call me Dami. Everybody does. And Ibiso will want you to call her SoSo" Damisi replied. The other twin girl walked to her grandmother, who picked her up without hesitation.

"Got it."

"So Ebele, how much longer do you have in school?" Mrs. Danjuma asked.

"About three months, Ma. After that, I want to get a job in the UK before coming back home and establishing something. But with Kam, I'm still up in the air."

"I still can't believe that Kammy found someone to tame him." Damisi shook her head.

"He's not that bad," Ebele said.

Both ladies gave each other a knowing look and laughed. "That's all right. Defend your man," Damisi encouraged her.

"Hey, family, I heard our wife is here *o* ... where is she?"

Ebele looked toward the foyer puzzled. No one had made an appearance yet. Wife?

"That's SoSo. You'll love her," Damisi reassured her.

"Oh ..." Ebele responded.

"Yohance, go and play with your cousins. Nkechi, please,

come and help me put these things in the kitchen." Ibiso's voice rang out again.

Seconds later, Ebele saw a little boy make his entrance. *Gosh, these children are too cute.* He was a cute, milk chocolate chubster with a mohawk haircut.

Damisi stood and walked in the direction of Ibiso's voice. Seconds later, a woman of medium height, with dark mocha skin and a short haircut appeared. There was no doubt she was the mother of the boy that just walked in.

So this is the Ibiso Danjuma, chef extraordinaire.

"Sis, how now? Where are my babies?" Ibiso asked Damisi as they hugged. Ebele watched their interaction. They were like sisters.

"They're fine. My boy ran right past me to his grandma," Damisi responded when they broke from one another.

"That's how it is. *Oya* move, let me say hello to our wife. I love you, but you're now old. It's been a while since we went to Kenya to pay your bride price." Ibiso shooed a laughing Damisi out of the way so she could get to Ebele.

Mrs. Danjuma laughed as Ibiso walked closer to them. Ebele stood up. Ibiso smiled at her but went to greet Mrs. Danjuma first.

"Mama, good afternoon." Ibiso knelt in front of the older woman.

"My daughter, how was work?"

"It was fine, Ma. You know all hands-on deck for your party." Ibiso winked. "It'll be the talk of the town. I have the *aso ebi* in the car. Let me say hello to our wife first." Ibiso walked over to Ebele.

Ebele stretched out her hand. "Hi, I'm Ebele. Please, call me Ebi."

"*Abeg jare,* give me a hug. Anybody who can tame Kammy is all right by me." Ibiso squeezed her tight.

"We told her that before. She's over there talking about he's not that bad," Damisi said, retaking her seat.

"Hmmmm, okay *o*." Ibiso sat and pulled off her shoes. "Mama, do you have anything to eat, or you want me to make something for family dinner?" She paused and looked around like she'd just realized someone was missing. "Where are your sons, Ma?"

"They went to see the site for our house," Damisi said.

"Oh, okay. So, Mama, what's up? You need me to cook something?"

"I think Nkechi is already frying some goat meat," Mrs. Danjuma said.

For the next couple of minutes, Ebele watched the three women interact. Even a blind man could see the love and respect they shared for one another. She longed to be a part of a family like this. She thought about her and Kamal. She absently put her hand on the necklace he gave her. She wasn't even engaged to him, and his family treated her like she was his wife. For that she was grateful.

The women decided to cook simple white rice and stew with goat meat and a choice of plantain or moi-moi. Mrs. Danjuma advised against cooking anything elaborate as they'd have a lot of leftovers from the party on Sunday.

As they were about to head to the kitchen, another beautiful woman entered. Instantly, Ebele knew it was Halima. The women squealed and hugged.

"This is our wife, Ebele." Ibiso, who was the true leader of the pack, introduced her.

"You keep saying that." Ebele giggled. "It's nice to finally meet you. Kam talks about you a lot." Ebele hugged Halima.

"That's my *dan uwa na*." Halima beamed. "It's nice to finally meet you too."

"Your who?" Ebele asked.

"Ebi, don't bother. They're special. She calls him "my brother" like they're not all her brothers," Ibiso explained with a chuckle.

"SoSo leave her alone," Damisi said.

"Am I holding her? Hali baby knows I got love for her. She and I are in *Naija* together, so we roll tight. Don't come from Detroit and put sand inside our garri," Ibiso joked. She turned to Ebele, "*Ehen* Madam, you say why do I keep saying you're our wife? Let me count. Have you gone to his games?"

"Errr, no," Ebele responded.

"Did he go ignorant in your apartment when he saw another man there?" Damisi asked.

"Errr, yes. And?" Ebele asked.

"That necklace on your neck, did he stress for you not to take it off?" Halima asked.

Ebele rubbed the necklace. "Yeah."

"Okay, you *are* our wife," Ibiso concluded. "Let's go cook,"

The three women laughed and headed to the kitchen. Mrs. Danjuma had since retired to her room with the grandkids in tow. The house help, Nkechi, had finished frying the meat, so Ibiso told her to go and rest. Damisi oversaw the stew, Ebele cut the plantains for frying, Halima cooked the rice, and Ibiso made the moi- moi.

As they cooked, the two wives shared their love stories with their husbands. They also shared some things she didn't know about the Danjumas. Like Ibiso and Rasheed owned a center for boys and girls while Jabir and Damisi had a ministry called Helping Hands. Ebele and Kamal had talked a lot about things he'd like to do, but he wasn't clear on what direction he wanted to go yet.

An hour-and-a-half later, they were done and started to set the table. Rasheed had called and told Ibiso they were on their way.

"E, where you at?" Ebele heard Kamal's voice boom all the way from the kitchen. She shook her head, and the woman laughed.

"E?" he called again, his voice was getting closer.

"I'm here, Kam. Stop yelling," Ebele said.

The other three women leaned against the counter and

folded their hands across their chests. They'd teased her off and on all day, so they were ready to watch their interaction.

Kamal entered the room, and Ebele's heart raced. This man did something to her every single time. Every time she saw him, there was a new reason to love him. He walked over to her with a broad smile on his face. He cupped her face in his hands and brushed his lips against hers. He stared at her like she was the only one in the room. Their gaze held until they heard a clearing throat.

"What? I had to watch y'all do your thing for years. You, Ibiso got Stone Cold smiling for no reason. Only you know what's in those meat pies you're giving him to eat. Dami, don't get me started. Had my boy looking all crazy for six years. And you Hali, just because you cover up, don't think I don't know that you be in the harem with Danladi getting in pre-work." Kamal pointed at each one of them.

The women's mouths were open. They each picked up a dish towel and began hitting Kamal. Ebele wasn't letting her man go down. She picked up a dish towel and went to war for him.

"Get off my baby," Ebele said, to no one in particular.

"What's going on here?" a voice boomed from the entryway of the kitchen. All activity ceased, and Ebele knew that was Rasheed. Her man's twin went directly to his wife and did the same thing Kamal just did to her.

"They're in their feelings, that's all." Kamal pulled her hand. "Baby, this is Rasheed, and I know you know who that is over there with that suction action going on."

"Hi Ebele, it's nice to meet you." Rasheed gave her a side hug. "If this guy gives you any trouble, you know who to call."

"Oh, she and I already talked," Jabir chimed in. "I'll hold him down while she gets what she has to say off her chest." Jabir walked up to her. "Get in here." He pulled her in for a hug.

"E, you're plotting against me?" Kamal asked.

"It was for a good cause, baby."

"It ain't never a good cause to plot against your man. That's girlfriend 101." Kamal furrowed his brow.

"Well, girlfriend 102 – the advanced course – says, 'When said boyfriend is acting a fool, do what's necessary so that the couple won't be on the evening news,'" Ebele sassed.

"Oooooooo," came the response from the group.

"Ebi, although you were against us in the dish towel fight, for that one, you're all right. I'm impressed." Ibiso and Damisi chuckled and hi-fived each other.

Ebele laughed. Kamal stared at her, waiting for her response. "Why thank you, but FYI, I'm the only one allowed to hit him. Hit at your own risk."

Kamal gave a loud "*Chai.*" Then he knelt in the middle of the kitchen and put his hands up. "You're faithful, Lord. Thank you for the immunity you put in my baby against the plot of my family women. My baby is still intact, no contamination."

Everyone stared at him and laughed. Jabir and Rasheed tried to smack him across the head but missed. Ebele helped him up and leaned into him as they all left the room.

Over dinner, everyone joked, talked, and had fun. Then they played a spirited game of Scrabble. Halima kept the scores, and at the end of the game, Jabir and Damisi won. Kamal complained all the way. When Halima, Rasheed, and his family left at about ten p. m., the rest of them headed upstairs to sleep. Kamal kissed her good night and turned the corner to his own room.

Ebele took a shower and dressed for bed. She lay on the bed and savored the memories of the day. Then she prayed a prayer of thanksgiving. Growing up, she spent so many nights praying for a big family. What she experienced tonight was beyond her. She blessed God for how He continued to blow her mind.

Chapter 27

K amal's feet hit the floor, and the strange feeling he'd been fighting all night came back. He ran his hand down his face and looked at the time. It wasn't dawn yet. Seated on the bed, he put his forearms on his thighs and bowed his head. He was restless and didn't know why. He picked up his Bible. He'd been studying it more. A lot of the willpower he had to remain joyful despite Pete giving him bad news each time they talked came from the grace of God through his growing faith. He had fewer bad days and was clinging the best he could. One day after the other. He even followed some Twitter handles for Christian athletes and some pastors he could relate to.

He was in his fourth month post-surgery, so his therapy now included some actual sports training. However, each time Pete called, he told Kamal he couldn't get any team to give him a chance to try out and possibly get a contract. He hadn't shared the effects the rejection was having on his mind with Ebele. Maybe he was just another washed up athlete.

Kamal turned on his bedside lamp and opened his Bible. He had no idea what he was looking for or going to read. As he flipped through, it dawned on him why he was feeling in the dumps. The anniversary of when his father walked out on them was around the corner. It was on Monday – the day after his mom's birthday. In retrospect, he didn't know whether it was intentional, but it's how it played out.

When he was younger, the day was a somber one for Kamal, but he'd learned to block it out. So why was he thinking about it today? There was an unsettling in his spirit. He stopped flipping the pages when he came to Isaiah 55. He decided to read the chapter. At first, he wondered how it applied to him. But then maybe it didn't. What was he supposed to get?

He read it a couple more times and focused on verse eight and nine. *"My thoughts are nothing like your thoughts," says the Lord. "And my ways are far beyond anything you could imagine. For just as the heavens are higher than the earth, so my ways are higher than your ways and my thoughts higher than your thoughts."*

Kamal closed the Bible and turned off the light. In the darkness, he began to pray, "I'm sorry Father. For so long, I've harbored pain and resentment on how I thought things should go with my father and in my career as opposed to trusting Your plan and how they did go. I didn't know better then, but now I do. Thank You for bringing Ebele into my life. As painful as it is to admit, if I didn't get injured, I might never have come to this understanding. Father, open my eyes to what and who I'm supposed to be to Your glory. Help me surrender totally to Your will in this season and the future. In Jesus' name, Amen."

Kamal realized, in that moment of prayer, he'd never forgiven his dad. There were so many things he wanted to say. He'd suppressed it instead of dealing with it. He knew what he had to do. He picked up his phone. Day had broken, so he typed a text to Ebele.

Hey, Beautiful, you up?

Good morning, Babe, yes. Just finished prayer.

Get dressed. I need you to go somewhere with me.

Okay, give me 15 mins.

You got 10. I love you.

Kamal shot up from the bed, took a shower, and got dressed. Placing his baseball cap on his head, he picked up his sunshades and left the room. He got downstairs, and his mother was returning from morning Mass.

"Mama, good morning."

"Emeka, how are you?" He was the only one their mother called by his Ibo name.

"I'm good. Mama, where was daddy buried?"

His mother's shocked face was expected, but he had to do this for him. He was the one that had suffered in his own hell, and this was the only way he knew to let it go.

"*O di kwa nma*? Is everything okay?"

"Yes, Ma, it's all good. I need to go there." He wasn't in the mood to talk much. His emotions were flaky, and he didn't want anyone worrying; neither did he want anyone trying to fix it. Ebele was coming because he needed her.

"It's in Kubwa Cemetery. Madu can take you there. He's outside. Is Ebele going with you?"

"Yes." He smiled at her. "You like her, *abi*?"

"Yes, she's very pleasant and, most of all, doesn't allow you get away with murder. From what I have seen, she loves you deeply."

"She's my world, Mama. I'm glad you like her." He looked at his watch and was about to say something when he saw his angel glide down the stairs.

"Didn't I tell you ten minutes, woman?"

"Good morning, Ma." Ebele curtsied. She turned and looked at Kamal. "And I know I told you fifteen." She gave him a warning look. He pulled her to him and kissed the top of her head.

"Good morning, my dear. How are you?"

"I'm fine, Ma. How are you? Did you sleep well?"

"I'm good, my dear. Yes, I did. My joy is overflowing. My whole family is here with their loved ones." Kamal saw his mother tear up. Anger rose within him. He knew exactly what she was thinking about. Their yesteryears.

"It is well, Ma," Ebele offered.

"Mama, we'll be back soon." He grabbed Ebele's hand and walked out. "How was your night, baby?" Kamal asked.

"It was fine and yours?"

"Restless. I'll tell you about it in the car." Kamal looked around and saw Madu, his mother's driver. "*Oga* Madu."

"*Ah, I never reach o. Oga* Kammy, good morning. *You don wake?*"

Kamal laughed and nodded. "Adamu open the gate. Madu, please take me to Kubwa Cemetery."

They got into the car and took the ride to the cemetery. On their way there, Kamal filled Ebele in on everything that happened in the early hours of the morning, including his struggles with Pete finding him a team.

"Kam, sometimes God doesn't restore us to our default setting because He has something greater," she said when he was done. "I'm so proud of you. You increase my strength."

"I'm a better man for loving you. You center my world and make me believe I can do the impossible," he responded.

For the rest of the ride, they slipped into a comfortable silence. When they got there, they made their way to where his dad was laid to rest. The closer he got, the quicker his heart beat. He hesitated. Ebele squeezed his hand, encouraging him to keep going. When he got to the headstone, Ebele hugged him and stepped back.

"You can do it," she whispered.

Kamal stood in front of the stone for a few minutes. His lips quivered, and tears threatened to fall. His mind travelled back to when Rasheed and his mom came from Nigeria with the news that their father had another family and wouldn't be coming home. The heart-wrenching pain. Then he thought about the good times. Trips to the park, camping, and picnics. Good memories that had been suppressed by painful ones. Both experiences battled each other as Kamal dropped to his knees.

"Hey, Dad, it's me. You remember? Kamal. I'm several years late, but I'm here." He paused. "I think for almost two months after you left, I sat on the steps in front of the house every day. Every car that passed by, I stretched my neck to see if that was you. You promised that when you came back, we'd play for that match I lost. I waited with my football in my hand. I waited every day. What Rasheed and Mama said couldn't be true. You loved us, right?" Tears rolled down his cheeks as he remembered those days as a six-year-old. His friends would laugh. He refused to get up in case he missed his dad's arrival.

"You took my heart when you left. You left me, a six-year-old boy, with the broken pieces, and damaged trust, and confidence. How do I heal when the one meant to protect me, destroyed me? I was left for ten years with so many unanswered questions. By the time you came back, I couldn't afford to trust you. I used to regret not asking you questions then. But would it have made a difference? Why, man? I want to know why? Why didn't you fight for us? How could you leave us starving with no help? Why didn't you want us? How could you make the decision to leave? You left me … left us." Kamal placed his hands on his face. He turned his baseball hat backward. It was getting hot. He reached for his face towel in his back pocket, wiped his face, and the back of his neck. He stared at the headstone and continued.

"Do you know what that did? Rasheed couldn't love, Jabir refused to trust, and I felt I wasn't good enough. Why would I be? If you, that helped create me didn't want me, why would someone else? That's what you did." Kamal let the tears he'd held on to for so long flow. He planned on marrying Ebele, and he needed to be whole, not just for her, but for himself as well.

"But we struggled. Underneath it all was the need for you to see us, not be ashamed of us. For you to think we were worth more than money. So we made money, my brothers and I. More than we need. But what good is the money when we were damaged souls?" He wiped his eyes and stayed silent for several moments. He begged God for strength to purge. Once he left this place, that would be it.

He continued, "We were broken." He paused when he felt two hands on his shoulders.

His brothers. He looked at them, Jabir on his left, and Rasheed on the right. They knelt with him. He looked back and saw their wives standing with Ebele.

The brothers looked at each other for a few seconds before turning back to the headstone.

Rasheed took his turn. "Why? I've asked that question so many times. You took my childhood from me. You left me to be a man when I hadn't even mastered being a boy. I had to be Mama's rock and a guiding figure to my brothers. No one was there to guide me. I took on so much because, in my mind, I couldn't be another person to let the family down. I wasn't ready, and you left me naked. Father, you did that to me, so for years, I built a wall to cover myself. But God loves me and sent me someone who taught me how to cast every care on Him." Kamal noticed Rasheed's voice was low and shaky.

Jabir spoke to their father next, in a whisper, "How do you trust love when as a boy you're exposed to its wrath? You said you loved us, but you couldn't have even liked us and treated us with no regard. Rather than expose myself to love that could do to me what it did to Mama, I closed my heart. I thought I could control my own destiny. People only have the power to hurt you when you give them access. I nearly lost my heart because I was afraid to give it away." Kamal glanced at Jabir, and his eyes watered.

Kamal spoke again. "Today, I'm—we're letting go of the need to know the why. I'm freeing myself from the hurt your actions caused. I'm letting go. I'll cherish the good memories, and by God's grace, overcome the bad. With Christ confidence, I'll …" Kamal stretched out his hands. His brothers put theirs in them. "We'll head to the future. We're good men and will no longer live in the residue of your rejection but in the fullness of God's glory. Bye, Dad. Rest in peace."

Kamal stood, and his brothers followed. The three men hugged each other, reminiscent of when they were boys, and Rasheed would huddle them together to reassure them that everything would be all right. This time, Rasheed said a short prayer. After the prayer, they walked away in silence to meet their women.

Their embrace gave them the strength they needed after they had let go of the weight they had carried around for years. At least, Kamal knew that's what Ebele did for him. They all got back in their cars and headed to the house. Kamal leaned his head back on the headrest and exhaled the breath he'd held since he was six.

Chapter 28

E bele sat in a chair in the living room as a lady did her makeup and tied her *gele*. Damisi stood to her side, scolding the lady about being late. She still had to get to Ibiso's house to do her *gele* and makeup. The women had decided on a blue lace with a white and blue *gele*. Ebele had been hesitant on wearing the *aso ebi*. How could she wear the matching outfit that designated that she was family when she wasn't a wife yet? She wasn't even a fiancée.

But the other women wouldn't hear of it. Ibiso went as far as saying they would ignore her the rest of the trip if she didn't wear the *Aso Ebi*. When she conceded, they got their tailor to make her dress in twenty-four hours. The style she chose was an off-the-shoulder, fitted dress. It hugged her in all the right places. Her waist was encrusted with white studs, and a cape flowed from it.

Ebele looked in the mirror and couldn't believe this was her. The makeup artist had skills, but at six thousand Naira a person, she'd better. Ebele checked her watch. They had about two more hours until the ten a.m. Mass Mrs. Danjuma attended.

After she finished her makeup, she'd check on Kamal. She

hadn't seen him yet. The previous day had been draining for everyone. After they drove back home, he refused to eat breakfast and dragged her into his room. They'd sat in comfortable silence until he drifted off to sleep. She left him there after ensuring his comfort and headed downstairs to help prepare for the festivities the next day. Ibiso's team cooked at the back of the house under her direction. The quantity was too much to use the kitchen indoors. Ebele and Damisi supervised the people who set up the canopies in the compound. Everything turned out great. Now to get to church and start the celebration.

"It's so beautiful, gosh. Thank you," Ebele said. She got up from the chair. "Do you know Ibiso's house?"

"Yes, I've done makeup for her before," the makeup artist replied.

"*Oya*, go there. The driver is waiting to take you. Thank you very much." Ebele headed up the stairs while the lady packed up.

As she walked down the hallway, she heard Jabir fussing at his girls for making their mother upset.

Ebele smiled and rounded the corner to Kamal's room. She knocked gently.

"Come in," his voice came through the wooden door.

"Hey, baby, good morning."

He was in front of his mirror trying to slant his red embroidered cap on his head. "Hey, beautiful. Good morning. You look gorgeous." His eyes roamed over her, causing her insides to quiver.

For Kamal and his brothers, the tailor-made white kaftans. The outfits were embroidered with blue on the cuffs, ankles, and down the middle in an intricate design.

"Sit on the bed. Let me help you," Ebele instructed.

Kamal did as he was told. Something was off with him. His mood was somber. She didn't know if he was processing what went on yesterday or if something else was bothering him. After helping him with his cap, she cupped his face in her hands.

"Baby, are you okay? Talk to me."

"I'm good, E. I promise. How are you? Did you sleep well? Have you eaten?"

She looked into his eyes to gauge his sincerity. "You keep worrying about me. I'm trying to find out about you."

He stood and stroked her cheek. "I'm good, baby. Now get out of my room. Let me finish getting ready. It's becoming harder to be with you in closed spaces alone."

"I know. I'm gone. I love you."

Several hours later, the Danjuma family was seated in the first two pews in front of Saint Augustine Catholic Church. This was Ebele's first time in a Catholic church. The interior was magnificent. The stained glass had what she could tell were specific scenes from the life of Jesus. Mrs. Danjuma was flanked by her grandchildren on both sides. Nkechi sat next to her to help keep the children occupied. In the second pew was the rest of the family.

After a short homily from Mark 5:25-28 about the woman with the issue of blood and her faith in Christ, the Reverend went back to his seat. Ebele rubbed the back of Kamal's hand. The rest of the Mass breezed by, and they were done in two hours.

Ebele loved the thanksgiving portion. Mrs. Danjuma had so many friends; it was ridiculous. Depending on the women's club she belonged to, they wore a different color *Aso Ebi*. Ebele counted four different groups. When it was time to dance to the front of the church with their offerings, Mrs. Danjuma insisted her daughters as she referred to her, Damisi, and Ibiso stand behind her. Behind them were her sons who carried a kid each. Everyone else danced behind the Danjuma brothers. The fanfare was overwhelming, but Ebele was so grateful for the experience. The Reverend blessed the family and soon after, the service was over.

Several hours later, the party was in full swing in the Danjuma compound. Food was in abundance, and the DJ was great. Ebele got to meet Moji, Damisi's cousin, and Boma, who was Ibiso's best friend. Halima joined them after Mass. Her mother, however, was on another trip to Dubai. Ebele walked in the house to trade her heels for some slippers. She'd since taken off her *gele* and combed her hair out.

"My daughter, come. Let's talk," Mrs. Danjuma said to her as she reached the top of the stairs. She'd changed into her second attire for the evening. She stretched out her hand, and Ebele took it.

"Okay, Ma." Ebele followed her into the sitting part of her bedroom. Kamal's mother told her to sit.

"Ebele, I know you'll be heading out tomorrow evening. I'm thankful for your presence but most especially for coming into my son's life. Emeka needs a woman like you. You see past the façade he puts on, camouflaging his pain. He has changed so much in this short six months since I have seen him last. When he got injured, it took everything for me not to get on a plane. Especially when the news reported he'd never play again. Jabir assured me he had someone to keep him in order, and he wasn't wrong. Thank you for everything. I know you love my son, but apart from that, thank you for helping him. Don't ever let his presence overshadow you."

Ebele gave her a faint smile and lowered her eyes. "I love him, Ma. It was no problem."

Mrs. Danjuma laughed and stood. "It's Emeka. He can be a problem. I know him, but you can cover for him if you want."

As they walked out of the room, Kamal was coming up the hallway. "Isn't this a wonderful sight? Hang on." He took out his phone and took a picture of them. He walked up to them and kissed his mom on her cheek. She left them standing there and went to join the party.

"I missed you." Kamal wrapped his arm around Ebele's waist.

"I missed you too. You okay?" she put her hands on his chest.

"Yeah, thank you for coming with me." He kissed her forehead.

"I enjoyed it. Thank you for inviting me."

"Let's go dance."

———

KAMAL LOOKED OVER AT EBELE. HIS BABY WAS EXHAUSTED. They had been flying for two hours. She was knocked out the minute they settled in their first-class pods. He reached over and massaged her scalp. The action usually soothed him and her. However, now for him, it wasn't doing the trick. He bounced his knee as his nerves got the best of him. The velvet box in his inner jacket pocket seemed to emanate heat wanting to be let out. He'd bought the ring months ago – the day after they confessed their love to each other. He was still struggling with what to say to her. He knew he joked around about her already being his wife, but he was no longer laughing. She was everything he needed but didn't even know he wanted. He didn't want another month or two to go by without her having his name.

A few minutes later, Ebele stirred. He continued to massage her scalp until she opened her eyes. She sat up, and her eyes met his.

She frowned. "What's wrong? Why are you looking at me like that?"

"You're mine. I'm still in awe of that," he said.

"Aww, that's sweet, baby. Did you get to sleep?"

"Nah." Kamal kissed her forehead. He looked ahead to make eye contact with the hostess. She nodded, and his heart skipped a beat. He felt Ebele's eyes on him. He gave her a weary smile. On cue, the saxophonist he had arranged to have on board stood and started playing Michael W. Smith's "You Belong to Me."

Ebele looked at him; confusion etched all over her face. Then she turned to him as the saxophonist walked over to them and stopped in front of her. She looked at Kamal, her eyes surprised, and misted. He didn't know if she remembered, but it was exactly six months ago, they both were seated on a British Airways flight.

"Ka—"

He placed his index finger over her mouth. A while ago, Ebele was playing one of Michael W. Smith's songs, and his voice intrigued him. She educated him on who he was, and since then, he'd become a fan. He knew that whenever he proposed, this would be the song that expressed what he didn't think he could aptly express in words. Kamal could feel all eyes on them, but he only had eyes for her. She lowered her head. As the song ended, he knelt on his good knee. He felt a little discomfort, but nothing was going to stop him from doing this right.

"Ebele Vanessa Ashiedu, the day I met you, I knew I'd never be the same. Until I met you, I lived a loveless life. You taught me that a life without love isn't one worth living. You mended my damaged heart with your love, showing me how not only to receive love but give it. With your help, my life has found meaning. I can't guarantee you a fairy tale. As a matter of fact, I can guarantee I'll get on your nerves. I know for sure you'll get on mine. But what I do know is that I'll work every day, with God's help, to put a smile on your face. I told you before, when God created you, He was looking out for me. Please, baby, marry me. Let's walk together, through the light and the dark. I promise I'll never let you go."

Ebele was in full cry mode by the time he finished. Her hands hid her face as she lowered her head. The cabin was silent, everyone waiting for her response. It was like time stood still.

"Err ... baby, I'm still down here. You know I'm injured," Kamal whispered.

His voice jolted her from her trance. She jumped up. "Oh, yes! I'm sorry. Yes! Yes! I'll marry you." She helped him up, and he slipped the three-karat, cushion-cut, Tiffany diamond ring on her finger.

Kamal kissed her repeatedly as the cabin broke out in applause. The hostess brought them the bottle of wine he had chilling. The pilot announced their engagement over the speakers. Ebele left her seat, sat in his lap, and they settled in for what was left of the flight. Before he drifted off to sleep, he took a picture of them. Her head was on his chest; her hair covered her face. Her left hand was placed on his chest showing her ring. He uploaded the picture to Instagram. He captioned it, *I found my rib, and she's the best part of me. Mrs.KD #OffTheMarket*

Chapter 29

Three weeks later, Kamal walked into his kitchen and poured himself a cup of coffee. He had several meetings lined up. Pete was back in the UK, and although he still didn't have any favorable team news for him, he had some endorsement deals he wanted him to go over. After that, he'd meet up with his lawyer, and a business consultant. His last meeting would be with a major publishing house – Inspired. His life had taken a complete three-sixty degree turn from where it was at the beginning of the year, but he was going along for the ride.

When he got back from Nigeria, he threw himself into therapy and prayer. There were so many opportunities in front of him that he wanted to make sure he was going after the right ones. The most important one was what he was meeting his lawyer for. Kamal got into the car and headed to his first appointment. His phone rang with the ringtone he set for Ebele.

"Hey, beautiful," he said, with a smile on his face.

"Hi, baby, how are you? Are you on the way?"

He could feel her smile through the phone. "Yeah, you pray for me?"

"Always. Guess what?"

"Wassup, E? It's too early for the guessing game."

"You're no fun."

"I can be anything you say as long as you're ready to go in exactly three weeks."

"Are you still on that?"

"Yes, wife."

"I'm not your wife yet, Kam." She chuckled.

"Yeah, you are. Before you were formed in the womb, God knew you …"

"Kam, you know that's not what that verse means."

Kamal laughed at her. She always got on him about interpreting the Bible wrong. He did it to mess with her, and she fell for it every time. "I'm serious E, in three weeks we leave for Mozambique. On the plane, I told you five weeks. You pushed it to six, but that's all you get."

"Kam, between school, exams, and my final project paper, I'm trying."

"We've discussed this before. Tell Nse what you want. I'll work with her, but I need my wife now." He paused. She didn't respond, so he drove his point home. "My folks have already gone to your folks to get the traditional stuff together. We both agreed to a small intimate wedding. So, we'll get on a plane, go get married and be back in a week. Why are you stalling?"

"I want everything to be perfect."

"It will be. Now fix your face. I can sense your frown. What was your good news?"

"My dad called. He said while I was in Nigeria, he told his other two kids about me," she said, excitedly.

He wanted to be happy for her, but he was apprehensive at the same time. It had been over a month since he talked to Mr. Watson, and Ebele hadn't heard a word from him. He wondered what happened. Mr. Watson had insisted that the relationship between he and Ebele was fine. Changing like that didn't sit well with Kamal. But he wouldn't tell his girl that. If this was genuine, he didn't want to put doubts in her heart.

"That's great, baby. When? Do you need me to come with you?"

"This afternoon. No, I can handle it. If I need my super-man, I'll call."

"And I'll be there, cape, and all. Keep your phone on and have fun. Are you coming over for dinner?"

"I won't miss it."

"Okay, see you soon. Love you."

"I love you more." She hung up, and Kamal said a quick prayer over that meeting.

———

SEVERAL HOURS LATER, KAMAL SAT BEHIND A MAHOGANY DESK in his lawyer's office. He sat back as he listened to the presentation the project manager put together. Kamal was excited about his new venture. He'd met with his mentee, Chris, a couple more times and was getting to know the young man. Then one day, Chris came to the center with a friend, Ken.

Ken was in the same condition as Chris – young, injured, and totally clueless on where he was going. Soccer was what he intended to use to help his family out. A light bulb went off in Kamal's head as he talked to them. Their attachment to soccer was for different reasons, but it was the same thing Kamal had gone through.

And thus, Beyond the Sports was formed. He and Ebele fleshed out the idea, and she told him he needed a business lawyer, project manager, analyst, campaign marketer, and web designer.

"We'll start by selling the idea to training camps for young athletes across the UK. Our vision would be to develop the well-rounded athlete, whose identity isn't only in what they can achieve on the soccer field. As time progresses, we'll expand to other sports, and veteran athletes reaching retirement. Our mission would be to train athletes mentally, spiritually, and socially. Ensuring that at the end of their career, no matter when that is, they have the life skills they need off the field of play to succeed," the project manager explained.

Kamal clapped. "Great. I love it. You captured my idea perfectly. I'll leave you to hire who you need to get the business off the ground. I want to be actively involved. Great work."

The team packed up to leave, and Kamal was left with his lawyer. He stood and buttoned his jacket. He still had two more stops before he was done. Adam, his lawyer, stood also. They were going together. As they walked out, Kamal told him what was on his mind.

"Adam, I want to set up a foundation named Kam Kare. I want to partner with rehab centers to offer full coverage of medical costs, and care for the immediate family during recovery. The recovery time must be the one recommended by the doctor. My wife-to-be will head the charity. She doesn't know it yet, so I want to get the ball rolling before I tell her."

"Sure thing. I'll get the paperwork started. So, this publisher, you sure you want to write a book?"

"I don't know. They approached me, so at least let me see what they're talking about. Right now, I have nothing but time. Maybe that's what God wants me to do."

"Wow. Kamal Danjuma, I never thought I'd see the day. You're a totally changed man."

"I'm a new creature, my man. You either get with it or get left behind."

———

Ebele sat tapping her finger on the table as she waited for her siblings to arrive. They were fifteen minutes late.

"Are you sure they're coming?" Ebele asked her father.

"Yes, they will. I want us all to be a family, and I told them about you. They weren't pleased, but they're willing to give this a fair shot," her father explained.

Something twisted in her stomach. He might have meant well, but the way he said it sounded like they were doing her a favor. She remembered Nse telling her to make sure she gave this a fair chance, so she remained silent. Her father looked down at his phone and smiled.

"They're here, parking the car," he said.

Ebele nodded and took another sip of her soda. Her mind drifted to Kamal. She was so proud of him and couldn't wait to hear how everything went. She felt movement and lifted her eyes. She couldn't believe who was coming her way. A tall, gorgeous blonde and a tall, equally handsome blonde man were walking straight toward their table.

She turned her head and felt her breath hitch. Okay, maybe she was here to meet someone. Did Kamal know she was in town? As those thoughts circled through her head, her mind tried to justify what her eyes were seeing. The guessing game stopped when the duo stopped at her table, and her father stood. He and the two new arrivals embraced one another in turn. Then she became the center of attention.

"Brandon and Brittani, I want you to meet Vanessa, your sister," her father introduced them.

Brandon remained silent but extended his hand after a few moments. Brittani, on the other hand, looked at her with daggers in her eyes. Ebele had never had a confrontation with Brittani, so she wondered what the problem was. But then she remembered Kamal was splashing her picture across social media almost on a daily basis, so maybe she'd seen them.

Brittani's evil eyes travelled to Ebele's ring. She turned her nose up in disgust.

"Your existence has ruined my life. Even when I didn't know about you, your evil preceded you. Your mother took my father from mine. The diagnosis was cancer, but I know she died of a broken heart." Brittani seethed.

She looked at her father's shocked face and sneered. "Oh, daddy, don't look at me that way. I never knew who or what it was, but I knew you cheated on her. I had no idea that you had a child." Her face was filled with hatred for her father. "I blamed you for my mother's death. That's why I went to the US, leaving you, and this place behind. Now your black baby is back, and she stole my man."

Brittani turned back to Ebele in a rage. "Are you and your mom that pathetic that you have to take what belongs to others?"

At the mention of her mother, it was as though Brittani had poured cold water over her. Ebele stood. "Listen, as long as you live, don't talk about my mom. *Our* dad knew he was married and still chased her. Another thing—your man? The one you walked out on when you thought he could no longer play? The one I mended? I catered to. I calmed his wrath. I wiped his tears. I shared his fears. And I could care less whether he plays or not. Because unlike you, my soul is tied to the man and not the football star."

"You changed him. You put him under your spell. The man I saw no longer wanted to fight for what he wanted. You changed him!" Brittani looked at her with pure disgust. "My so-called sister stole my man."

Ebele looked around and noticed phones being whipped out and people recording. She had never been so embarrassed in her life. She needed to get out of there. In no way was she defending herself to this woman. She looked at her father. He stood there silent, looking at his shoes. She didn't know why she expected him to say something – to come to her defense. He had never been a father to her before, so why should he be one now?

Brittani continued calling her names from homewrecker to joy stealer. She even put part of the blame for her mother's death on her. Ebele quickly packed up. She was saved but wasn't going to be too many more homewreckers.

"Brandon, for what it's worth. Nice to meet you. Father, see you around." She turned to Brittani, "You, get some help." She walked out of the restaurant with her head held high, but her heart was broken. She hailed a taxi and got in.

Her phone rang. It was Kamal. She sent him to voicemail. Right now, she needed to gather her thoughts. This was supposed to be the reunion of her dreams, but it had gone terribly wrong. As she rode to Kamal's house, her phone chirped again. It was Nse with a text.

How did a lunch with your dad end up with you on the number one gossip blog? With a client now but check In The Know's website NOW!

With shaky hands, Ebele checked the site. Brittani's tirade made the center portion of the page. The caption read, "*Bad Boy Soccer Star Trades One Sister for Another*. Her heart sank. She read the article. Apparently, one of the blog's editors was at the restaurant, and Brittani decided to give an interview. Ebele was painted as a homewrecking opportunist. She and the tabloids – not again!

———

LATER THAT EVENING, KAMAL MOVED HIS BODY TO "MIGHTY God" by Joe Praize featuring Soweto Gospel Choir as he cut the onions. It had been a great day. He could feel the presence of God everywhere he went. The publishers turned out to be Christian. They wanted to give him a hefty advance to write a book about his life. They claimed someone gave them a backstory on his childhood, so they explored him further. They agreed he could write a book of hope and healing. Kamal already had the idea in his head.

Pete came back with two endorsement deals, one was for a knee brace company of all things, and the other one was a brand of alcohol. That he turned down.

Kamal heard the front door open. A few seconds later, his beautiful fiancée entered the kitchen. He felt the energy in the room shift. Something was wrong. He walked up to where she sat on the barstool by the island.

"What wrong, E?"

"You know how I wanted to meet my siblings so bad?" She spoke in a soft tone that scared him.

"Yeah, so how did it go?"

"Remember apart from me, my father had a boy and a girl."

"Yea, what does that have to do with why you're crying? E, Talk to me. You're killing me."

"Brittani is my sister." She looked up at him.

Kamal jerked his head back. "Huh? How?" He sat in silence as Ebele narrated the story to him. She even showed him the news tabloid from one gossip rag.

"Wow. I never would've thought that. Wow." He couldn't seem to get his mind around it. His ex-girlfriend was his fiancée's sister.

Kamal walked back to the stove to stir the sauce. He looked back at Ebele. What he saw gave him an instant headache. She was turning the ring on her finger as though she wanted to take it off.

"E, what's going on? I agree this is crazy. Like really crazy. But Brittani has nothing to do with us. You know that, and I know that."

"Don't you see how it looks?" she asked.

"How what looks? What are you trying to say?" Panic shot through his body.

"I'm just saying, two sisters. Maybe we should take some—"

Kamal didn't want to hear the rest of her statement. "Nah, baby, it doesn't work that way, No take backs. Besides, didn't Jacob marry two sisters? So, it's Biblical." He hoped that his joke would calm some of her anxiety. He tried another joke. "Our families have already done the traditional introduction stuff. All the drinks my family took over there for the first and second visitation, you know your greedy people have finished it already. Are you gonna buy them back?"

When she remained silent, he struggled for breath as his panic increased. His angst was overshadowed with confusion.

"Are you for real? You're thinking about not marrying me for some false allegiance you have with a sister you've known for two minutes?"

"Stop putting words in my mouth, Kam. That isn't what I said. In fact, I haven't said anything because you won't let me speak." She raised her hands in exasperation.

"Then speak, Ebele." He folded his hand across his chest and walked closer to her. There was a long pause between them, then she spoke.

"What I'm saying is … let's hold on, at least until all this dies down." Her eyes pleaded with him. He'd give her anything she wanted, but not this.

"And if it doesn't?" He knew the news cycles always changed when something new came along. She should know it too. The bigger issue was their ability to bear unfavorable cycles together, not apart.

"You don't know that it wouldn't."

"And if it doesn't?"

"Kam—"

"Baby, I understand you're sad, and this is a storm neither of us expected. You've wanted to be accepted by your father for so long that this development is a blow. I can't fill that void, but I promise to protect and love you as long as I have breath." He pulled her close and wrapped his arms around her. His hand went up and down her back in a soothing motion. Ebele began to cry. His heart couldn't take seeing the love of his life in so much pain. He could relate all too well to what she was going through. If he could, he'd bear the pain for her; he would.

He picked her up and by reflex, her legs went around his waist. He carried her to the opposite side of the island and sat on the barstool.

"Look at me. Please, stop crying," he said.

She sniffed and looked at him. Her cheeks were wet. He kissed her lips.

"You know I can't take your tears. You gonna make me cry too, and you know you don't want your man looking like a punk out here."

She gave him a faint smile.

"I'm not belittling your pain and disappointment, but you need to find a way to get over it. I'll help you. Don't let your father and siblings rob you of your happiness. Our happiness. Don't let them take something else from you."

Ebele remained silent, and Kamal felt his unease return. He placed her on the stool and went to turn off what he had been cooking. He walked back over to her, and she spoke.

"Kamal, I hear everything you're saying, but I need time." Her voice, barely a whisper.

"Time for what, E?" She was calling him Kamal and not Kam. He was about to lose his mind. He battled between shaking her to force her to see that punishing them wasn't the answer and being the loving fiancé, giving her the space she needed.

"I'm in the tabloids again because of a man—"

"Don't you dare compare me to that clown." He seethed.

"The look my father gave me let me know he'd already picked sides, and it was that of my siblings. Fixing his relationship with them means more than having one with me." She got down from the stool and picked up her purse.

Kamal felt his heart constrict. Ebele was the air that he breathed, and she dared not leave him breathless.

"Don't do this, Ebele," he pleaded. "E, Ebele …"

Ebele gave no response and walked with calculated steps toward the door. He leaned against the island and watched her. He had pleaded but refused to chase after her. He couldn't force her to do anything she didn't want to.

She got to the door and turned to look at him. "I'll call you soon, Kam."

He stared at her but didn't respond. She was hurt, and he was supposed to be her shield, but she was pushing him away.

The sound of the door closing was like a hammer coming down on him. He looked around his house, and although she didn't live with him, it felt cold. He went up the stairs for a shower and a bath. Food was the furthest thing from his mind.

Three days later, his empathy had turned into anger. He sat on his bed and looked at the phone again. He had been sent to voicemail for what had to be the millionth time. He'd given her twelve hours, which Tega had to talk him into. Kamal figured that the longer she stayed away from people who loved her, the more she'd think and let her emotions run wild. Since then, he'd been trying to get to her. He just got back from her apartment some minutes ago, but she wasn't there.

He blew out a harsh breath and ran his hand over his head. Ebele, of all people, knew how hard it was for him to give his heart away. He gave it to her and now wasn't sure if he could trust her with it. She taught him about selfless love, but she was robbing him of the opportunity to show it to her. She wasn't the only one suffering. The scandal his love life had turned into was being splashed all over the tabloids and hurting his chances of getting a new team.

Kamal picked up his phone to send her a text. After this, he was done. They were a little over two weeks from their wedding. She would have to come to him.

I'll be at the terminal like we previously planned. I pray to God you'll be there. If you're not, then I know where we stand.

Kamal hit SEND and went about his day. It was now left to her.

Chapter 30

"You look terrible, and you stink. Get yourself up. I'm not playing with you," Nse fussed. She picked up the clothes strewn all over the floor of Ebele's apartment.

Ebele pulled the comforter over her head. She felt Nse pull it down. Ebele had been in zombie mode for nineteen days. All she did was go to school and return to her flat.

Nse put her hands on her hips. "You see, back home they would say, I won't stand there and let another person puts soap in my eye. You, on the other hand, put the soap in your own eye. Why are you crying now that it's uncomfortable?"

"I was confused," Ebele whined.

"About what? That man loves you like no man's business. Sometimes watching both of you is sickening. You allowed a non-factor like Brittani confuse you?"

"I didn't say I didn't want to marry him. I wanted all the attention to die down, and I needed to think."

"Sweetheart, what were you thinking? Granted, you had to take it all in —but you guys should have processed together. You should've let him help you. He probably feels you don't trust him enough to shoulder your pain. Kammy has changed a lot. You need to have more faith in him."

"Why can't anyone see I needed this?"

"I'm not saying you didn't. Just not alone. Let me ask you this – when you get married, and you run when there's an issue, or he runs when he has to deal with something, what kind of marriage would that be?" Nse asked, with her hands on her hip.

Ebele remained silent. Put that way, she did have a point. He was her fiancé and not just a boyfriend.

"Ebi, your father hasn't even reached out to you. Don't let them win and take your happiness. As far as the media goes, Kamal has bent over backward to shield you. But it's time you step up and be the kind of woman a man like him needs. He's a celebrity; you know that. If you get confused at the first sign of trouble, maybe you're not what he needs."

Ebele sat up, and her face turned red. *How dare she say that to me?* "Look, I agree; I made a mistake. I had a lapse in judgment, but I'm what he needs."

"Can he trust you in good and bad?" Nse shot her brows up in challenge.

"Yes!" She shouted.

"Stop yelling it at me. You should be telling him."

"I tried. I reached out to him some days after I got his text. But he won't talk to me. He won't respond to my texts or calls."

"Three days after? Were your fingers broken? *Ehen*, you know your man. He's saved but hasn't been delivered from pettiness. You'll have to wait out your punishment. The flight to Mozambique leaves in two days."

"How do I know he'll still be there? He has never frozen me out completely before."

"Well, you live and learn, girlfriend. You live and learn. Now get up and go take a shower. Let's see what we can do about those big zits on your face from all this grease you've been eating." Nse grumbled. "I can't believe you. They gave you the palace, but you want to play on the roadside with people that don't even like you." She walked out of Ebele's room, dragging a hamper full of dirty clothes, and slammed the door.

Seconds later, Ebele heard the washer start. She ran her hands through her sweaty hair. The August heat peered through the curtains of her room. She scooted to the end of her bed. No one wanted to try and look at it from her standpoint. She told her mother about what happened, and she went completely off. She scolded her for retreating from Kamal.

Brittani, on the other hand, was on a rampage. Almost every day, there was another twist on the story of two sisters sharing a man in the tabloids. In all this, Kamal remained silent. She wondered how he was doing and regretted she was the cause of the pain in his eyes. Nse was right – a man like him needed a woman who wouldn't collapse under pressure. She could be that woman, and she'd show him. Her father and Brittani couldn't win. She was getting her man back.

Two days later, Ebele rushed down the airport terminal. *Oh, Lord, please don't let him leave.* Everything that could go wrong that morning did. Because she hadn't slept in days, she overslept. Next, she couldn't find her keys. As she was about to leave, she got an alert on her phone – an email from her professor. Part of the paper Ebele submitted was missing. In her haste to get it submitted by the deadline the day before, she'd made an error. Ebele knew that if the professor didn't know that it was unlike her to make such a mistake, she'd be failing that course. She called Kamal, but he wouldn't answer the phone. She couldn't get Nse either.

Ebele was still determined not to let anything stop her progress. This was all her fault. She looked at the time on her phone again as she pushed her way through. Five minutes to departure. Luckily, she had no bags to check in. Before all this, Nse told her that everything she'd need Kamal would carry with him. She finally got to the gate breathless but two minutes late. She ran up to the kiosk.

"Hi, I'm supposed to be on that flight."

"The cabin door has been closed," the kiosk attendant told her.

Ebele watched through the window behind as the plane started to move. "No, please, I have to get on that flight. My life is on that plane." She sobbed. "I'm supposed to be getting married, and my fiancé is on that flight. If he leaves, he won't marry me anymore, and my life will be ruined. I'll be playing outside with those that don't like me. Where would I get the money to return the drinks that his people bought? If Tina starts coming around him, I'll just die, because that should be my palace. But I was so stupid. I picked up the soap and rubbed it in my own eyes. Who does that?" Ebele rambled.

"I won't have anyone to call me E, or rest their forearm on my head when they're tired. Then Brittani and Victor will get together and have a victory party. My life is over." She used her hand to wipe her tears, shaking her head.

"Miss, I didn't understand a word of what you've said, but let me see your boarding pass," the attendant said.

Ebele handed her the document. Seconds later, the woman took off her glasses. "Young lady, your flight leaves from two gates down in twenty minutes. There was a change in gate and time."

Ebele wiped her eyes, thanking the lady profusely. She then straightened up and speed-walked to the correct terminal. Kamal was inside the lounge, reading a newspaper and looking unbothered. She went in and stood in front of him.

"I'm sorry."

"Don't let it happen again." He didn't make eye contact.

"I'll make it up to you."

"Yes, you will." He folded the paper, put it down and looked up at her. His smile calmed her nerves.

Ebele got in his lap and laid her head on his shoulder. He held her close. She was at peace again.

———

"With the power vested in me, I now pronounce you man and wife. You may kiss the bride," Pastor Ricardo said.

Kamal stared at Ebele. His heart overflowed with emotions he couldn't put into words. The last two weeks had been so painful; he'd nearly lost his mind. He didn't doubt Ebele loved him, but the possibility of her having a change of heart about marrying him wasn't something he could deal with. After he waited three days for her to respond to his text, he had lost all sensibility and began to question if they were ready for marriage. He knew she was hurting but to shut him out, hurt. Completely cutting her off after that was for him and her. He needed her to be sure he was want she wanted without his influence. He always teased and pushed her, but she had to endure the unkind spotlight and still come to him on her own. He needed to be sure she'd be able to stand.

Kamal lifted her veil and kissed her with earth-scattering passion. She wrapped her arms around his neck, and he picked her up.

"Ladies and gentlemen, I present to you Mr. and Mrs. Kamal Danjuma."

Kamal faced the audience with his new wife. They were on the beautiful white sanded beach of the Vamizi Island in Mozambique. It was an intimate ceremony, exactly what they wanted. The people that came were those who mattered the most. The Danjuma family jet brought their mothers, her Uncle Ezi, Halima, and Rasheed's family from Nigeria. Jabir, his best man, flew in from Detroit with his family. His boys, Freddie and Princeton, were also present with their wives. Tega had flown with Nse, Ebele's chief bridesmaid. Ebele's dad called to congratulate her, but he and her brother opted not to come in loyalty to Brittani.

The couple danced in to an elegant but intimate ballroom, that had what he knew to be her favorite colors: orange and crème. Everyone celebrated with them and had fun. He watched Ebele's face as he unveiled one surprise after the other. The highlight of her night was after they cut the cake, Kamal and his boys danced a choreographed routine to Larae's "I Love You."

Nse had to move the couple's first dance to the end because Kamal's surprise was late. It still worked out because Kamal wanted that to be the end of the reception for them. They'd be leaving to another part of the island where they would stay for a week.

When the lights dimmed and Nigerian recording artists, Flavour and Chidinma, entered the hall with their hit song "Ololufe," the hall went crazy, and Ebele started to cry. She was such a crybaby. Kamal went to her, and they danced to the serenade.

"Oh, my gosh, baby, this is fantastic. The best wedding I've ever had."

"It better be the only wedding you'll ever have," Kamal teased.

"You know what I mean."

"E, your old man pays too much for you not to know how to speak English." He kissed the top of her head.

"Stop teasing me, Kam."

He chuckled and held her close. If he must say so himself, he'd outdone himself. He and Nse put all this together including Ebele's custom-made wedding gown. It was fitted lace with stripes of Ankara on the side. What he designed that day with his sketchpad on the couch looked so good on her. He had on white linen with the same Ankara patches on the collar and pockets.

When the song ended, Kamal held her hand and thanked

everyone for coming. He told them to keep dancing and eating, but he and his wife were out.

Over the next week, he and Ebele went on every adventure available in their honeymoon package. They learned the local dance, swam, kayaked, despite all of that, they had spent most of the time in bed. It was now the last day of their stay – time to head back to reality.

Kamal's phone rang as he put the last piece of luggage on the cart. He answered the phone.

"Hey, Pete. What's up, man?"

"Congratulations to you both. I know you're still on your honeymoon, so I'll be quick. I got a call yesterday from two major teams. One is here in the US, and the other is with the Premier League in the UK. They wanna come watch you train."

"Oh, for real? That's great. Let me get on this flight. We'll talk when I land. Good looking out, man." Kamal ended the call. He sat on the bed and ran his hand down his face. He felt Ebele move until she was standing between his legs.

"What's up, baby?" she asked.

"It was Pete."

"I figured. What did he say?"

Kamal placed his head on her stomach. "He said two teams want to come watch me train in October. That's two months away."

"Okay, that's good news, right? Potential for a new contract. You get to play ball again. That's what you want, right?"

He remained silent.

She lifted his head. "Right?"

"I don't know. Suppose I'm no longer as good as I used to be? Maybe I don't want to play. Does that make me a quitter?"

Ebele cupped his face. "Look, my husband is far from a quitter. You don't want to play because you have other focuses, fine. But don't you dare say you're not good enough to play soccer. That's fear and a lack of confidence playing tricks on your mind. That's not the man I met, and it's not the man I'll allow you to become."

He smiled at her. "Have I told you I love you?"

"Every day, without fail."

"And it will be that way for the rest of my life."

"I'll hold you to that.

THE END

Epilogue

Three Years Later

KAMAL SAT BACKSTAGE AT TEDX STUDIOS IN THE CITY OF London. He squeezed the hand of a very pregnant Ebele. He didn't want her to come, but the whole family was here to watch him speak, and she wouldn't be left out. That didn't matter to him, though. The only reason he allowed it was that the studio was only an hour away from their house in Essex. Over the last three years, **Beyond the Sports** had grown. He'd spoken at many training camps and various platforms but never TED.

Rasheed and Ibiso flew in with Yohance and their six-month-old daughter, Jumai. They'd been in the UK a couple of weeks now. Kamal was proud of his sister-in-law. She'd opened her first international branch of Bisso Bites in Leeds, UK. So she visited at least once a quarter. His mom had been staying with Jabir and Damisi in Detroit for the summer. She was helping them take care of their new son, Idris, while the couple packed and got ready for their relocation back to

Nigeria later in the year. Jabir's clinic in Lagos was finally ready. In addition to Mosaic blog, which was now a magazine, Damisi had started a web series called *Woman at The Well.*

The brothers lived very busy lives year-round but took every summer off. All of them still maintained their homes abroad but were based in Nigeria. Kamal and Ebele came back to the UK the month she entered her second trimester. He'd been traveling back and forth, and he didn't want to leave her in their Abuja alone. He was so proud of his wife. She was the owner of her own rehabilitation center, Mended by E. He'd developed the design he created and had it built. It was a struggle, but she finally let him help her. Between that and heading his foundation, Kam Kare, she was happy and quite busy. He stopped all that after her third month of pregnancy. Anything she couldn't do without minimal stress, the manager they hired did. Ebele fussed, but he told her that if the manager couldn't handle it, then they needed a new manager.

Kamal caught her rubbing her stomach in his peripheral vision. He frowned. "Baby, you okay? Momsie can go back home with you." Her mother had been with them for two months now.

"I'm good, my love. You know we're so proud of you." She pouted her lips, and he gave her a kiss. They were having twins, a boy and girl.

"He needs no introduction, but I'm going to give one anyway." The moderator's voice boomed.

Kamal stood. "He's the two-time MVP for the MLS, winner of the MLS Supporter's Shield. He is also the recipient of this year's Man of the Year award from the Philanthropy UK Foundation. The best-selling author of the book *Anchored Wrong,* CEO of Beyond the Sports, and along with his wife, he owns the Kam Kare Foundation. Despite his fame, he was once a broken soul. Ladies and gentlemen, please help me welcome Kamal Danjuma as he tells about his journey from sinking sand to solid rock."

The theatre broke out into applause. His brothers patted him on the back. He kissed his wife and walked out on stage.

"How are y'all doing this afternoon?"

The crowd screamed their response.

"As you know, I retired from professional sports after a knee injury. I did get the offer to sign for two new teams. Even though playing again is what I wanted, I didn't want to try out because my direction was somewhere else. Truth of the matter was that although my focus was indeed elsewhere, lack of confidence and fear were the root of my hesitation. But with my wife's encouragement, I did it. To beat fear and prove to myself I could. After I got the offers, I declined. I want to talk to you today about being anchored wrong. That's the title of my book. By the way, I'll be signing copies at the back after this. My twins got to eat, so I need the money." He paused for effect.

The crowd laughed.

"I'm kidding y'all. Anyway, an anchor has one job, and that is to steady the boat. Through the storms, the highs, the lows, pain, and gain, you must have an anchor that doesn't shake. It doesn't sway with the times. That, ladies and gentlemen, is what God's hope does for us. After my injury, I drifted, but a woman, who is the center of my world – my wife – helped me. She mended me physically with love, but that's not all. She also worked on my mind. She showed me I couldn't be anything by myself. As an anchor steadies the boat from the outside, I needed something outside of me to steady me during my storm."

For the next thirty minutes, Kamal taught on a topic close to his heart; hope and readjusting to life after sports. When the talk ended, the crowd gave him a standing ovation. Kamal walked to the waiting room, thanking God as always for the opportunity.

"Oh, baby, I'm so proud of you," Ebele said moving from side to side.

"Thank you, baby. But calm down, my kids might be sleeping." He steadied her.

"Good job, bro." His brothers patted him on his back. His mother and mother-in-law also came around to hug him with his sisters-in-law right behind them.

Kamal walked back over to his wife and held her close. Her face crumbled, and he felt water seep onto his Ankara loafers.

"E, you peeing on me? Oh, man. I knew you should've stayed home. I can't have people talking about you." Kamal whispered louder than he intended. He felt all eyes turn on him.

"My water broke," she said, softly.

Jabir came over. "Sis, how long have you been having contractions?"

"For a while, but I wanted Kam to finish speaking."

"Are you serious, right now?" Kamal scooped her up and headed for his car. The family got in their cars, and they all headed to Broomfield Medical. "When my kids get here, we gonna talk about your punishment. My kids trying to get out, and you suppressing them for some speech."

Ebele started to sob. "Baby, you sound ignorant, but I'm sorry. I just wanted to be there."

He put her in the car, "Momsie, please, stay with her in the back."

"Nah, baby, that crying won't work. I love you, but you still gonna be on punishment," he said as he sped out of the parking lot.

Five hours later, their son, Nasir, and daughter, Nafisah, came into the world. Once the babies were cleaned up and returned to their parents, the family entered, offering congratulations. Soon after, they left, and Kamal stood in the corner of the room and looked at the three humans, who made up his world. The babies were cradled in Ebele's arms. He walked over to them and picked up his daughter. Ebele smiled up at him, and he caressed her cheek.

"Three of you are the reason I look forward to the next day. I thank God; I had the sense to give my heart to you. Thank you. I love you with every part of my being," Kamal said.

"Aww, I love you, baby. I thank God I had the good sense to demand I be put on that flight."

Kamal chuckled and kissed her forehead.

Discussion Questions

----

1. Kamal was your typical celebrity, spoiled and entitled, what do you think of his growth by the end of the book?
2. What are your thoughts on Kamal and Ebele's instant romance?
3. Ebele craved the same love from her father that Kamal sought from his. Do you think her pain was more or less because her father's attempt at reconciliation was not complete?
4. The Bible places no condition on forgiveness, but Ebele's seemed to be based on the action of her father. Discuss.
5. Forgiveness doesn't mean reconciliation. True or False?
6. Kamal was the typical alpha. Were his actions toward Ebele when he was still dealing with Brittani fair?
7. Kamal hid behind his career and couldn't deal with it when it was abruptly interrupted. Do a self-examination, are you anchored in things that can pass away?

Final Note

Thank you for reading Kamal & Ebele's story. Please consider leaving a review on the platform you purchased the book from. I greatly appreciate honest feedback. They really go a long way. The number of reviews a book receives greatly improves how well it does.

If you liked this story, I trust you might like some of my other titles. But before we get to those, never miss a sale, new release announcements, or freebies. You can ensure that by joining my mailing list. I'd love to stay connected.

As you know, the Danjuma Brothers have a sister, Halima. Her story is told in Redeemed Through Love and you can order it here.

Also by Unoma Nwankwor

Stand Alone Books

An Unexpected Blessing

He Changed My Name

When You Let Go

The Ultimatum Series

The Christmas Ultimatum

The Final Ultimatum

Sons of Ishmael Series

A Scoop of Love

Anchored by Love

Mended with Love

Redeemed Through Love

Mixed Tidings

The Invisible Shackles Series

To Live Again,

To Breathe Again

The DuBois-Arazi Family Novels

A Promise Fulfilled

Destiny Fulfilled

The Billionaire Pact

Vegas Nights

Second Shot

Pretend Bae

Away To Africa

New Year's Kiss (Prequel)

Rent-A-Bae

His Makeshift Fiancée

A Suitable Wife

www.ingramcontent.com/pod-product-compliance
Lightning Source LLC
Chambersburg PA
CBHW061644190726

48289CB00006B/1742